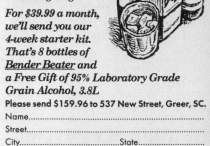

"'Madame Bovary c'est moi,' Flaubert said. Recognizing her illusions and struggles to grow up, we all might say, 'Iris is me.'"

—*BOMB*

"Instant favorite . . . hilarious high jinks."

—*O, The Oprah Magazine*

"A modern Joyce, a Portrait of the Artist as a Young Woman."

—*Rumpus*

"Iris Smyles is my spirit animal."

—JAMES ST. JAMES

"Delightful, dreamy, witty, sad . . . makes one think of one's own youth and folly, and all the folly yet to come, because maybe the unspoken message of this story—and one I agree with—is that we never really grow up."

—JONATHAN AMES

"A series of serious one-liner gems, laugh-out-loud hilarity, 'no-she-didn't' moments of vicarious embarrassment, and truly intelligent philosophical observations. The most believable untrue autobiographical treatise on life, love, liquor, and literature you'll have the pleasure of reading this year, or maybe ever."

—*Coast*

IRIS SMYLES'
DATING TIPS
FOR THE
UNEMPLOYED

Iris Smyles'
DATING TIPS

for the

UNEMPLOYED

A MARINER ORIGINAL
HOUGHTON MIFFLIN HARCOURT
BOSTON   NEW YORK   2016

Library of Congress Cataloging-in-Publication Data
Names: Smyles, Iris, author.
Title: Dating tips for the unemployed / Iris Smyles.
Description: Boston : Mariner Books/Houghton Mifflin Harcourt, 2016.
Identifiers: LCCN 2016009605 (print) | LCCN 2016015866 (ebook) |
ISBN 9780544703384 (softcover) | ISBN 9780544703681 (ebook)
Subjects: LCSH: Smyles, Iris — Fiction. | Young women —
New York (State) — New York — Fiction. | Dating (Social customs) — Fiction. | Self-
realization in women — Fiction. | BISAC: FICTION / Humorous. |
FICTION / General. | GSAFD: Autobiographical fiction. | Humorous fiction.
Classification: LCC PS3619.M95 D38 2016 (print) | LCC PS3619.M95 (ebook) |
DDC 813/.6 — dc23
LC record available at https://lccn.loc.gov/2016009605

Book design by Mark Robinson

PRINTED IN THE UNITED STATES OF AMERICA
DOC 10 9 8 7 6 5 4 3 2 1

The following chapters were published previously in a different form: "Socratic Dialogues," "Dating Tips for the Unemployed and Unsuccessful," "Literature, Sex, Monopoly, Gin," "Monsters," "Adventures with My Parents," "Dispatches from My Apartment," "Dengue Fever," "Phatso," "The Family Politic," and "Talking" in *Splice Today*; "The Great Lawn" in *BOMB*; "MENU" in *Guernica*; "The Friend Registry" in the *New York Times*; and "Large Hadron Collider" in the *Atlantic*.

"Book 1: Athena Inspires the Prince," from *The Odyssey* by Homer, translated by Robert Fagles, translation copyright © 1996 by Robert Fagles. Used by permission of Viking Books, an imprint of Penguin Publishing Group, a division of Penguin Random House LLC. Excerpt from *You Can't Go Home Again*, copyright © 1940 by Thomas Wolfe. Copyright renewed 1968 by Paul Gitlin, C.T.A., Administrator of the Estate of Thomas Wolfe. Reprinted with permission of McIntosh & Otis, Inc.

THIS IS A WORK OF FICTION. ALTHOUGH PORTIONS OF THIS NOVEL ARE INSPIRED BY REAL EVENTS, THE CHARACTERS ARE FICTITIOUS, COMPOSITES DRAWN FROM SEVERAL INDIVIDUALS AND FROM IMAGINATION. THE ADVERTISEMENTS IN THIS NOVEL ARE ALSO FICTITIOUS.

To Russ Smith,
for giving me my start

+

To Irene Skolnick,
for helping me find my way

Caveat Lector

Sing to me of the man, Muse, the man of twists and turns
driven time and again off course . . .
Launch out on his story, Muse, daughter of Zeus,
start from where you will — sing for our time too.

— HOMER, *The Odyssey*

Dear Kermit,
Wocka, Wocka, Wocka!
But seriously . . .

— FOZZIE BEAR, *The Muppets Take Manhattan*

Originally a medical term, "nostalgia" was coined by the German scholar Johannes Hofer in a 1668 paper to describe a severe homesickness in soldiers, whose terrible longing in combination with battle wounds sometimes proved fatal. The word is a compound of the Greek words "nostos," meaning homecoming (used by Homer to describe Odysseus's return in The Odyssey), and "algos," meaning pain.

On the assumption that home is a place left behind, nostalgia is commonly understood as a yearning for the past. But for many a young person seeking their place in the world, home is an idea with stronger ties to the future, embodied by a person or place not yet seen, making nostalgia an equally apt diagnosis for the strange ache that often defines early adulthood.

In his twenty-four books of The Odyssey, Homer relates the story of Odysseus, literature's earliest nostalgic, on his long journey home. Spanning ten glorious, miserable, lusty, drunken, mistake-filled years in its hero's life, The Odyssey is a catalog of ill-fated romances, parties, daydreams, grief, feats of daring, and experiences that very often lead to nothing but the next one. It's a lot like those first, lost, adventuring years when you're just starting out in the world.

Older and much changed by his experience, Odysseus does eventually make it home. And though The Odyssey ends before he has a chance to look back, it would be a mistake to assume that he regretted any of it, that, recounting his tale in quieter times, Odysseus would wish he'd arrived any earlier. "The sea was tough," I imagine him telling his son, "but strangely, sometimes, I miss its cold."

Homer, the great poet of nostalgia, began his odyssey in the middle. I begin mine likewise.

BOOK I

It takes a lot of nerve to have nothing at your age.

— ELAINE MAY, *Ishtar*

SOCRATIC DIALOGUES

ON THE AIRPLANE, I sat next to a sixty-two-year-old Greek American woman named Kiki who got married at thirty-seven. She told me so within five minutes of my sitting down, before adding that it's not too late for me either. By the time I got up ten hours later, I knew all there was to know about the struggles of Kiki's son in AP Physics, his engineering degree from Cooper Union, the car accident four years ago that rendered Kiki unable to wear stilettos, how Kiki met her husband at church, how he scuba dives like her, about her father's shipping company where she worked before marrying, and recent renovations Kiki oversaw to her house in Astoria. I told her my name when she asked upon landing. I said, "It was nice talking to you, too."

The drive from Athens airport to the bus station took an hour. I took a taxi and the young driver helped me with my bags. Tired from the last ten hours of talking, I pretended I couldn't speak Greek, hoping this would exempt me from polite conversation. "Is okay. I speak English very good." He told me the islands were very nice, have I been? That if I wasn't married, I shouldn't worry; this summer, here in Greece, I might meet the love of my life. "You are a kind girl, I can tell," he said. "My business is peoples; I know." After being riddled as to why Greece is better than America — "I love the quiet," I answered — we arrived at the station, where he proceeded to overcharge me ten euro. And because I didn't want to talk anymore, I gave it to him.

My parents picked me up five hours later from a connecting bus station in Volos. Eager to make conversation, they said, "How was your trip?" I told them about the bathroom attendant at the bus stop, a little old lady with a tip jar on a folding chair outside the door, dispensing wads of single-ply toilet paper from a lone roll. "No cologne." I told them about the porcelain footprints inside the stall, the elegant hole in the ground over which I squatted. "It got me thinking; I should have my toilet removed back home. Go minimal, modern, make a statement."

"How long will you stay?" some friends of my parents asked over the roar of the boat's engine the next day. A small party of us was motoring to the island of Skopelos.

"I'm here for the month of August," I yelled back.

Tired from my trip, I was at first excited by the roar of the engine, anticipating a few hours' lull in conversation.

"She doesn't talk much, your daughter!" our host yelled to my father.

"What?"

"She doesn't talk much, your daughter?"

"What?" my dad yelled back.

Then they put the radio on, turning the volume high enough for it to be heard over the engine. Then they raised their voices so they could be heard over the radio. They talked about the view, about the sea and the sky. "It's so relaxing," they yelled in agreement.

Back at the house, every room is filled with guests—aunts and uncles and cousins and friends. In the afternoon, after lunch, I slip off to my room for a nap. Drowsy from the midday heat, I shut my eyes and listen. Eventually the voices fall away. I dream of a long conversation, but when I wake, remember none of what was said.

In the early evening, I step onto the front patio and find Dimitra, my cousin's four-year-old daughter, dancing before an audience of our family. They clap and laugh as she wiggles from side to side. They call her "*i micrí*," which means "the little one." It's what they used to call me. My mother stops clapping and says she doesn't like my dress. "What's wrong with it?" I ask, looking down.

"It looks old."

With Dimitra, conversation is easy. When she stops dancing, she sits next to me and I ask, "What color is the sky?" She says, "Blue." I ask, "What does the rooster say?" "Koo-koor-ikoo," she sings. "And the dog?" "Ghav, ghav," because Greek dogs bark in Greek. Then she, Mamoù (her stuffed monkey), and I sit for coffee. Mamoù drinks too much too fast and becomes sick. I tell him I understand; sometimes I drink too much coffee, too. The *micrí* reprimands him, and I jump to his defense. I say, "Give the monkey a break, *i micrí*! He's had a long day."

In the kitchen my aunt flips on the radio, and the voices of a Greek talk show waft out. Dimitra jumps up and begins dancing to an argument about the Greek economy—Dimitra can dance to anything. Eager for some silence, I head down to the beach and stare out to sea. The wind is loud. The trees, too. The leaves rustle furiously as if urgently relating an opinion; everyone's got something to say.

I take my bike into town after and am stopped by a flock of sheep occupying the narrow path that leads to the village. I stand and wait for them to pass.

When they see me, all the sheep *behh*; they disapprove of my outfit — I should have worn the green dress. "Sometimes, Iris, it's like you don't even want to get married," the sheep say. Then the sheepdog emerges from the crowd, a big shot barking orders.

An old mustachioed shepherd watches silently in the distance. *Single?* Eventually they pass and the road is clear again. The sheep clink off with their ears marked for slaughter.

"You don't have forever," the last sheep tells me, before he turns away.

I shrug. "Neither do you. You're gonna die, you know," I say. "And your jacket's old-fashioned."

I spin through the olive groves and the wind fills my hair. How old am I?

I pull my bike across the gravel path an hour later and find my parents on the porch with their feet up. I join them. Dimitra sits beside me and asks why my feet are so large.

"To match my nose."

My mother complains that I'm antisocial, that I should make more of an effort to see my friends in town, to talk with them, or else "they might stop talking to you, too. You don't want to become a hermit," she warns. She says, "Why don't you go out tonight?" the same way she used to say, "Must you go out every night?"

The road to and from our house is less a road than a narrow dirt trail cut out from some trees, which leads to a clearing by the beach where our house rests. The "road" passes olive groves, orchards of plum, pear, and quince, and farms with chickens and roosters and their guards—more asshole dogs. After an evening at a café in town talking with friends, the sky is black and littered with stars like empty soda cans and the embers of discarded cigarettes.

I drive back in a gold 1982 diesel Mercedes we call "the Tank," which my parents shipped here ten years ago. It is the car with which I learned to drive, the car I took to and from high school in Long Island, the car in which I had sex with my first serious boyfriend. The Tank rolls slowly through the trees, pushing rogue branches out of the way with its nose. A few horses grazing near the "road" see headlights and approach. They, too, want to talk.

I roll down the window. The one that looks like Julia Roberts in *Pretty Woman* sticks her head in. She thinks I'm lonely. She asks, "You lookin' for a good time?" She wants to be taken up to my penthouse. "I don't have a penthouse," I tell her. She wants to be saved. "I don't have a penthouse, and even if I did, what do I want with some hooker horse?" I honk a few times to usher her out of the way, but she's stubborn and thinks I'm honking compliments. I nudge my way past and see her in the rearview mirror, watching me leave. She'd look better with less makeup. Someone should tell her.

My dad likes to listen to opera in the morning, but my mom never lets him because she thinks *Turandot* sounds like yelling, which makes her jealous; she prefers to be the one raising her voice. It's not that she's angry, but that everyone in my family alternates between two volumes—yell and scream. I'm the black sheep because I alternate between whimper and cry. As a result, no one understands me. They yell, "What?" I whimper, "I didn't say anything." They scream, "What?" I sniffle, "May I have an aspirin?" "Turn down that racket!" my mom yells at my dad, losing her patience with "Nessun Dorma."

Yesterday my dad insisted on hearing his songs and so, together, mischievously, we barred the door to the front terrace where normally my mother and aunt sit together to peel vegetables and gossip about the people they know—those who are not married and not getting any younger, those who are getting fat, those who've failed again to earn college degrees, and those who they suspect might be gossiping about them, too.

My dad's not antisocial like me, but every now and then he requires some peace and quiet. He achieves this by turning the volume up high, so high that the sound of his stereo drowns out all others. Like that, all dogs, all insects, all birds, all sea, and all wind, any and all conversations are swallowed by the rush of music.

Yesterday my dad turned the volume up on *Tosca*, and we sat side by side with our feet up, looking out to sea. For a few minutes, we said nothing.

The lonely voice of the jilted Maria Callas (divorced and then ditched—"a kind girl, such a shame") whirled around us, drowning out the voices of the rest of the family, who, relegated to the back terrace, continued their conversations in convivial screams. From their Greek staccato and sotto voce sighs, I could almost make out their measure, their firm agreement, this time about me: now that I've completed my second master's degree, what I really ought to do is find a man and get married. And quickly, too, before I gain any more weight, before I get too old, before people start to talk.

BOOKS II–XVI

If at first you don't succeed, failure may be your style.

— QUENTIN CRISP, *The Naked Civil Servant*

DATING TIPS FOR
THE UNEMPLOYED
AND UNSUCCESSFUL

YOU ARE UNEMPLOYED, at best very unsuccessful. Yet you go to parties. Parties where you meet people who ask, "So what do you do?"

You live with your parents. You share a one-bedroom with three roommates. You consider ramen a food group. You update your Facebook profile daily.

Your job has no title. You work within a department. You're an unpaid intern. You're assistant to the intern.

You stop people on the street and ask them if they like comedy, then push ticket packages to the "best comedy club in New York!" You stop them and say, "Excuse me, may I ask you a question about your hair?" You hand out free soap samples; nobody wants your soap samples.

You don't read the newspaper; it's expensive and the news is never good. Instead, you pick up the free alternative weekly. You skip straight to the comics and read without laughing. You could do better, you think. That is, if you drew. You blame your parents for not recognizing and encouraging your artistic potential early on. You remember when you were ten, you'd sketched some pretty realistic-looking horses. You skip to your horoscope:

"Inside you is an untapped power source, Pisces. Tomorrow, Libra, a great opportunity will present itself. Be prepared, Gemini, the rest of your life is about to begin. Leo, stop living in the past, the future is right in front of you!" You throw the paper away before you get home and forgive your parents for not buying you pastels — they did their best.

You call your mom, and she asks you about the weather. You lie and say it's colder than it is. You want to say something interesting. "We've a wintry mix today, Mom." When she says, "You sound depressed," you say you got a flu shot yesterday, just as she instructed, that it might have infected you. You feel so tired all the time lately. "Wear a hat," she says.

"I'm wearing one right now, Mom!"

"Hold on, I'm going to put your father on."

"Drink plenty of liquids," he says. "And cheer up!" he commands, before hanging up.

You take a job answering phones in a husky voice. It was funny at first, and all your girlfriends had a good laugh. You told them, "I'm going to learn what men want and then share it ALL with you!" After your first day, you met them for cocktails and they asked you what you found out. "Men want sex," you said, too demoralized to go into detail. The reality wasn't nearly as funny as the idea. "They never call in to talk about art or politics," you joked. But no one laughed, something about your tone. You lie and tell your parents you're a cold caller for the Ballet at Lincoln Center. You tell them all your friends are jealous because they let you work from home; you say, "A commission is even better than a salary, Mom!"

You log on to Facebook and update "favorite movies." You

take out *Rocky*. Put it back in. Then take it out. Then you add *Rocky I, II, V, IV, VI,* and *III* in that order. "*Rocky IV* gets priority and could switch places with *V*, though *V* is actually a superior film, as *IV* has a sociohistorical significance and represents in many ways the apotheosis of the Cold War experience in America," you've been known to say on first dates. "You will lose," you once said in an Ivan Drago accent, to a guy just before he kissed you, before he didn't call you back.

You log on to Facebook and scroll down your ex's wall.

Your college internship comes up at Thanksgiving dinner. Your mother says, "Why don't you apply there, honey?" You can't tell her that you've dated everyone in the office, that you can't possibly go back now, what with Jed, Field, Gibb, and Markus all over the place. You're too pretty or too easy, have low self-esteem or a superiority complex—you're not sure what's wrong with you, why you did what you did. You dated Jed because he said you were beautiful. And then Markus had kissed you after you drank too much at the holiday party. Gibb you went out with because Jed dumped you, and then Field after Gibb because you could do whatever you wanted, because you were above caring anymore. You say, "I'd like to try something different, Mom. Maybe teaching." You tell her about the ads in the subway about making a difference.

You attend a birthday party. The host brings out Milton Bradley's Operation, and everyone cheers when she extracts the spleen. You fail to extract anything. Later you overhear someone ask her in the kitchen, "What do you do?" You watch out of the corner of your eye as she replies unselfconsciously, "I wait tables." Perhaps you, too, could wait tables, you think the next morning, as you stand still for thirty minutes, naked before an NYU drawing class, a class you took yourself a few years ago, before you graduated early. What was the rush?

You found your own T-shirt company. You are president and sole employee, and your apartment is filled with the unsold stock from the street fair where you ran into an ex and a former professor all in one day. They fingered your goods and neither of them bought anything. "I was in your class! I make them myself!" you said too quickly. Your ex said he liked the one that said SECOND BASE and was trying to gauge whether or not it would fit his new girlfriend. He got her on the phone to ask her size, but then she didn't want one after all, he explained, before winking at you and saying he had to go.

You get a job at a trendy restaurant you once went to on a date. You thought it would be fun to work at a place so chic. But your uniform is not chic and the wait staff, they correct you on your first day, must enter and exit through a special door in the rear. An older waiter who always gets the best tables, an actor who's worked there for twenty years, takes you under his wing, shows you tricks with the ice machine, and tells you not to worry, that you'll get used to it. You thank him with a mixture of gratitude and horror. You don't want to get used to it.

You type forty words per minute, you lie. You believe you can learn PowerPoint. On days between job interviews, you smoke pot and watch *Jerry Springer, Judge Judy, Judge Joe Brown, Dr. Phil, Oprah, Tyra,* because "it's so bad, it's good," you tell someone at a party. You call your parents to ask for more money. Your life, you think staring at Dr. Phil, is so good, it's bad.

You avoid your friends. The successful ones make you feel

ashamed, and the unsuccessful ones avoid you, too, for fear that all together you give off too strong an odor of failure. You prefer the company of strangers, those middle-aged drunks at the bar around the corner from your apartment, about whom you've decided to write a novel. You have the title and the last line already. *Nowhere Is a Place.* "Because you can't leave nowhere unless nowhere is a place." It's about desolation and redemption at a bar around the corner from your narrator's apartment.

You check your email: nothing. But then, a message from your parents: "We just got email! How's the weather?"

You think of responding with a link to a weather website, but then worry it might destroy the delicate balance of your relationship with your parents. What would you talk about? "Mild with a chance of rain," you write back. You want to write something hopeful, some bit of good news, something they can feel proud of. You want to tell them that things are looking up, that they shouldn't worry. You type, "I got one of those new Sonicare toothbrushes you told me about. It's revolutionized the way I clean my teeth." You sign it "love" and press Send, unable to shake the feeling that your mom thinks you're a loser. And no, it shouldn't matter. But it does. It starts to.

"Getting a date," a woman says on morning television, "is just like applying for a job." This makes sense; no one will go out with you and no one wants to hire you.

You've heard a rumor that there is someone for everyone but are starting to worry that the one for you is ugly and stupid. What if you don't like the one for you?

You've begun to take seriously magazine articles offering dating tips, when you come across an article entitled "Dating Tips for the Unemployed and Unsuccessful." You read:

Singles comprise two distinct groups: the Miserable and the Non-Miserable. Recognizing to which category the object of your affection belongs is your first step toward establishing a a healthy romantic life.

RULE #1:
Never date someone more or less miserable than you.

Your ideal partner is just as miserable as you are, though early on this may be difficult to discern. For in the beginning, you'll both put on a good show, disguising your misery with a sprightly off-the-cuff wit (this has been rehearsed). Thus charmed by one another's astonishing élan and the unusual receptiveness you've found with no one else, you'll both begin to fall.

Now, having successfully tricked one another into believing you're both happy, laughing persons, one of you will suggest that you share that happiness exclusively. You eagerly agree, and are thrilled to find yourself the object of a love you suspect you do not deserve. *She/he is just so great!* you think, until you discover that your partner, whom you'd thought was way out of your league, whom you'd thought you'd stolen from the high shelf, was only faking it, just as you were. He or she, it turns out, is just as miserable as you are. At first you are angry, but then anger gives way to relief. At last, you can share everything, including your misery. That is until one of you (you pray it's not the other) achieves some modicum of success and leaves you even more miserable than before. But don't despair—there are plenty of other miserable fish in the sea!

RULE #2:
You will never fool anyone with your self-conscious quips about what you do.

Your wit will be your giveaway, as the most miserable in work are the most creative in their responses. Individuals who are happy with their profession have no need for whimsical replies. They answer plainly, "I'm a bonds trader." "I'm a teacher." "I'm a doctor." "A journalist."

If someone answers, "I'm a blowfish," rest assured this person is narrowly holding on. Furthermore, it will never work between the bonds trader and the blowfish. For just as you are suited to misery, the non-miserable are suited to one another. Even if you do manage a few dates with the bonds trader or any other non-miserable bachelor or bachelorette, your misery and the air of failure you've attempted to mask will eventually become apparent through the desperation of your wit and near-compulsive charm.

"Why must everything always be a joke with you? I asked you a simple question. What did you study in college?" the non-miserable boyfriend may ask during your final argument. "I told you. Theory and Engineering of Sweet Meats!" you answer devilishly, not wanting to tell him the truth: Medieval Poetry. "Why can't you ever be serious?" he growls. "Are you suggesting my major wasn't serious?" you purr.

Once you have disabused yourself of any notion of dating a non-miserable, the next step is learning to navigate among your miserable peers. The key to a lasting union lies in finding that unhappy single whose misery best matches your own.

Online dating sites are a treasure trove of the sad. Match, OKCupid, and Facebook are all great places to begin your search for a kindred loser. Once you've located a few nice pictures, scroll down their profile to where it says "Occupation." Learn to decode these often figurative descriptions, and you'll be well on your way to finding your perfect match. Let's practice:

See Christine! Blond hair with a pretty smile. She has written under Occupation: "Being Christine." This is to imply that Christine is down-to-earth, that she understands in a deep way that being herself is enough. Christine is lying. The truth is Christine hates being Christine, but feels she must get used to it; "everyone else is taken" she once read in a fortune cookie. At the corners of Christine's smile lie curls of defeat, but isn't that what you found so charming in her photo?

John is smiling beside a sock puppet in suit and tie. Scroll down to Occupation, which reads: "I make toast in space." John is deeply unhappy, so much so that he has mistaken it for happiness. He blinks a lot and is frequently confused, sometimes crying inexplicably at the conclusion of knock-knock jokes—he'll claim he is crying because he is so happy to find "Orange" at the door. If you go to a diner with him, he will make the beaker of milk talk until you laugh out of awkward politeness, which he'll take for encouragement before continuing with the sugar packets.

Watch out for those who write "Secret Agent." These charmless charmers are quick with ready-made phrases borrowed from the sitcoms and movies they favor, as a way of imbuing their steady stream of nervous chatter with the personality they fear they lack. "How you doin'?" the Secret Agent will ask you repeatedly in his best Joey Tribbiani voice, no matter how many times you answer that you are "fine."

Longing for intimacy and eager to drop his disguise, the Secret Agent can morph into "the Real Me" in a matter of minutes. You'll recognize the change when he begins talking of your "getting to know the real me," as the primary characteristic of the Real Me is endlessly alluding to "the real me." Other catchphrases of the Real Me: "I thought we were beyond that" and "I don't play games." What the Real Me means is "I am bad at playing games. My saying I don't play games is actually my best game. My Secret Agent secret weapon! 'Yeah baby!' Please be gentle. I'm very vulnerable right now. I can't find a job and have had to move in with my parents."

Need more help? Here's a chart:

Occupations Decoded

If someone writes this:	He/She really means this:
"I breed chinchillas with the hope of one day creating a super chinchilla."	"I'm studying for my real estate license and live at home."
"I make pasta necklaces. Would you like one?"	"I'm a barista and spend my free time training my fine blond hair into dreadlocks. I'm applying to graduate programs in 'art therapy.' My parents send me checks weekly, but I'm always 'broke.'"
"I'm writing a screenplay about the psychological blocks of a gifted twenty-something male with a trust fund who is writing a novel about a gifted twenty-something male with a trust fund who is unemployed."	"I've been in therapy since my fifth birthday party, when my psychiatrist parents diagnosed my constipation as 'withholding.' Therapy takes up all my time. My parents send the rent directly to the landlord."
"I'm pursuing an MFA in creative writing."	"I like the flexible hours of graduate school. Those years I spent working were really cutting into my drinking schedule. I hate my parents. My grandparents pay my rent."

Occupations Decoded

If someone writes this:	He/She really means this:
"I'm in the book trade."	"I'm a bookstore clerk and scoff at the titles successful customers ask me to find and correct my coworkers' grammar in order to deflect attention from my own insecurities, which you'll find are numerous and fascinating should I open up to you. But you have to earn it. I share a one-bedroom with five strangers I found on Craigslist and resent my friends whose parents pay their rent."
"Freelance."	"I sell knives. I call my mother's friends and ask them if they'd like to be able to cut a quarter in half without breaking a sweat. Born and raised in Manhattan, I've attended all the best schools. My parents moved me into the top-floor apartment of a building they own in order to get rid of a rent-stabilized sponge. I'm just doing them a favor."
"Somali pirate"	"I plunder ships on the open seas."
"Professional cow-tipper"	"I update my Facebook profile every hour with a new fake occupation. This is a good one. Ach! I just got poked! I love it! I'm gonna bite back with this cool Vampire app! I live in the basement."

But back to you! "What do you do?" That is, what are you going to answer when the question comes up at that party tonight?

Feeling like you can't face it? Like you might just stay in after all? Maybe stay in every night until you finish your novel? Until you've diagnosed the ills of your generation and found their cure in prose, so that when you do go out again, you'll know who you are, and it won't matter anymore how you answer, but it won't feel too bad either when you say: "Novelist!"

Yes, you think, looking in the mirror, as you throw on a comfortable sweatshirt. *Stay in, it is!* But to the deli first to buy a six-pack! And then, yes, of course, to your destiny in front of the computer, to your blank Word document entitled "The Novel."

You crack open a beer and type a few paragraphs before deleting them. You don't know what you're doing, what should happen next, what's important, if any of it is. You consider making the novel about desolation at a bar around the corner from your narrator's apartment. You finish your last beer and consider going to the bar around the corner from your apartment for some research. But then you don't; you're already in your underwear and, besides, that lonely five-dollar bill in your wallet needs to last the week.

You stare at the blank document, a broad open boulevard inviting you to pass through, a door to your new life. The light from the screen reflects back on you like a spotlight.

You decide to go online awhile, just a little while, and log on to Facebook, where perhaps you and I might meet.

Look me up! I'm Iris. I have long brown hair, an uncertain

smile, and become nervous when questioned directly about what I do. Scroll down. Under Occupation my job is listed as "You!" Which really means: "I like writing and talking about myself in the second person. If you go out with me, I'll tell you *all* about yourself."

What disturbs and depresses young people is the hunt for happiness on the firm assumption that it must be met with in life. From this arises constantly deluded hope and so also dissatisfaction. Deceptive images of a vague happiness hover before us in our dreams, and we search in vain for their original. Much would have been gained if, through timely advice and instruction, young people could have had eradicated from their minds the erroneous notion that the world has a great deal to offer them.

— ARTHUR SCHOPENHAUER

LITERATURE,
SEX,
MONOPOLY,
GIN

MY APARTMENT IS ABOVE two restaurants and made of some kind of red clay, which causes it to burn like an oven come summer. I'm in my underwear. For the last hour, I've been lying on the living room floor, cooking.

There's a fly above me, dancing with the ceiling fan. Nearly all of my windows are broken, and the bugs come in through the missing glass panels. I can't call the landlord though because my name's not on the lease. Officially, it's my brother's apartment. I moved in after he bought a fancy high-rise with views of the Hudson. He made a lot of money in computers and moved to the top of a luxury condo in Midtown where he sits alone, watching C-SPAN, afraid to spend another penny. He sits on the floor, as he hasn't bought any furniture yet. He wants to make sure he gets all the right pieces. That was three years ago. Anyway, that's why I can't call the super to come fix my windows. He might try to kick me out or raise the rent.

It's not so bad in the winter. The radiator just under the window hisses hot and can't be adjusted, so the broken windows, through which freezing air spills, balance everything out. Sometimes I'll sit by the window and pretend I'm submerged in an outdoor hot tub in Aspen, surrounded by husband material. While my body burns, a cool mountain breeze caresses my forehead and lets me see my breath. *What me, marry?*

Traffic out front. Deliveries. Buses starting and stopping. People chatting.

I'm trying to whistle. I'm practicing the look-at-the-golf-sticks-on-that-toothsome-retirement-plan, I-wouldn't-mind-wrapping-my-mouth-around-his-soft-manners whistle one hears so often at the entrance to squash courts and charity galas—the intermediate skill level I'm stuck on. I want to whistle lonesome country tunes in perfect vibrato, but the best I can do is mimic a sick bird. Where is my recorder? Back in Long Island with my parents, in its green sleeve. In my old bedroom, I suppose. Probably under the bed. I used to be pretty good at that. I should find it next time I'm home, bring it back with me, start practicing again.

Sunday.

I'm trapped in my apartment with a crippling hangover and no way out. This happens all the time. It never occurs to me to use the door. Because I know that beyond the door is just more of the same. No. There is no escape. The only thing to do is wait. Or jerk off. But I've done that three times already this morning. I'm not a compulsive jerk-off or anything; I just find it helps with hangovers. But I don't have it in me to do again now. Plus, lately when I do it, I'm possessed of a weird vision. I'll try to picture myself having sex with someone, when suddenly all the dimensions get warped, and I get this image of myself as a giantess, and the man I'm imagining as some tiny minutia whom I can barely see between my mountainous thighs. It's disturbing and makes it very hard to come.

On the ceiling, a series of images: all the idiotic things I've ever done, all the idiotic things I've still to do and, more specifically, all the idiotic things I did last night—the Scotch tape fight with Felix, the disgusting mouth of that guy I kissed at the bar, the water balloons, the neighbor knocking at 5 AM, my tap-dancing back and forth on the coffee table in time to marching band music.

I got this album, *Popular Marches,* from a street vendor a while back and like to play it when I'm drinking. Something about the drums and horns inspires me. When Souza fills the room, I feel as if my drinking were a heroic act, as if each full glass were a threat to America, as if it were all up to me to knock them back. I'm very patriotic. That's my problem.

Maybe I should stop drinking. Maybe I should marry Jacob. So what if he's shorter than me. I need a boyfriend. Someone sensible for whom I could cook sensible dinners. I should stop going out. And stop staying in and tap-dancing on my coffee table. Stop defending my country all the time. Another vision from last night: that guy I danced with, his sweaty face coming toward me.

In the kitchenette, flies circle the sink like buzzards over a body. The sink is full of dirty dishes from the party I threw Friday: a quiet dinner for thirty. It was supposed to be a small affair, but then I couldn't stop inviting people. What happens is you invite so-and-so and then realize you can't invite so-and-so and not so-and-so, so you invite so-and-so, too, doubling your list. And then you realize you've invited almost all men and so have to double *that* list by telling each of them to bring dates or be dead to you forever, and then the next thing you know, the neighbors are complaining about the noise pouring out of your intimate soiree, which you ended up hosting on the roof because you couldn't fit everyone in your apartment, despite the fact that your roof is not coded for entertaining, according to your complaining neighbor, as if it's your fault the builders didn't lay any kind of tile or wood over the melting tar destroying your shoes as you offer him a conciliatory meatball. It was fun, but still.

No more banquets. Just sensible dinners for two with my boyfriend Jacob, who wears lifts in his shoes. He and I could stop drinking together. We could experiment with healthy low-fat recipes and, after sharing balanced meals, sit on the couch and take our blood pressure before opening our respective mystery novels in order to read with our feet touching about the cold world and its thrilling crimes.

But I don't want a boyfriend! I want to be independent! What I want is to finish my own novel. I'd be much more attractive if I published a bestseller, a book about papal conspiracies with a raised font on its cover, or a nonfiction tome about how dairy created the modern world. Something bankers would enjoy. I should land a boyfriend who's vice president of something, that's what I should do. Then we could get married, and I wouldn't have to work anymore and could stop pretending I'm modern and interested in having my own identity apart from his. I could get my hair and nails done biweekly, have parcels from my shopping trips delivered to the house, where they'd remain unopened, their tissue paper clogging the hallways of our baroque mansion's western wing, in the far end of which I'd recline, miserable, bloated on high-grade whiskey and pills, yelling between massages whenever the fink dare ask me about my spending—"Why don't you ask the nanny where the money's gone, you Vice President of shit!"—get married and start living the good life.

Under my coffee table I spot a few pot seeds, the burned paper of a roach, a bottle cap—"Drink Coke, Play Again"— and an uncapped Magic Marker from when we played the let's-throw-Magic-Markers-at-my-ceiling-fan game.

A broken cigarette; I put it in my mouth. No light.

I hoist myself up, pad over to the stove, and set the thing on fire, nearly singeing my eyelashes in the process. *Need the lashes, Ms. Smyles! No vice president is going to marry a lashless freak.* The cigarette burns my throat. I never enjoy cigarettes, yet I continue to smoke them. If only I could apply that kind of discipline to my writing.

My book. Yes, the book. If my book were really good, I might skip marriage altogether. I could live alone, clothe myself in lavish silks and turbans. Start penciling in my eyebrows. I could pay servants to act as my friends. I could stage elaborate tests to see who of my friends/servants truly care for me and who are just in it for the trickle-down of my wealth and status. And then when I found out, fire the true friends. I could become very eccentric, stop clipping my fingernails, let them grow long and curling, never leave my bedroom, take to peeing in jars. I could get a small dog and fill the estate with oil portraits of him dressed variously, in a spacesuit, on a clam shell . . . I should get to work.

But I can't write now. Not in this heat. Not with this hangover. Tomorrow, once my head is clear. Tomorrow. Another vision from last night: Reggie's face. He was so mad when I brought all those guys to his place. But I made it a party! Why did I kiss Jess's friend Tom? Because his face was right there. Jess is never going to call me now. Which is good because I can't afford to be in a relationship, and if I go out with Jess that's exactly what it will turn into, and I need to stay focused on my book right now. The book is the key! Thank god I kissed Tom. Kissing Tom was really the best thing.

I can't breathe; the cigarette tastes stale. Perhaps I should go to a tubercular sanitarium, like in *The Magic Mountain*. Convalesce for a while, write my book on the horizontal. I don't have the stuff to get into Yaddo, but a sanitarium might accept me if I did enough damage to my lungs. Must build up to a pack a day.

I should do something. Writing is out of the question, but I can't lie here all day either or I won't be able to sleep tonight, and then tomorrow will be a wash, too. Tomorrow, I'll put pants on as soon as I get up. First thing. Nobody changes the world in their underwear. I'll say that in my *Paris Review* interview when I talk about my process. I'll tell them all about my collection of slacks. I should go for a walk, that's what I should do.

Outside, the heat hits me like a rogue wave. But then, there is a slight breeze, and it feels altogether much better than it felt upstairs. Why didn't I leave earlier? Why all that stewing? Why always surprised by the very same surprises?

I overthink things is the thing. And in all that thinking, I just can't see my way around the present. A hot day feels like it's going to last forever. Like there was never any day before, and there will never be a day after, so I might as well just stay very still and try to get used to it.

You know those people you see in the hot car on the subway? You know how in the middle of the summer, when you board the subway in the middle of the day and the car is stiflingly hot because the air-conditioning is broken, and so the compartment is all but empty, empty but for a few weirdoes who are sitting by themselves, staring and sweating, and they kind of watch you as you go through the double doors to the next car, which is cool and fine and normal? That's me. The weirdo looking at you as you leave. I stay in the hot car. I just figure once I get on, that's my lot.

I don't need an island; I could get stranded on a desert square inch. There could be a mini-mart around the next corner, but I'd just lie down, telling my thirsty companion, "Take whatever's left of the water and go! Leave me here to count my time upon the sand. But if you do survive, tell them my name. Let my memory live on through you and your children—tell them I was pretty!"

But now I'm at large in the city! Free! Turning destiny over in my pocket like loose change. A summer day, the air like "free soup with sandwich after 5 PM," moved by a light breeze as if some good god were blowing on it with poised spoon. Not bad at all. And the sidewalks, lively with bright-eyed pedestrians, the streets full of eager cars, and restaurant doors opening and closing, offering cool air-conditioned gusts to passersby. Vendors set up along the curb, and there's an ice cream truck and all sorts of wonderful things, and already I'm feeling much better.

I pass a blanket laid out with some fine merchandise on one of the sidewalks not too far from my apartment. I'm accustomed to my neighborhood's regular roundup of vendors, but this guy's new, so I stop to get a closer look at his wares, when something colorful catches my eye.

How to Make Sex Fun, a videocassette. Part 3 in the series *How to Make Sex Fun.* This particular segment involves board games, I'm startled to find as, turning over the box, I'd braced myself for something considerably less literal. But then, why not? Why shouldn't sex benefit from a little Battleship?

I inquire with the store's proprietor, the guy lying next to the blanket presumably, about the contents of the companion videos. "What did *they* offer as fun tips?"

He supplies a quixotic "oh yeah" and lies back down.

He has a point. What could possibly be more fun than board games?

I don't buy it, though I want to. I decide to think about it more instead, get it on my way home if the interest still holds. I don't want to act on a rash impulse. I'm too much lately a bundle of rash impulses, tied together with the string from an old box of cannolis. I want to try—I don't know—to improve myself through a strict protocol of careful consideration. I want to give more thought to this matter than I've given to all previous matters, to matters last night, for example. Balance things out a bit the way I do with cabdrivers, tipping some in small change and others in whole bills, knowing this makes it all even in the end.

I keep walking, keep considering, and the questions arrange themselves like this: Is sex fun? The makers of the video assume not and offer a remedy for that via Jenga. It's an interesting supposition and I tend to agree that it's not fun, but more . . . sexy. Still, I could stand to learn a thing or three. I decide to make the purchase. Add it to the sex library I keep next to my bed for like-minded guests intent upon their education. I'll put it to the left of *Libido Theory* and to the right of *Disorders of Sexual Desire,* or should it go between *The Hand-Job Handbook* and *Living Sober*, a book I read from time to time, from cover to cover, on long nights of drinking alone. By the twelfth step, I usually pass out and upon waking find that someone's trashed my apartment.

I'm imagining all kinds of sexy fun in the future. This video might really leaven the bread. "Look what I've got, Vice President!" I'll sing, waving the videocassette and a pack of Chinese checkers.

I follow the same streets home and purposefully stop by the blanket boutique, excited now to make this very thoroughly considered purchase. Scanning the blanket though, I see no tape.

No tape!

Not next to the blow-up electric guitar, not next to the single baby diaper, not beneath the gently used Hallmark cards, not under the pile of scrunchies and broken answering machine.

I ask the man lying on his side, his head propped up on his hand. He's more alert now than he was before. He watches me search. "Where is it?" I ask again. "You had a VHS tape."

"That's a good little answering machine," he answers. "Have the same one at home."

"Did you sell it?"

"I might have," he says cryptically, like one of the witches Macbeth meets on his return from the battlefield.

"This is terrible! I really wanted that," I say, wanting it now even more than when I could have had it. "I needed it," I double-down.

"Shoulda bought it when you had the chance," he says, not bothering even to prophesize my coronation.

"Unsex me now," I say, just because I want to say it, though really it has no bearing on the situation. But if I wait for an appropriate situation, it might never arise, and haven't I just learned a bitter lesson about waiting?

"How 'bout a phone card," the man offers. "I'll throw in this toothpick; still in its wrapper," he says, holding both before me like ingredients for the cauldron.

"No," I say, crestfallen, and continue home.

I look up. Rain is on the way. A summer storm. I round Bleecker and approach my building. Climbing the steps to my apartment, I feel dejected, ravaged again by fate's obvious proclivity to step around me. Once inside, I proceed to the kitchen, reach under the sink, and pull out my jug o' gin. Night is upon me, or cocktail hour anyway. Hugging the bottle, I proceed immediately to my bedside library.

"This book does not offer a plan for recovery from alcoholism," I read. I look over at the darkened TV screen that is not doling out "fun" bedroom tips and take a long slug from the bottle. I read on, skipping to my favorite chapter. "Sorrow is born of the hasty heart, an old saw goes. Other troubles, including an alcoholic bout, can be too."

The page is worn from use, the type blurry from spills. I put the book down momentarily to attend to my stereo. *Popular Marches* is still on the turntable. I turn the volume all the way up, strip down to my underwear, and lie back on the floor because it's hot. It will always be hot. The drums of routine pound out the rhythms of Souza.

My person was hideous and my stature gigantic. What did this mean? Who was I? What was I? Whence did I come? What was my destination? These questions continually recurred, but I was unable to solve them.

— MARY SHELLEY, *Frankenstein*

MONSTERS

LAST NIGHT I WENT TO a costume party dressed as Doctor Who. There are few experiences less rewarding than running into your ex and his new girlfriend when you're dressed as a 750-year-old Time Lord, and she's dressed as a sexy nurse. It was the first time I'd seen him since the last time I saw him, and it felt exactly like that.

Luckily, I was being romanced by a Klingon and turned, just at the last possible moment, to become very interested in what he was saying. He loved *Doctor Who,* the Klingon told me, as the two of them passed by, mellowly holding hands.

"Let's go to the roof," my suitor then suggested.

I nodded and let him lead me up the stairs. There I sat down under a great blanket of starless sky and cried. The Klingon sat next to me. "Don't cry, Doctor," he said, and gave me a Tootsie Roll.

"Whose party is this anyway?" I asked, chewing.

Then we kissed and I said, "I don't love you, okay?" and we went back downstairs and danced to "Thriller."

When I was a kid, my parents owned and operated a party store. On weekends, when other kids went with their family to church or temple, I went with mine to the shop. My mom would set the price gun, then direct me toward a group of Miss Piggy paper plates, Super Bowl–themed cups, or Smurf tablecloths. Prancing through the aisles in vampire dentures and fairy wings, I'd vigorously attack the party supplies. I loved "the store" and loved working, especially at the end of the day, when I'd be allowed to choose my preferred method of payment—three precious items almost always selected from the novelty aisle.

The novelty aisle was filled with wonders: spider rings; finger puppets; red capsules that exploded in your mouth for a bloody effect; wax lips; rubber pencils; tiny pills that, when plunged into water, expanded into planets or dinosaurs; fake mustaches; bubble gum that could be squeezed from a tube; chattering teeth on little plastic feet . . .

Between the odd items my brothers and I took home and the free samples suppliers were always sending my parents, our house was suffused with a bounty of strange treasure: Slime in a variety of colors, a pile of fake shit, a cupboard full of Silly String . . . For most of my childhood, you couldn't sit down without activating a Whoopee Cushion. Inured to the "novelty," our eyes passed right over the giant rubber rat guarding our foyer, and were it not for the screaming Jehovah's Witness who pointed it out, we might never have even known it was there.

Every year, beginning in elementary school, I threw a big Halloween party in our basement and backyard. Always a few friends would come over to decorate, mistakenly thinking this would be fun. But my father, a professional, took party decorations seriously. Running the team of merriment like a drill sergeant, he'd assign each of us specific duties, give mini-lectures on the art of the fake cobweb, the proper inflation of balloons, and lose his patience completely when his helpers lacked what in our house was deemed common sense.

"Iris!" he'd yell across the room, to where I was busily arranging the hair on a severed head. "Show your friend how to do streamers. This is ridiculous!" he'd snap, motioning to the limp ribbon Jason Birnbaum had just hung. I rushed over to demonstrate the correct technique, while my father went on, oblivious to poor Jason, on the verge of tears. "Flat streamers look like toilet paper," my father told the gathered children. "They mock the room, whereas we want to decorate it!"

My mother, in charge of refreshments, put out Dunkin' Donuts Limited Edition Halloween Collection, which were covered with orange sprinkles and little candy ghouls. We had a witch piñata, which, at the end of the night we drowned in the pool by way of trial, and prerecorded screaming to welcome guests as they came down the driveway.

The kids arrived in the usual disguises: Dracula, Spider-Man, and Darth Vader stood awkwardly by the grape soda. One year all the boys were ninjas. Another, the girls all dressed as Madonna—a dozen ten-year-olds shouting the lyrics to "Like a Virgin." Sometimes kids came without costumes and then bore the penalty of my painting their face however I liked. Others, especially later on as high school fed their insecurities, donned prescient but slight costumes—they were accountants carrying a pocket full of pens from their dad's firm; they sprayed their hair pink and wore chain-link belts and called themselves hookers, or else drizzled pretty sparkles on their faces and said they didn't know who they were. They were nurses all in white; they were plumbers with their pants dipping low in the back; they were one of the guys who hung out in the parking lots of nearby Deer Park Avenue drinking beer and looking for a fight on most weekends following high school graduation.

There were a few years, though, when I didn't throw the party, as I had no one to invite. In middle school I was picked on and, eager to avoid being seen, ate my lunch alone in the library. Like Frankenstein's monster, I'd flee the crowded cafeteria and take refuge in the wild, deserted stacks. Except on Halloween when at last I could blend in. In a room full of monsters, what was one more?

The new season's catalogs arrived every spring, giving my parents time to order their stock well in advance and me the requisite months to plan my costume carefully. The catalogs were organized according to age, and I begged my mother to let me choose from the grown-up section. At nine years old, there was nothing I wanted more than to be a Sexy Mermaid. When I imagined myself grown up, I imagined myself in costume.

Was there anything as sophisticated as a Sexy Cavewoman with a bone through her nose and a hot animal pelt covering her privates? Would I ever be a Sexy Witch and have a handsome husband dressed as a Jailbird? Staring at the gently lascivious She-Devils and Harem Girls, I projected my fourth-grade self, my undeveloped figure transformed through the magic of Halloween.

But by the time I hit puberty, I'd lost interest in sexy costumes. Why would I want a coconut bra, when I already had a real one? With time, I graduated from the catalogs, moving on to costumes that required great thinking and planning. As Picasso's style evolved over the course of his life, giving way to Blue,

Rose, and Cubist Periods, so is my costume history defined by distinct epochs.

Historical

With aviator cap, leather jacket, scarf, and high-waisted trousers, I was Amelia Earhart.

Pop

It was easy to become Cameron Frye from *Ferris Bueller's Day Off* by wearing a Devil's jersey, penny loafers, and a bowl-cut wig.

Macabre

With a flesh-colored bodysuit I just happened to have lying around, the contents of my Jug o' Blood spattered liberally over it, and a wire hanger looped around my neck, I was an aborted fetus.

Literary

As Charles Dickens's beloved Oliver Twisted, I dressed in period rags and begged, "Please, sir, I want some more anal penetration."

Then there were the couple costumes: I've been the Damsel in Distress, tied to a short stretch of train tracks that I built myself. My then-boyfriend Martin—dressed in black, twirling his sinister mustache—was the Villain. My college roommate May and I were a crime-fighting duo, the Siamese Superheroes; we wore blue tights and red trunks, and shared a cape and one shirt with two neck holes, on the front of which we printed a double S. The year before that, my college boyfriend was Popeye, and his brothers, visiting from Arthur Avenue, were Bluto and Wimpy. I was Olive Oyl and May was Swee'Pea; we put her in pigtails, bought a stroller from the Salvation Army, and filled baby bottles with whiskey. I rolled her around all night, as we passed the baby bottle back and forth.

Group or couple costumes I've found are the most fun. How wonderful to imagine we're all part of the same plot, that all our ill-considered utterances are actually dialogue. Once I was Burt Reynolds from *The Best Little Whorehouse in Texas*—May was Dolly Parton. And then another time, I was Tommy Chong to May's Cheech Marin.

Sometimes in the last minutes before a masquerade, friends will show up at my apartment, costume-less and desperate, knowing that with all the vintage clothing I've collected over the years, the bevy of old dance recital ensembles, and a hodgepodge of wigs and feather boas, my apartment is a better version of the Halloween Shop on Broadway. I can make a last-minute costume for anyone at any given moment and have. Last year, in just a few minutes, I turned Reggie into the Credible Hulk (green all over like the Incredible Hulk, but with smaller muscles so that it's believable).

This year I put off my costume planning until the last minute. First, I didn't know if I'd be invited to any parties and being all dressed up with no place to go takes on an even more desperate air when you're dressed like a bunch of grapes—easy to pull off if you attach some purple balloons to a leotard. And from experience I know that costume choice is a delicate matter, that the wrong costume could even trigger a breakdown:

You're at a party drunk; it's a few months after college graduation, and you're dressed as a giant baby. You repair to the bathroom where you stare at your reflection and then, gripping the sink with both hands, you yell, "A big unemployed baby, that's what you are! When are you going to grow up?"

I settled on Doctor Who, I'm not sure why.

A lot of people didn't get my costume right off—sometimes the better costumes don't look like costumes at all. On the street, on the way to the party, strangers called out, "Annie Hall!" "Oscar Wilde!"

"Doctor Who!" I corrected them. "I'm the Fourth Doctor played by BBC's Tom Baker from 1974 to 1981." I pointed to my hat and colorful long scarf, my curly hair, my big nose. "I roam alone through time and space."

Halloween is an opportunity to exteriorize one's desires, to explore remote curiosities, and to confront one's fears. We play at death, at gender-bending, at celebrity . . . at fictional characters and historical figures, weaving the stories that compel us into our own. What touched the lost Amelia Earhart when she met Dr. Frankenstein's monster at a party, when he confessed next to the stereo, "I have the heart of a madman and the mind of an accountant." Why did we go home together?

Our regular clothes project what we do—practice law, deliver mail, nurse the sick—while costumes project what we want, think, fear, like (the TV shows we watch every Monday, the books we read before bed, the things that make us laugh or scream). Costumes are a public display of a person's most private self, which is perhaps why donning one is by some so vehemently refused.

My ex-boyfriend hated dressing up. He didn't "want to be anything," he huffed when I asked after his Halloween costumes past. Remembering this should make it easier; obviously he was all wrong for me. But it's only easier if I believe someone else out there is right.

That's what I was thinking on the roof and then again later on the dance floor, when I saw my ex-boyfriend walk out the front door, his new girlfriend, in sexy white, two steps ahead. He was dressed as himself; I almost didn't recognize him.

I'd just finished the "Thriller" pivot where you sort of turn around on one leg with both of them bent, and was doing that terrifying squat walk with my hands pressed into my knees when he turned suddenly and found my eyes right on him. He waved. And before I could catch myself, I waved back.

I stayed to the end of the party—the Klingon had already gone, having had better luck with a Witch of Eastwick—and then decided to walk home alone. The streets were filled with monsters but I wasn't scared. I had a pocket full of candy, which I ate as I walked.

Who will you be tonight?

ENTER THE WU-TANG

I MET PHATSO IN 1997 at my college dorm's security desk on my way in from Dialects I. I'd just workshopped a monologue from *Ma Rainey's Black Bottom* to mixed reviews and was trying to decide how I felt about it when I spotted him — short, overweight, and picking something from his teeth with a near-poetic confidence, as if what he were searching for were simply the right word.

He was there to see his friend Donald, who'd introduced us at a party months earlier. Would I mind signing him in?

"Sure!" I said, a little too brightly. I had a crush on Donald.

We walked in silence to Donald's room.

Phatso knocked.

After a minute, I turned to him. "I guess he's not here."

"I like your shirt," Phatso said, staring at it.

"Thanks. I like yours, too." I was wearing a wifebeater without a bra. So was he. "I don't normally dress this way," I explained. "I'm actually conducting an experiment. See how I have this huge disgusting zit on my chin?" I pointed. "I'm hypothesizing that my not wearing a bra will draw the eye down, making this thin tank top even more effective at masking my blemish than a dab of thick concealer."

He continued staring at my chest and then redirected his gaze to my face. "You're right," he marveled. "I didn't even see it." Then he asked for my number.

• • •

Phatso loved hip-hop music, being Italian, and employing the phrase "I'm Italian," though sometimes he'd say, "I'm Sicilian," to shake things up. The fact that he'd never been to Italy or Sicily, had never met anyone who'd ever been to Italy or Sicily, and could not speak a word of Italian or Sicilian did not enter into it.

He also loved movies, specifically Italian and Sicilian ones, which is why one Saturday night — before going over to his place for one of our standard at-home dates of watching a movie, having sex, smoking pot, followed by my rapt staring as he performed a bizarre vaudevillian puppet show starring his penis and an E.T. doll — I rented a few of my favorite Italian films: *Cinema Paradiso, Seven Beauties, La Strada*.

But Phatso wasn't interested in *this* kind of Italian cinema, he told me, and took off mid-screening to heat up Italian-style Hot Pockets in the microwave just next to his cardboard cutout of Robert De Niro in *Casino* — Scorsese was his favorite director, he explained.

Among his many ambitions — Phatso wanted to be a comedian, an actor, and screenwriter — he also wanted to direct movies and, instead of going to college, had moved to Manhattan to make it happen ASAP. When I met him, he was ASAPing all over the place. With his two older brothers — fatter versions of Phatso, who together owned and operated a pawnshop back in the Bronx — he'd already written, directed, and starred in his own film. The movie was called *Manners* and was all about the importance of being polite. People who didn't say "please" got whacked.

They submitted it to film festivals all over the country and to any and all prominent Sicilians they could think of. When it was accepted to a festival in Manhattan, we all got dressed up for the screening. I wore a white feather shrug, long black gloves repurposed from one of my old dancing-school costumes, and an understated diamond-encrusted evening gown. Phatso wore a fake mustache I helped him glue on, and a Hawaiian shirt, so he looked like my bookie. His brothers wore matching T-shirts that said "Get the Papers."

With us in the audience that night was almost all of Arthur Avenue, the Bronx neighborhood where Phatso grew up. Phatso's parents had bused them in, leaving only a few seats for the other filmmakers. After the screening, the thirty of us filled the lobby, chatting boisterously as we waited for the votes to be tallied. We cheered when *Manners* won the "Audience Choice" award and celebrated with a trip to Little Italy.

It was because of stuff like this, because Phatso didn't just "talk shit" but had actually gone ahead and made a "dope" movie, because Phatso was "mad talented" and his beat box was "illin'," because his drawing "skills" were "money" and his cable access show "off the chain," that Phatso was king among his friends, a pack of toughs from the streets of his hometown.

Throughout the year, members of his Bronx "crew" came into Manhattan to pay tribute, which meant their bringing him a sign they'd swiped from a Costco that read DOLLAR DAYS and sleeping for a few nights on his living room floor. Once, when Phatso's "crib" was full, I let two of his "homies" crash at my place and in the morning found my coffee table covered in graffiti. Because I couldn't make out the handwriting, I didn't know who to blame, so I blamed Phatso.

Viewing this as a teachable moment, Phatso pointed to the scribble and explained that the most illegible "tags" are regarded as the most "pimpin'."

"Like the handwriting of doctors and teachers," I said studiously.

Phatso had his hands full with my education. Being a sheltered suburbanite, I was always getting things wrong, proclaiming that I was "up for anything" when I was supposed to be "down," and saying "peace in" when I entered a room. It was from Phatso that I learned "fat" meant cool if you swapped the "f" for a "ph," and that creative spelling was a style with which all the rappers were rolling. Looking through his collection of CDs one night, I discovered a rapper named "Ludacris" and another called "Makaveli." Excited to drop my knowledge, it was then that I christened him "Phatso," owing to his illin' brand of obesity. Before that, he'd been called "Joey." "Come here, Phatso," I cooed all gangsta-like, before pulling him in close for an "off the heezy" kiss.

One weekend, when we were all on the roof belonging to the bitch of Juice (Juice's girlfriend had gone to see her parents in Scarsdale and had asked Juice to housesit), and the boys were busy "tagging" her water tower, I got in on the act, too. Grabbing a can of hot pink spray paint, I found a blank wall and drew a heart, then wrote inside of it *Iris loves Reagan*. Then I "bombed" another wall with pictures of my eponymous flower and the words *Repeal the Income Tax!* in an elegant script.

Being part of an inner-city gang was pretty exciting and, having finished my graffito, I expressed my enthusiasm by tap-dancing up and down the roof to the rhythm of Phatso's beat box, while his friends, forming a tight circle around him, one at a time, commenced their dope rhymes.

After a few minutes, I tossed my hat in, too. Time-stepping

toward them, I began, "Yo, yo, yo . . ." The other guys always began this way, I noticed. Phatso would be beat-boxing, and then
one of them would start in with the *yo-yo*s. It's like if you're a
hobo trying to hop on a moving train, you can't just jump on
the boxcar straightaway, but have to run with it awhile. "Yo, yo,
yo . . ." I went on, running alongside their boxcar, watching the
others nod their heads rhythmically, as they waited for my next
words.

"'It is an ancient Mariner, And he stoppeth one of three. "By
thy long beard and glittering eye, Now wherefore stopp'st thou
me? . . ."'"

It hadn't been my intention to recite the entire "Rime of the
Ancient Mariner," I just got nervous and, seeing the group grow
impatient, said the first thing that popped into my mind. I'd
hoped to break off into my own direction after a few lines, once
I got comfortable in the spotlight, but then it just started sounding so good that I ended up "freestyling" all seven parts.

Back at Phatso's, Gary, whom everyone called Juice—"because I'm really into fruit juice"—asked me about my rhymes.
I stopped spinning. Phatso's apartment had linoleum floors,
which made it excellent for practicing my pirouettes. "I borrowed the bulk of it from Coleridge," I confessed and, standing still, began reciting once more, "'"God save thee, ancient
Mariner! From the fiends that plague thee thus!—Why look'st
thou so?"—With my cross-bow, I shot the ALBATROSS.' Isn't
it funny how the archaic language makes the speaker sound like
he has a lisp?" I asked Juice.

High from the blunt we'd just smoked, I began talking at a
frenzied pace, telling him all about how the poem was written,

how according to his friend Wordsworth, the idea sprang from a conversation he and Coleridge had while hanging out. "So it's sort of like freestyling," I finished.

"How come you have it memorized?" Juice asked.

I jumped in the air and performed a scissor kick. "I went through a phase in high school where I read it every day. I was kind of intense back then," I said, performing an air split, high kick, a back bend, and shimmy to the ground. "I was also into Byron for a while, but the only one of his I memorized is 'When We Two Parted,' and that's not nearly as tough sounding. You know it?"

Juice shrugged.

I performed another scissor kick, this one with a midair pivot. "The mariner is cursed to wear the albatross around his neck in penance for having killed it," I went on, "like Flavor Flav has to wear that clock in penance for having killed time. The other thing is that he is cursed to keep telling his story to anyone who'll listen, which sucks because it's so long. Seven parts and something like fifty stanzas. Can you imagine?"

"You were going for a pretty long time," Juice answered.

I explained about the poem's poor reception, how the critics of his day panned it for its archaic language, which prompted Coleridge to add "a gloss," explanatory notes, in a subsequent publication ten or so years later. I went on, surprised by my rather profound grasp of English Romantic poetry. Why didn't I have this much authority back in AP English? Why was it only clicking for me just now? I could have gone on for another hour had Juice not interrupted me.

"Yo, Phat!" Juice yelled. Phatso was in the kitchen with the others, smoking Marlboros and playing a drawing game called Exquisite Corpse. "Your girl's buggin' out again."

I sat on the floor and tried to calm down. "I'm sorry for bugging, Juice," I whispered feverishly. "I just got excited. Listen, what do you think about my rapper name being 'Busta Rime of the Ancyent Marinere'? I could use the medieval spellings of 'rime,' 'ancyent,' and 'marinere' the way Coleridge does. Methinks it would be quite gangster, aye?"

Permit me my enthusiasm. A middle-class suburbanite from the North Shore of Long Island, I found their street lives fascinating. Their stories of Biggie Smalls were to me as exotic as tales of the Dutch Sinterklaas and Scandinavian Yule Goat. Like a child, I riddled them with questions about the California Tupac. "Does he have helpers?" "What's a cap?" To each they responded wearily, if patiently, first by suggesting that I "seriously, try to chill," and second by playing me an album called *Enter the Wu-Tang*.

If aloof in the beginning, Phatso's "crew" eventually warmed to me. Yes, I rolled my joints differently—borrowing skills from an origami class I'd taken in grade school, I'd developed my own technique, manipulating index cards into gargantuan animal-shaped filters—but they still pulled well, they had to admit, having successfully drawn smoke from a paper elephant trunk. And like this, one joint at a time, they softened. Gangsta by gangsta, they exhaled and said, "Y'a'ight."

Then I found out they were all graduates of the Wathen School, an elite preparatory academy in Riverdale, that their parents were dentists, lawyers, and the occasional financier, and that each was now enrolled at various private colleges in and around Boston. Their knowledge of the street had come from watching *Yo! MTV Raps*; their baggy pants, gifts for Christmas and Chanukah; and their stories of Biggie, gleaned from the album's liner notes. Having gone to public school, I had more street cred than all of them.

They were beyond excited when they discovered my low birth and asked, with real curiosity, if public school was anything like what they'd seen in the movies, if I knew any black people, and what it was like to be the daughter of immigrants.

Yes, my family spoke English at home. "No, only my mother is from Greece; my father was born here in New York." "I don't know," I went on fielding their questions, "if not having alumni in the family negatively affected my college applications." And then, before I went any further, I suggested they all calm down "and share of my chill pills." I opened a pack of Smarties and extended my hand.

Though Phatso had also gone to the Wathen School, unlike his friends who hailed from the tony Riverdale section of the Bronx, Phatso was from Arthur Avenue, an area known as the Bronx's "Little Italy" and the setting of Robert De Niro's mob movie, *A Bronx Tale.* "My fatha's a hustler," Phatso told my parents over coffee the first and only time they met.

Phatso's father hustled "surplus" out of a parking lot on 187th Street, which was nice for us, because whenever Phatso's mom visited, she'd bring leftover inventory from his father's store. One time she brought five pairs of discontinued Nikes and a giant box of Mexican jumping beans — the beans hadn't sold well. After she left, we emptied the box onto the kitchen floor and spent the rest of the day smoking pot and watching the beans jump quietly all around us.

"He sells sneakers, wallets, live chickens, basically whatever he can get his hands on," Phatso told my parents.

My mother blew on her coffee.

Sensing their disapproval, he added, "Mista Smyles, it's like dis: I'm in love wit' yaw dawta," which, of course, only made things worse. Trying to ameliorate the tension, I reminded my parents that I was dating a preppie, that, unlike me, Phatso had gone to private school.

After seeing all the trouble Phatso's older brothers had gotten into in the neighborhood, his parents had decided to send Phatso to Wathen. Though, if private school solved some problems, it introduced others. When Phatso struggled academically, his parents were encouraged to hire a tutor. And when Phatso's laziness was attributed to learning disabilities, they were encouraged to hire a doctor. To treat his attention deficit disorder, Phatso was prescribed a battery of medications, the last of which was Ritalin, which he was still receiving in the first months of our relationship.

We'd grind up the pills with a spoon, snort the white powder through a dollar bill off a hand-held mirror, and pretend we were Colombian drug lords. We'd yell at each other for hours in badly accented English. "Oh, no ju don't!" I'd scream when he failed to pass me the joint fast enough. When we tired of that, Phatso would move to the couch, where he'd throw pinches of salt at me in lieu of confetti, as I danced and sang Paula Abdul songs in the foreign accent I couldn't shake, having been born and raised in the Democratic Republic of Foreignia. "It's a small socialist dictatorship off the coast of Cuuuuuva!" I'd yell, out of breath, shaking my hips ecstatically. I'd go on dancing and explaining to him about my lonely childhood at the city orphanage where I grew up (having been secreted away following the assassination of my entire family, Foreignian royalty who'd perished in the peasant rebellion of 1978), where my only comfort had come from a single Paula Abdul cassette, which I'd played repeatedly until it warped. "Straight up, now tell me, is going to be you and me forever, oh, oh, oh . . ."

Phatso had been doing well at the Wathen School until his sophomore year, when a scandal broke around his tutor, who, it was discovered, had been writing all of his papers.

"The kid got the job done," his father told the headmaster, underlining the fact of Phatso's recent spate of As. "What's it matta' how?"

Expelled, Phatso moved to Manhattan and got a job in TV.

It happened like this: For the last year, Phatso had been coming into Manhattan every weekend to tape a public access show with his red-headed friend Allen, a Wathen classmate whose parents had recently divorced. Turning the custody battle to his advantage, Allen had agreed to move in with his father only on the condition that he'd have his own spa bathroom. There, the boys created *Pre-party with Allen and His Fat Friend*, a talk show taped "Live from Allen's bathroom!" in which Allen took bubble baths and interviewed his various toys and pets—a life-size Chewbacca doll and his mother's dog Mittens—while Phatso sat on the adjacent toilet reading magazines, laughing, and adding occasional comments like a junior Ed McMahon. As the show went on, Allen would wash his hair and apply a rejuvenating mask. Then, toward the end of each episode, Allen and Phatso would appear in terry cloth bathrobes and matching towel turbans, side by side before white marble his and her sinks. Like that, they'd introduce the final segment: a five-minute documentary Phatso had made during the week, featuring man-on-the-street conversations he'd conducted with the odd characters who hung around his father's "store."

Airing after midnight on Manhattan's public access channel, *Pre-party* quickly developed an underground following. With a vocal fan base of downtown scenesters that included Andrew McCarthy, Steve Guttenberg's brother-in-law, and the rapper Ice-T, news of the show soon reached executives at FOX, where the boys, two weeks after Phatso's expulsion, were offered a six-episode contract. Still taped in Allen's bathroom, instead of toys and pets, Allen now interviewed celebrities, while Phatso, leaving his neighborhood behind, began reporting live from exclusive events — concerts, video game festivals, movie premieres, and award shows all over the country.

Pre-party was a dream come true — one episode gathered the entire Wu-Tang Clan into Allen's bathroom; they brushed their teeth and trimmed their beards as they chatted with the boys about school supplies and bitches — that lasted three months. Despite its ardent following, like so many cult hits before it, the show was canceled, leaving Phatso adrift in Manhattan at seventeen.

I met Phatso a year and a half later and knew nothing of his brush with fame, nor the source of his confidence, which was as perplexing to me as it was attractive. While most persons his age, or any, are deeply self-conscious of their flaws, Phatso carried himself almost regally, as if to say with every gesture that he had a very good reason for being overweight, which was simply that he deserved more space than everyone else. And then, if there were boys more handsome (and there were — Donald from the dormitory), none were more fun. Whether lining his building staircase with pillows for us to slide down or wearing disguises to eat at the diner across from his apartment, Phatso and I always had a great time.

We laughed a lot.

Until we began to argue.

About stupid things. Like his refusal to believe that America had been settled by Europeans.

Because his tutor had been doing his schoolwork for so long, Phatso was startlingly uneducated, and his ignorance coupled with his confidence began to irritate me more and more.

"That's why it's called *New* York!" I screamed, red-eyed and frustrated, angry because he was ruining my high, "because there is an *old* York in England!"

"You think I'm dumb enough to believe that!" he yelled back, before taking a large swallow directly from a liter of Coca-Cola and burping the words "You're wrong."

"*New* Amsterdam—Amsterdam, *New* Orleans—Orleans," I went on, trying to prove my point, while he lay on the couch shaking his head stubbornly.

We dated for a hazy pot-infused year and a half. Or was it two? Our relationship ended around the same time mine did with weed. As the billowing clouds of marijuana smoke cleared, so, too, did my love for Phatso. After, we remained friendly. And I continued to smoke pot every now and then, too. But never again would I look at him or to the smoke with such wonder.

It would be a little while before I fell in love again and so, on lonely nights, I'd pick up a bottle of whiskey and pack up my collection of Slime—from the A&P nearby, I'd amassed multiple colors and kept them in their original plastic 25-cent globes

—and head over to his place. We'd joke around much as we had before and, much like before, he'd eventually start to chase me, pleading with me to relent and just have sex with him, though now, instead of ending up in his bed beneath him, I'd end up outside his apartment door alone, buttoning my coat in preparation for the walk home.

The trouble with us is that we stayed young too long.

— DOROTHY PARKER

ADVENTURES WITH
MY PARENTS

The Liquor Store

I ARRIVE BY TRAIN for a weekend in Long Island. My father pulls the car up, and I duck in from the rain. "We need to stop at the liquor store," he says. "If I forget, your mom will kill me."

We take Straight Path to Deer Park Avenue, where there's a big Crazy Billy's flanking the street. "Are Crazy Billy and Crazy Eddie related?" I ask.

"That's a good question, Iris." He thinks for a moment. The signal light clicks. "No."

We run through the parking lot, splashing through the puddles.

Crazy Billy's is huge with row upon row of every variety of booze: shots in test tubes, plastic rifles filled with rum, and chocolate scotch-filled bottles decorating the checkout counter.

My father immediately attends to the mission. Pausing in the entryway, he pulls a slip of paper from his pocket, dons his glasses, and brings the sheet toward him, then away again. Toward. Then away. Then he takes out a second pair of glasses, putting those on top of the first. My father layers glasses the way WASPs do sweaters. Prescriptions are a wasteful extravagance when you can buy a whole stack of readers at Wal-Mart and apply as needed. "Here we are," he says, finally able to make out his writing. He reads out the name of a fine $5.99 chardonnay, and an employee overhears him.

"Right over here, sir."

"Good, good," my father says, heading straight to the bottles. He looks them over carefully and engineers a plan. "All right, Iris. Let's tank up!"

He gathers five or six bottles in his arms, as many as he can hold—my father's not a big drinker but likes to buy booze the way he does spectacles—then puts them back down, deciding there must be a better way. He calls to the lady who helped us, "I need two cases."

Saturday Morning

"Mom! Mom!" my father yells. "Where did you hide my glasses?"

"How do I know where you left your glasses," she says in her Greek accent, which, because of its staccato, sounds always a bit menacing. "They're probably in the bathroom with your *Scientific American*."

"They're not. I checked. You did something with them!"

"Go look now! I'm cooking."

He disappears and returns a moment later, shaking his head. "No, these are my broken glasses!" he says, holding up the one-armed pair.

Mom brings a knife down on an onion.

"That's okay, I can fix it," he mumbles, looking from the broken pair to the trees beyond the kitchen window.

He puts on his shoes and goes out.

An hour later he comes through the kitchen door, walks over

to his desk, and rummages through a drawer. He pulls out a laser pointer, a handful of finger puppets, a pair of X-ray glasses, a rubber pencil, and some string left over from a box of cannolis —"Jackpot!" he says, holding up the string.

After twenty minutes, he puts his glasses back on. "There," he says, having used the string to fasten a twig in place of the missing arm. "Hey, Mom," he says. "Check it out!"

Knife suspended, she looks up. "You look ridiculous."

"I think it's cool."

He smiles and holds his *Scientific American* at a distance so as to demonstrate the utility of his work.

The Supermarket

My father pushes a shopping cart through the narrow isthmus of the produce section, his focus fixed on the list's next vegetable. In hot pursuit of red onions, he steps blindly in front of an elderly man several years his junior.

Rattled, the man looks up from a bottle of discount Metamucil. "Hey, what are you doing? Watch where you're going!" the man scolds.

My father regards him coolly as other seniors, tomatoes and squash in hand, turn from their carts to see the altercation.

"Calm down, Grandpa!" my dad says, laughing at his own zinger. My mom, pretending not to know him, watches from the other side of the aisle. "Crazy old men," she says to the woman next to her, before covertly motioning toward my father to meet her in the parking lot.

Jericho Turnpike

"Look out!"

"Look out for what?" my father says, jerking the wheel aimlessly.

"There, there. Red light!" my mother yells.

"You're gonna get us killed! I thought I was gonna hit a deer or something!"

Two minutes later:

"Stop! Stop! Stop!" my mother screams.

Without stopping, my dad narrows his focus on the road. Eventually he pulls over, turns to my mother, and says, "What's up, Mom?"

"We missed the entrance," my mother says, exasperated. "Why didn't you stop? Didn't you hear me yelling 'Stop'?"

"I thought you were yelling 'Pop,'" he says calmly.

"Why would I be yelling 'Pop'? What the hell does 'Pop' mean?"

"I don't know. That's what I was trying to figure out. I thought you'd lost it."

Ten minutes later:

"Shit! We're on the wrong side of the road!" he says, swerving.

"Huh?" my mom says, coming to from a passenger-side nap.

"It's a good thing one of us is awake!"

"Like it's my fault you can't drive!"

"You're supposed to be the navigator. I can't drive AND look at signs!"

"I don't know how I've put up with this man for forty years."

"Careful, Mom," he says, "or I'll trade you in for a thirty-five-year-old."

"Like anyone else would put up with you."

"Don't make me come up there!" I say from the back seat.

Saturday Afternoon

I appear in the living room, where my dad's watching TV with his eyes closed. Like Cassandra, I announce, "We're out of Whoopee Cushions."

My dad opens one eye. "Impossible!" He picks up the remote and shuts off the TV. "Let's get the finder!" he says, meaning my mom.

We repair to the kitchen, where my mom's listening to talk radio and cleaning a large roasting pot. She bangs it back and forth in the sink.

"Iris says we're out of Whoopee Cushions."

"What?" she yells, over her percussion.

My father turns down the radio and repeats, "Iris says we're out of Whoopee Cushions."

"Impossible!" She drops the pot with a loud bang, wipes her hands on a dishrag and, wordlessly, leads us into the office/laundry room, where she opens a large filing cabinet labeled "Taxes."

"Your mother's amazing," my father marvels. "She can find anything!"

Stopping on one of the folders, she reaches in and pulls out a brand-new Whoopee Cushion, still powdery in its bag. "Last one," she says, handing it to me.

I unwrap it, inflate it, and disappear into the basement.

The Basement

The TV's on and my older brothers are lying on the couch. Teddy, supine with his hands in his pants, is engrossed in an episode of *Star Trek,* while Alistair is seemingly asleep, though I know what he's doing — "reclaim[ing] a third of [his] life for Learning, Personal Development, and Self-Improvement."

In high school, Alistair bought a series of cassettes called *Learn While You Sleep.* By accessing his subconscious directly, they promised to improve his memory by up to 75 percent. "Suppose you could attain the knowledge you need and want without having to study for hours," it said on the box, above a picture of a man sleeping, his cranium translucent, his brain glowing blue and green. "With our proven sleep-learning techniques, you'll wake up refreshed AND smarter!" Once he got the tapes, his thirst for knowledge became unquenchable, and no one, not even my parents, could keep him from a nap.

I lie down beneath the Abdominizer — a device my dad bought when he couldn't sleep — and position the Whoopee Cushion beneath me. I set it off as I do a sit-up and look. Neither of them reacts.

I watch Captain Kirk perspire as he surveys the grounds of an alien planet, trying to ascertain if its inhabitants will be friendly.

"Alistair! Alistair!"

Alistair opens his eyes, then closes them again.

I stand up and start explaining the rules of Awakenings to him. The game's based on the movie with Robin Williams and Robert De Niro, which is based on the book by Oliver Sacks, which is based on real people who fell victim to a plague of "sleeping sickness" just before the Great Depression. In the movie, there's a scene where Dr. Sacks, played by Robin Williams, throws baseballs at his patients, who've been catatonic for decades and discovers that they are all really good at baseball. Though their faces and bodies don't change at all, when the balls come whizzing toward them, their hands shoot up, and they catch them with miraculous dexterity.

I take Alistair's socks, which he's discarded by the side of the couch, and roll them into a ball. Then I go to the other side of the room and take aim. A sock hits him in the face.

"What the fuck, Iris!" he says, blinking.

"It was an accident! I thought you were awake!" I squeal, and beat it back up the stairs.

Reappearing in the living room, I find my dad watching a program on suspension bridges, and my mom standing nearby, telling him to turn off the TV and cut the meat.

"Just a minute."

We stare at the TV in silence.

". . . Most people don't realize that the horizontal cables on the Brooklyn Bridge serve no physical purpose, but are merely decorative . . ."

"When's dinner?" I interrupt, raising a hand capped by five finger puppets. "The beasts are getting hungry," I announce, motioning toward my hand.

"I'm waiting for your dad to cut the meat," my mom says irritably.

"The show's almost over. My god, you have no patience!"

With my free hand I struggle to keep the snarling, snapping monsters from devouring me. "Back, beasts! Back!"

Coffee

"Oh, these kids," my mother says, looking at my two older brothers and me — bald, balder, and hung-over; ages thirty-one, thirty, and twenty-five, respectively. "Are we ever gonna see any grandchildren?" She shakes her head and blows on her coffee.

"I was thinking I might sponsor a child," Alistair says, yawning, referring to the TV infomercial his unconscious, blue-green brain accidentally absorbed earlier.

"We've given up on you two," my father says, motioning to the sloppy pair next to me. "You're our last hope, Iris."

"I could get knocked up, no problem. I mean, I wasn't planning on going out tonight, but if that's what it'll take to finally make you proud of me . . ."

"Oh, now, don't joke like that," my mom says. "First you need to get married." She takes a sip. "You're too picky," she says, looking at the three of us, slack-jawed and bleary-eyed from hours of VH1's *I Love the '80s* or, in Teddy's case, C-SPAN marathons in the basement. "No one is ever good enough for you!"

"I'm a Twixter," Alistair offers sprightly, as an all-purpose explanation for the twelfth time that day. Last week he napped in front of an episode of 20/20 that described "a new generation."

"You are not! *I'm* a Twixter. You're a Gen Xer," I shoot back, restarting our argument from lunch. I saw the same episode.

"You're wrong," Teddy says, lifting his eyes briefly. "You're both idiots."

"Anyway, you need to hurry, Iris. You don't have forever."

My dad reaches for Teddy's cannoli.

"Hey, what are you doing?" he yells, roused from his cup. "You already had two!"

"Tax," my father explains.

"You can't keep any food near him," Teddy complains. "It's like the event horizon; if anything gets within a certain proximity, he just sucks it up like a black hole!"

"God, you're so mean to your old man. You know I'm not gonna be around forever."

"Here," my mother says, offering Teddy her pastry. "Have this one."

The Fourth Dimension

"Is it cold in here?" my father asks before layering on a fourth pair of glasses.

Teddy sits beside him and draws a diagram of the sixth dimension—a fold.

"Can you stop breathing like that?" Alistair snaps from his end of the table. He's cranky, having just woken up from a particularly challenging nap—"I'm mastering string theory."

"Look," Teddy says to my father. "Since the ten dimensions are layered on top of each other, if we could travel through the sixth dimension, we could theoretically travel through time."

"Quick question," I interject. "Which is more realistic: *Back to the Future* or *The Terminator*?"

"Neither."

"I mean, in *Back to the Future,* Marty is forbidden from changing the past for fear of altering the future and thus upsetting the space-time continuum. Time travel in *Back to the Future* is treated as unnatural. In *Terminator* though, John Connor's best friend in the future is sent back in time expressly to change the past, and during this time he impregnates John Connor's mother with John Connor, making him his best friend's dad, implying that time travel is actually a natural part of human evolution."

"That's interesting," my dad says.

"Like *Planet of the Apes!*" Alistair adds. "Is Dr. Zira hot for an ape? I've seen the movie a zillion times, and I still can't tell."

"'Take your stinking paws off me, you damned dirty ape,'" I say, in my best Charlton Heston.

"'The question is not so much where we are, as when we are,'" Alistair answers.

"Do you mind holding off on your stupidity so I can finish explaining the ten dimensions to Dad?"

I shrug, collect my cold cup of coffee, and drift over to Mom, who's chopping vegetables on the kitchen island.

I lean down and rest my chin in my hands.

"Anything wrong?" she asks.

"I was thinking, maybe it's time to take down that picture of Ezbon." I motion toward the refrigerator, where there is an eight-by-ten photo of my ex-boyfriend's dog.

"But he's so cute!" my mother says.

"You can tell he sees a squirrel!" Alistair calls out. He took the photo himself and developed it in three alternate sizes on his Epson.

"But if it bothers you, sweetie . . ." my mom trails off.

"It's just—" I feel my voice start to shake.

"What, now you hate dogs, Iris?" Teddy breaks in. "What kind of horrible person hates dogs?!" he says, looking around to gather our parents' agreement. "And she's your favorite!"

"We love all you kids equally," my father says automatically.

"'Some apes, it seems, are more equal than others,'" Alistair interjects, raising an eyebrow, before opening a fun-size Snickers bar and arranging it beside two others on a Smurf-themed birthday party plate.

My mom goes to the refrigerator and untacks the photo from the Botero magnet I gave her last year on Mother's Day—a fat woman in a negligee, lying in bed eating a piece of cake. She puts it in a drawer. In its place, she hangs a photo of Ronald Reagan on his ranch. The sun is setting in the background as Reagan, in a cowboy shirt, stares off into the distance.

"You can't perceive the upper dimensions from the lower dimensions," Teddy goes on. I open a cabinet, count five glasses, and start setting the table.

Dinner

Alistair is on the verge of purchasing a new apartment.

"Of course, it doesn't have a dishwasher," my mother says, serving the mashed potatoes. "But you can put one in."

"Yeah, Alistair," I say, thinking of the mess awaiting me at home. "You'll definitely need a dishwasher."

"Or you can just get married," my father adds thoughtfully.

"Women are even better than machines." My father begins a retching sound from the back of his throat and pulls out a bay leaf. "Your mother's trying to kill me," he announces.

Dessert

I finish reading aloud from *Speaking My Mind: Selected Speeches* by Ronald Reagan, my last Father's Day gift, and my mother calls my brothers into the kitchen for dessert.

"My hands are warm. Can I put them in your ice cream?" Alistair says, reaching toward my bowl.

"Quit it!"

"Just for a second!"

"Quit it!"

"Oh, these kids," my mom sighs. "When are they going to grow up?"

Before my brother has a chance to explain again that he's a Twixter, the phone rings.

We all look at each other, frightened by the possibility of it being any number of our insane relatives. According to my father, "Insanity doesn't run in our family; it gallops."

"Should I answer it?" my mother asks.

My father waves her away. "Let the machine get it."

The ringing stops. A short silence. Then a long beep. "Theodore, happy birthday!" says my great-aunt Agnes.

"No shit!" my father says. "Is today my birthday?"

The rest of us shrug.

"Wow," I say. "Happy birthday, Dad. How old are you?"

"Uh, let me see . . . sixty-nine, I think."

"Weren't you sixty-nine last year?"

"No, I think I was sixty-eight," he says, furrowing his brow. "Get the calculator!"

My mom's already picked up the phone. "Theodore, Agnes wants to talk to you," she says, handing him the phone.

"When I think about it," Alistair says to himself, "I've never NOT been tired."

"Shhhhh," my mother whispers. "Your dad's on the phone."

My brothers and I retreat into the living room.

After ten minutes my father walks in to find Teddy lying lazily before the TV—a rerun of *Doctor Who* in black-and-white—and me playing with a Whoopee Cushion, squeezing it lightly beside Alistair's ear while he tries to nap. I apologize after each sound effect. "Sorry." Squeeze. "Oooh, sorry." Squeeze. "Did I do that?" Squeeze. "Must have been something I ate." "Sorry!" "Sorry!" Alistair swats me away without opening his eyes. I pause, wait for him to nod off again, then bring it back to his ear and gently squeeze. "No apologies." Squeeze. "Never say die." Squeeze—I look up.

"I can't believe it," my dad says, interrupting my symphony. He walks in front of the TV to get our attention. Alistair sits up.

"It turns out I'm only sixty-seven." He puffs his chest proudly. "Agnes did the math!"

"Isn't that something," my mother says, rushing to his side. She gives him a kiss on the cheek, then pats down the unruly gray wisps that make up his hair. She smiles. "And for two years now, you thought you were sixty-nine!"

HANDSOMELY CLOTH-BOUND FOR LIFETIME USE

The Big Book of Mold

Carnivorous Plants—How to Feed, Care for, and Cultivate Our Meat-Eating Friends

Felony: Make Money by Planning and Executing Large-Scale Crimes

Crafting with Cannoli Box String

Life Stories of the Great Motivational Speakers

40 Hangover Remedies

Acupuncture

Titans of Mail Order

Syphilitic Visions: From Nietzsche to Isak Dinesen—the Art, Philosophy, and Literature of History's Great Syphilitics

Become a Social Medium: Learn E-mail, Facebook, Blogging, and Twitter

Etiquette for Convicts: Getting Along in Medium Security Prison

The History of Soup

Multitasking: Learn to Write, Read, Listen to Music, Hold a Conversation, Masturbate, Have Sex, Prepare Dinner, and Meditate ALL AT THE SAME TIME

Prognostication and Procrastination

Curses and Casseroles: Revenge and the History of the Single-Dish Dinner

The Dark Truth About Mensa

10,000 Sconces

The Big Book of Sexual Disorders

Understanding Left-Handed People

Help! My Daughter's a Communist!!

Dressed to Kill: Time-Tested Fashion and Beauty Advice from 20 Serial Murderers on Death Row

Clinical Trial Disasters: Medical Research That Went Horribly Wrong

Guarding Against Spontaneous Human Combustion

Encyclopedia of Chins

The Moon Landing and Other Conspiracies

Prevent Masturbation

The Art of Social Climbing: History's Greatest Kiss-Asses, from Plato to Boswell to Kato

How to Quit Tobacco

Relax or Else! A Guide to Forcible Meditation

The Complete Book of Colds

More Colds

I whispered, "I am too young,"
And then, "I am old enough";
Wherefore I threw a penny
To find out if I might love.

— W. B. YEATS, "Brown Penny"

THE MOON AND THE STARS

I WAS IN GREECE for the summer and telling my Greek boy-friend Nicos about my exciting life back in New York, about Epstein my guard-plant and Herbert my stuffed animal—a medium-size golden Labrador my friend Reggie won for me in Coney Island.

"Reggie won Herbert in a shooting gallery. I'd been carrying him under my arm awhile when Reggie fetched me a plastic bag from one of the boardwalk shops to lessen my load. Then Reggie was telling me something or other, but I couldn't focus on what he was saying. All I could think about was how Herbert might not be able to breathe inside the bag. You're not supposed to put someone's head in a plastic bag! I tried to suppress the thought, knowing intellectually that stuffed animals don't require oxygen, but couldn't shake the idea and, after a few minutes, started to gasp in sympathy, like when you watch an underwater scene in a movie and unconsciously hold your breath.

"So, after a few minutes, I took Herbert out of the bag, apologized to him profusely, and spent the rest of the day feeling bad about what I'd done. Reggie tried to console me; he even bought me a beer at one of the boardwalk cafés. But I was beyond consolation, and it took five more beers and a couple of shots of whiskey before I started to feel even a little bit better. Reggie said I was being ridiculous. 'Think about it from his perspective,' I said. 'It's a stuffed animal!' Reggie reminded me. 'With a name!' I reminded him. 'How would you feel if someone put you in a plastic bag?' When I got home, I sat Herbert by the window in my apartment so he could look out. He's been with me ever since. I don't know what I'll do when he gets old. How can you throw something out when it has a face and a name?

"Coming here for the month, I worried about leaving Herbert and Epstein alone for so long. I arranged for Reggie to stop by once a week to water Epstein and say hello to Herbert, but still. On the flight over, it was hard to shake the idea of their succumbing to loneliness."

Nicos exhaled a long plume of smoke and passed me the joint. It was about midnight and we were alone at the beach. "You think too much," he said.

"People tell me that all the time. I've been thinking a lot about it." I took a hit and handed the joint back. I looked out over my knees at the dark sea, calm and shining under the moonlight.

"Look," he said, pointing to the light of the moon reflected on the water, a rippling line that began on the horizon and ended where we sat. "Why do you think the moon chose us?" he asked, and then motioned to another couple farther down the beach — "And not them?"

"Do you think they're having the same conversation over there?"

"You mean, are they saying, 'Why did the moon choose them'" — he smiled — "'and not us?'"

"Maybe the moon is a slut, Nicos, and she goes with everyone," I said, adopting the Greek style of assigning gender to objects. We'd talked about this earlier — "Why is a table masculine and a chair feminine?" I'd asked. "Why am I a man and you a woman?" he answered.

"Impossible," he said definitively. "The moon is a man."

"Well, what if the moon is a cad, then?"

"The moon is not a cad, Iris!" he said, taking me in his arms. "The moon loves us," he said, and kissed me.

It was August and I had been dating Nicos for nearly a month. I was living in my family's summer home at the edge of a small coastal village where I've spent most of my summers growing up. Though I already knew most everyone in town, Nicos I'd only just met, as he'd spent his previous summers elsewhere, careful to avoid inveiglement in his parents' business, a colony of rooms for rent at the edge of town.

It was at a seaside café owned by our mutual friend Dimitri where we finally met; we were sitting together at Dimitri's table, talking to Dimitri, but not each other. Dimitri had just taken off to greet some new customers when I addressed Nicos for the first time. "What happened to your shoes?" I asked.

"I don't like," he said, rubbing his bare feet together. "Is summer," he explained, then looked out at the sea, as if it had taken them.

He wore round John Lennon–style glasses, had dark eyes and long, thick, dark curly hair with a single dreadlock playing among the strands, which he usually wore pulled back into a low ponytail. He was tall, handsome, and remote. I asked him another question.

He told me about his studies, how he'd spent the last few winters in Germany, where he was studying accounting, though he wasn't sure anymore if he wanted to be an accountant. He said he was tired from work, managing the rooms his parents owned, that this summer he never had time for himself, but when he did, he took long walks. "Yes," I said, "I think I saw you yesterday afternoon near my house. I was on a hammock when you walked by. You must say hello the next time you pass."

Twenty-four to my twenty-six, Nicos liked classic rock and tying friendship bracelets from string, one of which he gave to me the day after we met. I was napping again in the hammock my father had tied between two poplars, and when I woke up I found a heavy stone, around which was tied a blue-and-green bracelet. He didn't want to wake me, he said when I saw him in the village later that night; I looked so peaceful.

He had a tattoo on each of his calves. On one was a skull lit from within by flames, and on the other, an angel in medieval armor who looked just like him—dark eyes; long, thick, dark curly hair; a square jaw—sat with his arms folded and his head tilted meditatively. Two large wings sprung up behind him. He said the tattoos were for balance. He said it was coincidental that the angel in any way resembled him, suggesting perhaps that that's just what angels look like—him.

He rolled his own cigarettes and kept the tobacco and papers in a fanny pack, which he slung over his arm or across his chest like a purse, a style that, on him, seemed very manly. He had a manly swagger, was proud of being Greek, and was, despite his hippie affectations, deeply old-fashioned. He believed women should be free with their bodies; they should go topless and have sex and get tattoos, but they should also do the dishes and laundry and only care for one man. He hoped to marry someday, far down the road, someone like his mother who was good with embroidery and cooking, and friendship bracelets of course. But not yet.

The day after we met, Nicos invited me to dinner. On the

back of his motorcycle, we drove high into the mountain, to a restaurant nestled under a trellis threaded with grapevines through which we glimpsed the moon. It was quiet, more romantic than the noisy restaurants in the village down below, which were always flooded with tourists. He said hello to the proprietor, whom he knew, and nodded agreeably toward a group seated at the next table.

The wine had just arrived when someone at the next table brought out a bouzouki and began to play. When Nicos asked if my friends back home played any instruments, I said yes, "but they tend not to bring them out in restaurants. You'd get thrown out, if you did that at a restaurant there." Nicos looked confused. "Americans don't like music?" I explained that in New York, if you want music, you finish dinner, go to a club where your friend's band is playing, and pay.

Nicos frowned, at first, I thought, at me, but then he motioned to the next table, where they'd stopped playing music and had begun arguing.

"Some people," he said after a full minute of silence, "drink too much and get angry instead of happy."

Infected by his gravitas, I nodded solemnly. This manner of exchange would become for us routine. Every once in a while he'd pause, as if on the verge of some serious pronouncement. Then, knitting his brow thoughtfully, he'd say, "Sometimes . . . at night . . . I feel tired" or "Should we . . . have an ice cream?"

After each of these aphorisms, he'd look up pensively.

I'd look up, too, responding with dual solemnity. "Yes," I'd say. "I'd love some ice cream."

Nicos was still frowning when, without a word, he rose and headed for our neighbors.

"What did you say?" I asked when he returned.

"I told them to be happy. We have the moon and the stars," he said, winking at me and then at the moon, which gazed back through the vine-covered pergola.

A minute later he stood up again, disappeared inside the restaurant, and returned with a guitar he'd borrowed from the proprietor. Sitting back down, he began to play. The argument at the next table ceased, as Nicos began to sing.

"Bravo!" they applauded after he finished "Stairway to Heaven," their anger cured by Nicos' musical prescription.

"I think," he said, holding my gaze with great intensity—I leaned in eagerly—"perhaps a sweet." Then, turning toward the kitchen, he gave the nod for cantaloupe.

He drove slowly around the mountain on the way down. Holding the handlebars with his left hand, he placed the right one over mine, which were linked around his waist. He was trying to warm me, he said, feeling me cold. At last, we arrived in our village.

He parked his bike away from the bustle of cafés and suggested we sit for a while at the beach where, eventually, he kissed me.

I began to see him every day. Every morning, I'd ride my bike to the bakery at the far end of town, passing his place on the way. Usually, he'd be sitting out front looking out to sea and, waving hello, would ask me to join him for a coffee. He was living that summer in a small apartment at the front of his parents' rooms. Every summer prior, his parents had stayed there, but this year they'd decided to go on vacation. It was time, his parents had told him, that he work.

While Nicos was technically a full-time student, he was also technically heading into his sixth year. His idea, he explained when I asked him why his studies were taking so long, was to stay in Germany for as long as possible, to extend his studies indefinitely in order to avoid conscription in the Greek army. There were rumors of the laws changing soon, he said, if he could only wait it out.

In the evenings, after he'd finish pressing the sheets and preparing clean rooms for new guests, we'd drink the wine his father had made from the grapevines in the communal area out back, and then get on his motorcycle and follow a path to a deserted spot in the woods. Standing in the dark among horses, chickens, and the occasional goat, Nicos would light a joint. Passing it to me in the pitch-dark, he'd point out stars.

"There, do you know that one?"

"No," I said. "What is it?"

"I don't know," he laughed. "That's why I asked you."

Realizing we both knew nothing of astronomy, we began to make up new myths.

"That," I explained, "is Orion's used condom."

"What a dirty mind you have!" he noted, before pointing out the giant cock on the horse just next to us.

The joint finished, we'd head back, and either sit at the beach, where we'd talk more nonsense, or else drink wine in his apartment, decorated with his mother's needlepoint tapestries and the black-light posters he'd hung over them to better reflect his taste. One night we bought ice cream in town and then went back to his place to watch an old Rolling Stones concert on his small TV, the famous one with the Hells Angels that ended in murder. Another night, we listened to a mix tape he'd made of his favorite Greek folk songs. Mostly, though, we'd sit out front on the beach, where he'd play his guitar under the moonlight.

The moon, the stars, soft breezes rustling the trees, and making love in a rainstorm—these were Nicos' favorite things. And he needed to be free to appreciate them. "I need to be free," he'd say sadly, throwing pebbles into the surf, as he referred to the dreary work with which adulthood had saddled him. "I am a man! Not a machine!" he would say, and bring his fingers to a point in the middle of his chest, offering his pitiful heart by way of proof.

Should he allow his heart to mark time in this life? Was it not wrong to treat it like a clock? Nicos would go on protesting that he wasn't ready to grow up, that he was still a child, that he would always be. And I'd tell him, as if I knew better, as if I'd accepted it myself, that we all have to grow up eventually. In truth, however, I'd been making plans not to. I'd begun looking into graduate school.

Our relationship progressed quickly. Soon he was even throwing the word "love" around. He'd bring it up in the abstract, wishing to discuss it philosophically, before asking me questions like, did I think I could love him? Sometimes, he said, he thought he could love me.

Sex is a wonderful thing. It's a wonderful, miraculous thing that two people should ever choose each other at the same time. What better way to describe it than "getting lucky"? Because it feels just like that, like getting double sixes in a game of Tavli, like being struck by lightning twice. Standing out in a field, your hands raised upward in the middle of a great storm, what the hell are the chances?

We'd do it in his apartment with *The Dark Side of the Moon* emanating from his cassette player. And he would come, of course, but I wouldn't. I didn't mind really because it doesn't always happen for me. At least, I have to be in love for it to happen. But then, after I have sex with a man, love isn't a matter of if, but when. And so, eventually, I began to wonder: *When?*

The thing is, after, Nicos wouldn't do anything. He'd just roll to the side and say, "That was beautiful," assuming that because it was over for him, it was also over for me. Finally, I decided to talk to him about it. Broaching the subject delicately, in the mysterious, veiled terms he seemed most comfortable with, "Nicos," I said, in a voice philosophical, "I haven't," I continued before pausing pensively, "come yet." He seemed not to hear me.

Another time I tried posing it in the romantic/scientific manner he'd once applied to ruminations on the tide. "Some say an orgasm is like a wave washing over you. Is that what it's like for you, Nicos? You know, there are many different causes for changes in the tide. The moon pulls on the sea, which I think you said is female . . ."

"The moon is beautiful," he said, still oblivious. "In Greek, the word for moon is *To Fengári*," he continued. "Say it for me, please. You must learn Greek so you can move here and we can stay together forever."

"Yes, Nicos, I understand. You don't want me to *come* to Greece. You want me to stay and *not come*," I answered.

One night, after dinner together in town, we returned to his apartment for the usual evening's end. I had to use the bathroom and excused myself as soon as we arrived. I closed the bathroom door, ran the faucet to disguise my tinkling, and was about to lift my skirt when, there, against the clean white porcelain bowl, I saw a frozen shit cascade that ended at the bottom of the drain.

My initial feeling was revulsion. But then, realizing that this was Nicos' handiwork, my revulsion was replaced by a very particular horror: I imagined him coming in after me, him seeing what I saw, him knowing what I knew about him. I imagined his shame, his humiliation, his pain. What could I do but shield him from it?

Leaping into action, I seized upon the toilet scrubber.

The work was difficult but not rewarding; it was caked on hard and thick, having been there perhaps all day.

At last, I was finished. I flushed, washed my hands, and rushed out into the living room to kiss him and make our love.

Nicos turned from the stereo where he'd been rewinding a Creedence Clearwater Revival cassette. He embraced me. And looking into his dark eyes — innocent of the pain from which he'd been rescued — I felt a special tenderness for him. I thought: *Perhaps I could love him.* We made our way to the bed, kissed passionately and undressed.

We struggled for a while through a variety of positions before he finished and rolled to the side as always. Next to me, his breath slowing, he stared up at the ceiling where he'd hung a large tie-dyed tapestry.

At last I took his hand. Trembling with love, I steered it toward me, but when it arrived at its final destination between my legs, Nicos recoiled and said, "No, not like that. I don't like it like this. I am romantic."

"I'm romantic, too," I said. "I'd prefer a happy ending."

"You make me feel as if you want me only for pleasure," he said, and then turned away angrily, disgusted by my selfishness.

I lay there for a while, wallowing in my selfishness, as I watched a small breeze ripple the tie-dye. Eventually I stood up, retrieved my clothing from the ironing board where he did the day's pressing, and prepared for the long walk home alone, beneath the moonlight, with the trees rustling and the stars shining and the sea lapping, surrounded by all of Nicos' favorite things.

"10,000 Dreams Interpreted OR What's in a Dream?"

FINALLY, *Gustavus Hindman Miller, renowned capitalist farmer and Miller Brothers Department Store impresario of Chattanooga, Tennessee, whose gifts of discernment have long been known to friends and family, has written a catalog of dreams and their meanings organized alphabetically for convenient reference upon waking.*

10,000 Dreams Interpreted or What's in a Dream? by Gustavus Hindman Miller

YOUR UNCONSCIOUS IS TRYING TO TELL YOU SOMETHING. ARE YOU LISTENING?

FROM "WHAT'S IN A DREAM"

COCKTAIL
To drink a cocktail while dreaming denotes that you will deceive your friends as to your inclinations and enjoy the companionship of fast men and women while posing as a serious student and staid home lover.

COCA-COLA
For a woman to dream that she is drinking Coca-Cola signifies that she will lose health and a chance for marrying a wealthy man by her abandonment to material delights.

COFFEE
To dream of drinking coffee denotes the disapproval of friends toward your marriage intentions. If married, disagreements and frequent quarrels are implied.
　　To dream of dealing in coffee portends business failures. If selling, sure loss. Buying, you may with ease retain your credit.
　　For a young woman to see or handle coffee, she will be made a by-word if she is not discreet in her actions.
　　For a young woman to dream of roasting coffee, it denotes escape from evil by luckily marrying a stranger.
　　To see ground coffee foretells successful struggles with adversity. Parched coffee warns you of the evil intentions of strangers.
　　Green coffee denotes you have bold enemies who will show you no quarter, but will fight for your overthrow.

And that's just the beverages!

Don't let your unconscious go to voicemail. Pick up the phone now and order Miller's essential home reference tome.

What boots it in these miffless times—

— ELAINE DUNDY, *The Dud Avocado*

DISPATCHES FROM
MY APARTMENT

9:30 AM

I seem to be getting worse.

I examine closely the image of two large soupspoons facing away from each other. Grasping my own two spoons in my right hand, I begin again frantically, bouncing the pair madly off my bare thigh—I'm in my underwear—until I'm out of breath. Resting, I indulge in a favorite daydream:

I'm at a swank dinner party and everyone's bored stiff. Then the soup arrives and I start in with the percussion. Ten minutes pass with all eyes on me as I click the spoons on my back and knees and, why not, playfully against my head. When I'm done, everyone applauds. I wave them off, saying it's no big deal. "Really, it's not," I demur, inviting everyone to ignore me, to please start on the lovely bisque provided by our elegant hostess, to whom I mouth "thank you" before blowing a kiss. Later, after quoting Shakespeare in Pig Latin ("Otay ebay, oray otnay otay ebay?"), I juggle the roast, a linen napkin, and a small candelabra. When I sit down, a successful husband-and-wife team compliment me on the elegance of my dress.

I look down at my bare legs—the spoon blows have impressed a polka-dot pattern across my thighs. I give up practicing for the day and go to the kitchen. Holding the freezer open,

I stare into it and let the cold pour over me. I remove the lid off a tub of ice cream and plunge one of my spoons into Breyers Neapolitan. I go for strawberry, the only flavor left, a mid-ocean ridge down the middle of the container. I think of plate tectonics and consider taking a nap. Then I look at my watch and decide against it as it's not yet noon.

10:40 AM

I'm trying to change the bag in my vacuum cleaner but can't figure out how to open it. I dreamed last night that I was discussing the problem with my friend Reggie, who, after, examined it with no better luck. He tried to vacuum with it as it was and then handed it back to me, remarking, "Yeah, no suction."

All of my recent nightmares have been similarly mundane. So much so that in waking life, I find myself often confused, thinking I've accomplished certain chores, about which I've only dreamed. Ten minutes ago, for example, upon noticing the still-full hamper, I threw up my hand. "Demon laundry! Why do you haunt me?" I cried, before pulling out a pair of pants to get dressed.

It wasn't always like this. I used to have dreams of far-flung fantasy. Often after closing my eyes, a masked lover would appear at my window. Bathed in moonlight—which is a lot like the light on my Timex when I press the side dial—he'd call on me in the smallest hours of evening and, from a part in the curtains, alight soundlessly, with a graceful tumble, into the interior of my apartment. Then, kneeling at the foot of my bed, dark cape slung sinister across his shoulders, he'd ask, would I mind darning his socks?—an obvious pretext for testing my marriageability. *No!* I'd say. *No!* And then I'd darn and he'd watch—his eyes, two flames, burning through me from behind his bandit mask.

1:20 PM

Someone saying he's a cop knocks on my door and asks if I've seen or heard anything suspicious.

I say through the door, "This seems a little suspicious."

My peephole is painted shut, so I continue the conversation through the closed door, warily. Apparently, yesterday, someone was robbed in the apartment just below mine.

"See anything on the fire escape?"

"No," I yell, straining a suspecting ear toward the muffled voice, thinking, *What if he is the burglar, and this is his trick— to pose as a cop investigating the burglary he's about to perpetrate! Perhaps the burgled guy living downstairs, if there is any burgled guy living downstairs, was robbed in just this fashion, and I am next!*

Terrified, I make sure the door is double locked, but continue speaking the whole time so as not to let on that I'm wise to him. My mind is racing. *What if he tries to force his way in? He'll see what I've been doing—nothing!* Quickly, I run to the TV and turn off *Soul Train*.

He keeps calling me "ma'am," the way cops do on television. But his slick "officer" impression isn't fooling me. I don't need a peephole to see him for the common thief he is. I imagine him dressed in one of those slim, all-black outfits burglars wear in movies and Edward Gorey books. *What a cliché! And yet, there is a certain sexiness to the ensemble: formfitting, sleek, hugging his sinewy muscles, showcasing his nimble maneuvers, as he slides through narrow hallways, pilfering jewels and negotiable bonds.*

In my reverie, I've neglected to answer his last question . . . *the way they sneak around in the shadows, cat-like and mal-intentioned . . .*

Softening to this image, I decide to invite him in. Hurriedly, I clear some space on my couch, then give my cheeks a few pinches in lieu of rouge. Perhaps I'll offer him coffee, reheat a few cups from the pot I brewed this morning.

I'm about to open up when I hear him knock on the door down the hall and, quite caddishly, begin posing the very same questions he just posed to me to my neighbor! *Fiend!* I bring a hand to my heart only to find it freshly missing.

3:48 PM

This guy calls me twice, asking for Ilene. He recites my phone number back to me, asking if he's dialed incorrectly. Ilene is the girl from the bar last night whose scribbled number on a napkin he is unable to make out. I begin to ask if he wants to talk about it, but he hangs up too quickly.

I really liked the sound of his voice and think about calling him back, saying something sharp and disarming like "Is this Ilene?" before I confess charmingly that it's just me again, the girl from before, and we share a good laugh over it. I imagine the whole conversation and decide I'll say yes if he wants to take me out for pizza. But then I end up not calling, worried he might be cheap and ask me to pay for my own slice, or mock my choice of diet soda. *Jerk*. For a minute I thought he might have been the one. I wonder if I'll ever love again.

A UPS package!

3:49 PM

The package is for the tenant in the apartment downstairs. I decide I've earned a twenty-minute nap.

5:37 PM

I write a poem in French. It's very difficult because I don't speak French and have to use an English-to-French dictionary that I found a week ago at a sidewalk sale. The poem is an existential meditation on the chicken that crosses the road repeatedly but doesn't know why.

> *Le Poulet*
> *Le destin est une question.*
> *Avec deux pattes, il traverse la rue.*
> *Sa vie est une énigme.*
> *Il marche pour trouver une réponse.*
> *"Pourquoi le poulet traverse la rue?"*
> *Il marche pour échapper de son destin.*

7:35 PM

I eat dinner and then record some fluctuations I've observed in the size and mood of my breasts. I'm something of an amateur alchemist when it comes to bust enlargement. I try out different formulas and report my findings in the daybook I've decorated with the catfish stickers I got from my parents' store.

In 1998, chest expansion occurred in direct proportion to Polly-O string cheese intake. Then, in the spring of 2001, records suggest a correlation between waffle consumption and swelling. In the fall of 2002, I believed I'd uncovered growth-inducing properties in corn dogs and various carnival foods. And just now — following a brief examination in my bathroom mirror and reviewing the activities of the last two weeks — I detect a relationship between increased size and cigarettes, whiskey, coffee, chicken parmesan sandwiches from Chez Brigitte on Eleventh Street, fumes from certain varieties of paint thinner (I tried to thin my walls in hopes of enlarging my apartment last Sunday), and the occasional mint Milano.

DAYBOOK, SUNDAY, NOVEMBER 2, 2004

Size: Enormous today! Possible side effect of daily spoon exercises?

Mood: Started reading *Crime and Punishment* last week and have detected a significant shift in the attitudes of both left and right subjects. They are brooding where they were once amiable. Catching sight of them in the mirror earlier, I noticed them eyeing me antagonistically. If they could speak, they'd bark: "The chicken crosses, so that I might kill and eat him!" But they cannot speak. Yet. Instead they sit squarely against me, peevish and silent.

8:23 PM

Worried about my finances, I take to the computer and visit my bank's website to stare at my account balance. Finding I am very much broke, I decide to stay home for the rest of the week in order to save money. Bored by the thought, I start clicking on pop-up ads I usually ignore.

One thing leads to another, and soon I am hot on the trail of a free iPod Mini, with just a few minor purchases. I use my credit card to join the Tie of the Month Club and Wine of the Month Club, but think twice when it's time to purchase an outdoor barbeque set. I have no room in my apartment for it—the paint thinner didn't work. *Damn! I can't afford to lose this deal!*

I pass a half hour in front of the computer. I lose the deal. I shut the computer off and lie on my bed. When I close my eyes, pop-up ads flash before them. I open them. *What demons possess me? What am I going to do with all these ties?*

. . . you looked as if you were tipsy; you drew a couple of breaths, then out it came, and you forgot everything else in the bliss of the sensation. . . . [Sneezing] was the sort of pleasure life gave you free of charge.

— THOMAS MANN, *The Magic Mountain*,
TRANS. H. T. LOWE-PORTER

HEY, HOUDINI

I WAS ON THE COUCH trying to work my mysteries when I spotted a cat close to the ceiling, staring right at me. Another, soundlessly, jumped up beside him and began eyeing me from the penthouse level of what Kevin, an emergency room psychiatrist and the man I was dating but hadn't yet kissed, called "a cat condo."

"I'm allergic to cats," I told Kevin, who was in the next room, getting our drinks.

"Not my cats!" he called back. He walked into the room and handed me a beer.

"Thanks," I said, and then, noticing a fifth of whiskey on his kitchen counter, added, "Maybe we should have some of that whiskey to wash down the beer."

Kevin returned with two highball glasses and a pack of cigarettes.

"I have some Benadryl in the medicine cabinet if you want. For your allergies," he said, sitting down beside me.

"No, thanks," I said, swallowing a mouthful of Scotch and then cracking the beer open and sipping foam from the top. "I try to avoid over-the-counter medications. Worried too much about the liver." I made my hand into a fist and knocked on my abdomen as if my liver were a cabinet I'd built out of wood. "Anyway, I can't stay long."

I looked at my watch: 6 PM. By 7 PM I would be out the door, I'd decided on the walk over. I needed to set a firm hour of de-

parture, so as to not accidentally stay too long and with that di-
lute my carefully constructed air of mystery. I took another sip
of beer then chugged the whole can.

It was Sunday evening and our second-and-a-half date. Half
because it wasn't an official date; I was only "dropping by" to
borrow his gorilla suit. On Monday, I'd be launching my new
literary magazine (in the future, everyone will edit a magazine
for fifteen minutes) and had organized a panel of well-known
writers to speak at Strand Bookstore. My plan was for the gorilla to sit silently among them. When I told Kevin of this, he offered his gorilla suit, leftover from Halloween when he dressed
as Robin Williams. "I just wore the body suit with a tank top,
pants, and rainbow suspenders," he explained.

"Suit yourself," he said regarding the Benadryl. He picked
up the remote and turned the volume up on the TV. Side by
side, we watched a Downy commercial in complete silence. I
started to wonder if maybe I should have declined his offer of a
drink instead of asking for two, if I should have just left after he
handed me the gorilla hands and feet.

"Shoo, shoo, shoo!" Kevin yelled, interrupting my thoughts.
The orange cat had sprung onto the armrest. I started from sur-
prise. "You have to be firm with them," he said, looking at me
hard. "Anything you want to watch?" he asked, directing his attention again toward the TV.

"I like the TV Guide Channel."

"Where they list what's on all the other channels?"

"Mm-hmmm," I said, suppressing a gag from the whiskey.
"It's my favorite," I announced, as a way of suggesting, *I can't
commit to one channel, no less one man! You'll have to battle my
commitment issues if you want to have a relationship with this hot*

ticket! It was my first time playing hard to get and I was struggling. I don't actually have "commitment issues," but I've met a lot of men who do, so I figured I'd pretend to have them, the way some girls pretend to be into sports, thinking maybe we could bond over it.

I stared happily at the TV. In the screen's upper-right corner, in a small box above the scrolling channel menu, was a rerun of *American Idol*, season one. I stared awhile more, pretending this was what I had in mind.

I lit one of his cigarettes and tried to look sexy and confident as I did so. Then I realized I lit the wrong end. He reached for the box and offered me another, but I said, "It's okay," and pulled my key chain from my purse and used the nail clipper on my mini Swiss army knife to cut the singed end off the filter. I relit it daintily and exhaled a long plume upward, like a sultry French actress in *Le Dragon Magique Puff*. I asked him about work.

He told me about the patients he had seen that day in the ER, how his job was simply to talk to them and ascertain if they were actually dying or only having a panic attack, which reminded me of the bemused look on another doctor's face when I visited the ER myself a few years ago.

It was a few weeks after college graduation. I'd just gotten high with my roommate when my generalized anxiety over what to do with my life manifested in an acute physical pain in my side and the firm belief that my insides were melting. My roommate walked me to the hospital a few blocks away, where I waited for eight hours for a very sarcastic doctor to admit me. After being examined by three more doctors and a small team of med students, it was determined that I had a yeast infection. They prescribed Monistat's one-day treatment and suggested I eat more yogurt. A few weeks later, I received a bill in the mail for $700 and, since I didn't have the money, had to call my parents and tell them about the yeast infection. My father reprimanded me about my wild lifestyle and told me I needed to get over these "commitment issues."

I imagined Kevin's face on the body of that sarcastic doctor and began to hate him, which naturally increased my attraction. I inched closer.

"Panic attacks can cause physical symptoms, like a raised heartbeat and shortness of breath, which contribute to the patient's idea that he or she is dying," he went on, as if giving a lecture. "Of course, the patient is not actually dying, but it can feel very real."

"Like love!" I interjected.

"Once I've ruled out the need for urgent medical treatment, I just talk to them for a while and try to calm them down."

"What do you talk to them about?"

"I'll ask a series of mundane questions, simple stuff to help ground their imaginations and focus their attention on what's real." He swallowed a few fingers' worth of whiskey and smiled.

"I once saw an ad in the back of the *Voice* about free experimental panic disorder treatments at Columbia University and was going to go—I had my coat on and everything—before I was like, wait, they want to subject me to 'test treatments'? My heart raced at the thought, so I went back inside, sat down, and practiced my breathing a while." I looked at him. "You know, I heard this story about some clinical trials they were running at a university medical center down in Texas. After being administered a new drug, the subjects began expanding, some of them doubling and tripling in mass before exploding!"

"Medicine's a grizzly business," he said, taking my cigarette, which now had a long ash. He tapped it over the ashtray, took a drag, exhaled, and smiled at me again, which is when I asked him about the possibility of my obtaining a prescription for Xanax, Klonopin, or any other fun anxiety suppressant. He shook his head, but I knew what he meant—the way I withhold sex from a man until I have his heart, he was withholding Paxil from me until he had my body. I sexed him with my eyes.

"What do you think is causing your panic attacks?" he asked, handing me back my cigarette.

"My liver," I said. "It's all I think about. I don't take Tylenol or Advil or Benadryl anymore because I don't want to agitate it. I endure the most horrific hangovers as a result, and sometimes this causes the attack. I'll be hung-over and start to think my liver hurts and begin poking around and pressing on it."

"You can't feel your liver, you know."

"Exactly. The fact that I can feel mine is what has me worried. Also, I have trouble breathing, especially when I try to sleep. When I close my eyes, my breathing feels uneven, which makes me nervous, and then my heart starts racing, and then I can't breathe and have to get out of bed and walk around."

He took my hand in his and looked at me. "Sounds like you have it."

"Sleep apnea?" I'd Googled the symptoms earlier.

"Panic disorder," he corrected me. "Just try to remember when it happens that you're not dying, you're just crazy." He laughed and let go of my hand and turned back to the TV. "*Law & Order* is on twenty-six and thirty-eight," he said, when, out of nowhere, the black-and-white cat jumped on my lap.

"Shoo, shoo, shoo," Kevin repeated and, coming to my rescue

again, picked the cat up and threw him to the ground. The cat landed on its feet and made a graceful exit into the next room. Kevin sat down. "Sorry about that."

"Most of the time I don't think I'm dying, but it's hard to know for sure because I don't have insurance. I try to examine my own urine sometimes, but I have no idea what I'm looking for," I said, feeling suddenly despondent.

"How sad," he said, placing a hand on my shoulder. He stuck out his bottom lip in imitation of mine. "A lonely girl and her urine."

"A lot of people mind being called 'poor thing,' but not me."

"You poor thing," he said, feeling my cheek and forehead with the back of his hand.

"Do I have a fever?"

"No. But I could take your temperature just in case," he said, finding my eyes. "I could give you a checkup if you want. I *am* a licensed MD."

"Really?" I said, brightening, happy at how well the half-date was going.

"I'll get my stethoscope." And with that he disappeared into the bedroom.

"Actually," I called out to him, "I'm not sure I want you to look at my urine just yet. I mean this is only our third date." I stood up, feeling suddenly shy.

"Second and one-half," he called back.

"I can do other tests," he said, reentering the room with a stethoscope around his neck. He touched my back lightly and motioned toward the couch. "Lie down."

First he checked my heartbeat against my chest and back. Then my lungs by asking me to "just breathe normally." I gasped in and out. Then he announced he was going to percuss my liver. He began tapping my midsection, listening for sounds, and I had trouble not tensing my stomach each time. He told me I had to relax in order for him to be able to evaluate my liver. "But that's how Houdini died!" I said, thinking of the story my friend Veronica told me by the coat closet in the second grade.

It was just after a successful show during which Harry Houdini had performed one of his most famous tricks, one that required him to endure a fantastic blow to the stomach. Later that night, passing by the docks on his way home, a shadowy figure approached the famous magician and said, "Hey, Houdini!" and socked him in the stomach before he had a chance to tense up. He died of internal bleeding, his magic his undoing.

"How's my liver?" I tensed.

"Perfectly normal," he said, and disappeared into the bedroom. He returned with his reflex instruments. "I'm going to measure the response time in your knees, elbows, and wrists."

"What about my heart?"

"Testing the baroreflex requires a different tool."

I sighed.

He activated my right knee. "Rather than just sighing, I like to say 'sigh,'" he said, hitting it again. "And I like to actually pronounce the 'gh' sound. Most of the letters we leave silent were vocalized in Old English, you know. You need to lower the waistline of your pants now."

"Oh."

"I'm screening you for ovarian cysts. I'm going to press on your pelvis a little, and you tell me if you feel any discomfort when I do."

"Okay."

"I feel a special affection for the silent letters. Like the 'p' in 'psychology.'" He pronounced the "p" carefully. "That's how it's pronounced in Greek. Comes from the Greek letter 'psi,' so really it's incorrect when we Americans keep the 'p' silent. No letters should ever be kept silent," he said, looking at me. "It's terrible what people do."

"Yes."

"You're okay," he said, still kneeling.

I sat up. "What about my glands? I heard Parkinson's has to do with the happiness glands not closing properly. I read somewhere that each person has a finite amount of happiness and the danger of drugs like Ecstasy is that it floods your system with them instead of rationing them out over time. It's like a binge and then you have none left."

He made circles with his fingers behind my ears. "Your glands are fine," he said, gazing professionally past my face, just over my head, before shifting his eyes to meet mine. I smiled. "Don't smile so much," he said. "You'll waste all your happiness." He glanced quickly at my whole face before he straightened up and sat again at a polite distance.

"You're in perfect health!"

"Thank you," I said, both relieved and a little sad that the exam was over. "Aren't there any other tests you can administer?"

He paused. "I *could* screen you for breast cancer."

I thought for a moment. "My health *is* important to me." I looked at him. "Shall I lay back down or sit up for this?"

"You can stay sitting up," he said. "You'll need to remove your shirt, though."

I removed my shirt and then unclasped the back of my bra and folded everything neatly into a pile next to me.

He maintained a careful clinical eye on my chest and then blushed.

"Okay?" I asked nervously.

Applying his hands to my bare breasts, he began searching for lumps. I stared off into various ceiling corners watching his cats watch us. "Dr. Goldman usually does circles," I noted, as he pressed with two fingers in a more vertical brush-like pressure.

"You can do it either way."

"I was told once that you should never let a cat stare you down. That you should always make sure they look away first or they'll think they're your master. I always get stressed now when I look at cats." The orange cat looked at me and I looked away first. "I can't imagine dealing with that kind of power struggle on a daily basis. Do you always win with your cats?"

He sat back on the coffee table directly opposite me. "You can get dressed now," he said, looking at the ground.

"Thank you," I said, recovering my pink bra and T-shirt. I started to get dressed. "It *is* disconcerting to have no primary care physician," I said, before feeling suddenly embarrassed. What if he thought I was rushing things, that I wanted *him* to be my primary care physician? I blushed. "We probably should have made use of your paper towels during the exam. We could have wrapped them around me like a hospital gown, you know, to make it more official."

He sat down next to me, put the TV on mute, and looked at me. I looked at him and then at the TV, at Kelly Clarkson singing in the upper-right corner. Her mouth was stretched open really wide, as if she were moaning something like "help" or "love." "It's too bad you haven't any TB vaccines—"

Which is when he kissed me.

He lunged and his whole body was all at once on top of mine. I struggled to adjust myself; the remote control was stuck under my back. Noticing my discomfort, he shifted his weight onto his arms a bit. "Don't want to puncture your organs," he breathed hectically. After another minute, he re-removed my shirt and bra, and then, a few minutes after that, I started to have what I call the quarter-kiss crisis.

It's that moment after you've been kissing awhile when you start to think, *What now, what next, where is this going,* and you begin second-guessing your decision to have majored in English in college as opposed to something more practical like computer science, before becoming angry at the whole university system in general, its exorbitant prices and the fact that no one bothered to prepare you for the real world—it wasn't your fault you didn't know what to do when you graduated, that you still don't know what to do now. And you consider enrolling in secretarial school, some place nice and old-fashioned where you can learn to type forty words per minute on a typewriter while wearing white gloves, and then wonder if you wouldn't have been better off being born in another time, in another place, and then decide you might have wondered the very same thing then, too, and that it's not the year that's the problem, but you. I struggled to push these feelings aside and began kissing him more aggressively while also scratching an itch on my neck.

Kevin kissed away, oblivious to my career uncertainty, so bewitched was he by my mysteries, I suppose, or perhaps he was undergoing his own quarter-kiss crisis and was wondering if he should have majored in linguistics like he'd wanted to despite his parents' admonitions.

After another minute, I started to feel altogether too comfortable, which began to worry me further. *Only the dead are truly comfortable.* And so, with my left hand, I fished around on the floor for the remote I'd removed and tried to put it back where it had been—wedged between my lower back and the seat cushions—as a symbolic gesture, as a way of saying yes to life.

My heart was racing from the excitement of our first kiss and all its philosophical ramifications, and for a second I thought I might be having a panic attack. I considered asking Kevin to take my pulse, but decided against it for fear it would ruin the mood. Instead, I just let him kiss me and tried to breathe more evenly through my nose.

I arched my back so that my breasts brushed against him. His chest hair tickled wonderfully at first, but then it just started to itch, so I writhed against him more as an alternative to scratching. At last I managed to get my hand up between us to scratch my left breast. I gave a quick scratch to my right one too while I was there, and then higher on my chest, and then on my neck, and then on my shoulder . . .

"Oh, god, I'm so itchy!" I said finally, breaking away. "I can't stand it!"

He moved off to give me some air.

"You've broken out in hives," he said calmly, retrieving his glasses from the side table. He gave a good look at my neck and chest, while I went on scratching.

"What?" I scrambled to my feet and ran into the bathroom. "Usually this doesn't happen until after I've committed the love act!"

It's true. I turn phosphorescent during orgasm. I'm a lot like a poisonous jellyfish that way; my skin glows red and purple in spots, but only during the agitation, ex-boyfriends have told me. I return to my natural color immediately after.

I looked in the mirror. "Oh, god," I said, seeing myself red and puffy. I threw an arm over my face. "I'm hideous!"

Kevin came in, took my arm from my face, and gently placed it by my side. He looked at me in the mirror. I looked at him in the mirror. There we were, a portrait in the medicine cabinet.

"It must be the cats," he said calmly, and reached for the mirror, opening it as if he were opening my chest. Our image disappeared and was replaced by an assortment of bottles, pills, creams, and pastes. He removed a narrow tube of something and closed the door. I watched his reflection squeeze the contents of the tube onto his fingertips. "Here," he said, making eye contact with my reflection, before breaking it to look at me.

He began applying the ointment to my neck, my chest, and then my arms. "Don't worry," he smiled. I closed my eyes and gave myself over to the feel of the cream, which was cool and lovely against my welts.

What hath night to do with sleep?

— JOHN MILTON, *Paradise Lost*

DENGUE FEVER

1

MY DAD CAN'T SLEEP. When the sun goes down, his worries attack, and he lies in bed, nervous and awake. At 3 AM, "the witching hour," he'll tiptoe downstairs and turn on the TV; the witching hour is also the hour of the infomercial.

I can easily assess the severity of my father's insomnia by the number of odd items he has delivered to the house each month. Greek language tapes, Moving Robots (plastic disks placed under a piece of furniture you'd like to move before *effortlessly* sliding it to its new position!), the Pasta Pot (a pot whose cover doubles as a colander!), Space Bags (store bulky sweaters in this giant ziplock and then use your vacuum cleaner to suck out the air, reducing clutter by 75 percent!), and a knife that can cut easily through a silver dollar, though why you would want to cut through a silver dollar, I don't know. Recently his late-night purchases have hewn to a theme: fitness.

I can almost see him yawning before the TV, cruising the channels, when his attention is arrested by a promise of great change. The light from the TV flickers and a hazy vision of a new him comes into focus. There he is, muscular and trim, his large belly replaced by a set of chiseled abs. "Ordinary sit-ups are uncomfortable on the back. The Ab Roller eliminates lower back discomfort once and for all, making strong, toned abs just three easy payments away!" And there he goes dialing. Only $39.99! So small a price for so grand a transformation.

Every visit home begins with my father, physically unchanged, telling me excitedly about his most recent acquisition: the Bean, the Abdominizer, the Ab Roller, the Total Gym . . . I walk in and he rushes to fetch it. "It's in the storage room," he says, already descending the basement stairs.

Minutes later he's dusting the thing off and leading me to the living room to show me how it works. This demonstration will be the last time he'll use it. He shows me his ThighMaster, and I suggest that next time he can't sleep, instead of buying something new, he just use one of the many old things he has already. "That way you'll save money AND get in shape!"

"That's not how it works, Iris," he answers simply.

Having recently experienced my own bouts of insomnia, I know what he means.

Then my mother brings out a box of cannolis, and we sit around the kitchen table for coffee. I pick up the white and red string thoughtfully. "Twine left over from a box of cannolis," I say, paraphrasing a line of Hemingway's, "many must have it."

2

Summer in the city and the night falls late. I strip down to my underwear and throw my clothes in a pile on the floor beside the bed. The pile is high with yesterday's and the days' before. But I can't clean up now. Later. Always later.

My bed takes up most of the room, with a bathroom and

closet on one side and a bank of windows, most of them cracked, along the other. In the corner, where the bed and windows nearly meet, a heating pipe runs vertically from floor to ceiling. In winter it gets horrifically hot and the pipe clangs loudly, as if on another floor someone were beating it with spoons. In front of the pipe, I've squeezed a small nightstand that holds a little library of sex manuals — for reference during moments of passion — along with a lamp, an alarm clock, and my tip jar.

The tip jar is left over from a brief stint as a coat-check girl. I made it myself, taping a slip of paper to a cylindrical glass vase that came with a bouquet of flowers sent previously to convey an apology. The flowers died, and in purple curlicued letters I wrote: "Tips!"

Not knowing what to do with it after, I installed it on my nightstand, which led to an argument with the guy I've been seeing.

"Someone else been tipping you?" Philip asked, noticing that the once-empty jar now contained fifty suspicious cents.

I'd dropped the coins in myself, hoping to inspire a conversation about our relationship. Haughtily, I replied, "I'm thinking of installing a coin-operated condom dispenser, too. A little one above the headboard might really bring the room together. Plus, a quarter here and there really adds up." I told him I was inspired by the stories of self-made millionaires, teachers and postal workers who'd amassed great fortunes by saving their change. I'd seen a show about it. The UPN network airs reruns of *Oprah* at 4 AM on weekdays, and I watch it sometimes when I can't sleep. That or a disaster movie. Stories about great and glittering promise gone awry — a glass skyscraper on fire, a state-of-the-art ship sinking. I like *The Towering Inferno* and *The Poseidon Adventure* best. Yawning before the TV, watching the characters scream, I find myself somehow soothed.

On hot nights like this one, I sleep with all the windows open. A fan, oscillating in the corner, ushers a warm breeze. I have an air conditioner, but don't use it. It's old, weak; its icy wheezing no match for the hot air leaking through the cracked windows that surround it. No match either for the restaurant ovens three floors below, burning all day, cooking the entire building.

From the street, the sound of late-night revelers echoes up —bawdy drag queens commuting from club to club, drunken frat boys spilling out of sports bars, and girls searching for love or at least a free drink, their slurred cries punctuated by clicking heels. Every twenty minutes, the M11 bus stops out front, its engine slows, its brakes screech, its doors open and close, before it takes off east. Around 5 AM, the garbage truck arrives, and before or after a fire engine roars, a police siren whirls or else bleeps quick. A concert of irritants, the night plays on. Oh, but to live in the heart of Greenwich Village! So what if the heart of the Village beats loudly.

In winter I sleep with the windows open, too, to mitigate the unchecked heat pouring out from the overactive radiators and the scalding pipe next to my bed. Last winter a man accidentally touched it. It was 4 AM —isn't it always when one's sleep is disturbed?—when he woke me requesting ice. "Stretch your arm out the window and you'll be fine. There now," I said, kissing him. "It's snowing."

In summer the windows not only bring breezes, but bugs, flies, mosquitoes, and other winged things whose names I don't know. In summer my apartment becomes an "auxiliary circle of hell," what Dante cut from his manuscript shortly before publication. Just off the second circle, where the lustful are tossed in an endless gale, lies Dante's "3rd-Floor Walk-Up," where New Yorkers are made to carry their bikes up and down the stairs during the hot summer months, which last for all eternity.

But one can get used to anything, even hell, and eventually come to appreciate its fiery vistas, which do, after all, cast a fine light. And so, I've grown accustomed to my apartment's small menaces and consider the noise, the bugs, and the heat all part of its charm. Charming, until recently, when into a nightmare, I awoke.

3

I can't sleep! Or I can, but only for an hour. Then sweating, panicked, blinking into the dark, *Where am I?* Staring into nothing, I try to untangle myself from the sheets, with which I've somnolently formed a cocoon. *Is this the beginning of my metamorphosis? To become . . . become . . . become what?*

In F. Scott Fitzgerald's *This Side of Paradise,* Amory Blaine dreams of becoming a great football star, of becoming the youngest general in the world. He lies in bed dreaming always of "the becoming, . . . never the being." Fitzgerald had trouble sleeping, too. In his autobiographical book, *The Crack-Up,* in a piece called "Waking and Sleeping," he describes his insomnia, saying how he tried everything, even sleeping "on the heart side," the left, as it's rumored to calm the body. After the book was published, Hemingway criticized his friend's decision to write so personally. To write about oneself was undignified, unmanly, said Hemingway. Years later, in his own memoir, *A Moveable*

Feast, Hemingway suggested that, in addition to being undignified and unmanly, Fitzgerald had a small penis. Their relative penis size is now the stuff of legend. Hemingway, I imagine, also suffered from insomnia. In "A Clean, Well-Lighted Place," he summarized the whole business in a line I paraphrase often: "Insomnia, many must have it."

With thoughts multiplying where I lay, I decide at once, *I must get out of bed!* I tear off the sheets, fling open the lights, and jump out of bed, gasping. *Why am I gasping? Sleep apnea? Why does my elbow itch? Flesh-eating bacteria?* I swat a fly that's flown through the window and landed on my bed, then pause to give its mangled body a closer look. *Is this a fly? Why no, it looks so strange! What is it? Dale Samsa, Gregor's younger cousin . . . Why can't I sleep? Why can't I sleep?* And then it hits me.

I sit down at my desk, turn on the computer, and begin to type.

I Google nine different diseases and realize I have all of them. I contemplate my relationship with Philip, which further fuels my worry. In Dante's hell, sinners are punished according to their sins. The lustful Paolo and Francesca are tossed, forever, in a terrible wind. Why should things be any different in my apartment? Philip and I try to protect ourselves with condoms, but what is latex against hell's furious variety? Is there really any way to fully protect oneself against the Clap? Chlamydia? Smallpox? Large Pox, Fun Size, and Jumbo? Against werewolves (I sometimes worry our cries might summon a demon)! Anything is possible! Everything is possible! Anything and everything makes sense in this bitter hour. Is it not called the witching hour for good reason?

When I've exhausted all STD research, I move on to sites

dedicated to menstruation, just to see if I'm normal. Naturally, I am not. *But how can I be both pregnant and in need of a hysterectomy? And how will I afford the medical bills? Moreover, how will I tell Philip? Twins sit lower on the stomach—what I'd thought during the day was a beer belly . . . What shall I name them? Am I too old to be sent away to one of those homes for wayward girls?*

A fly lands beside my keyboard. I execute it with a tissue. Unfolding the soft paper, I place the partially squashed bug under the light from my desk lamp to survey its constitution. I Google insects, just the rarest and deadliest. Terrified now for the health of my unborn twins, I rush from the computer and begin cleaning in a mad fever, certain that my apartment is infested!

I strip the bed, throw out the sheets, vacuum the rug, and scrub the floor. Assessing the tall pile of discarded clothes, I consider burning the whole lot. But then I think again of Philip and return to the computer. Bursting with regret, I compose the email one hopes one never has to send.

> To: Philip
> Subject: VD, many must have it.
> I think I have something.

I stand up from my desk and walk zombie-like to the bathroom before, on the toilet, I assume Rodin's *Thinker* position. Blinking back tears, I try to comfort myself by composing a top ten list of history's greatest syphilitics. I'm up to Nietzsche when I notice I've gotten my period, and my tears become tears of joy —my hysteria is not syphilitic but premenstrual! I am neither pregnant nor diseased, but merely "cursed"!

I return to the computer, happy until I see a reply from Philip. *What is he doing up at this hour?* It's then that I look out the window. The sky is breaking, and the morning light, faint, shows beyond the water towers topping the buildings across the street. Sunrise. A new day. I have made it to the other side. Like Dante seeing stars at the end of *The Inferno,* here is a sign that *Paradiso* awaits!

I click on his email.

> To: Iris
> Subject: Re: VD, many must have it.
> What are your symptoms?

Why! Why! Why did I write that email? I hit Reply and type carefully:

> My heart, it's red and swollen. I think you've infected me.

4

Dante's *Inferno* describes the poet's journey through hell. Naturally, his commute begins at midnight. Dante, very likely, couldn't sleep either.

If you've ever suffered insomnia, you know too well the relief that comes with the dawn. The birds begin their noisy off-key chorus, the garbage truck reprises its morning dirge, the commuters pile into the M11, and deliveries are made to the restaurants downstairs, while one truck backs up to the curb, beeping a parody of an alarm clock.

A new day commences, and the dark and all its horrors recede. The sun appears in the window, cutting through my apartment like an extraordinary knife my father saw on TV. And just as I've gathered all my belongings into the center of the room, just as I'm about to apply the lighter fluid generously, the dawn makes me pause. And it occurs to me: *Perhaps a simple wash and fold would do the trick?*

Like my father, I've developed my own insomniac pattern. On the bright side, the will to burn everything returns about once a week, offering in exchange for my night's suffering a clean apartment in which, during the day, I might convalesce.

5

I switch off the computer and go to the bedroom to lie down. In the light of a new day, I might finally get some sleep. I close my eyes and think of Dante and Fitzgerald and Hemingway, of my own great potential—a Towering Inferno in which I'm trapped at the top. I place myself at the end of a long line of great authors, a top ten list of literary insomniacs. Dante, Fitzgerald, Hemingway . . . What great works might I yet write? *I could become a great author! I could become . . . I could become . . .* I turn to lie on the heart side and look briefly out the cracked windows. *Perhaps the sun might also rise for me.*

But later. I'll get started on all that later. I raise myself up and draw the curtains to shut out the morning in order to better pursue my dreams. Exhausted, I settle into the first nap of the day. There will be many. *But when I wake up . . .*

The glitter of sunlight on roughened water, the glory of the stars, the innocence of morning, the smell of the sea in harbors, the feathery blur and smoky buddings of young boughs, and something there that comes and goes and never can be captured, the thorn of spring, the sharp and tongueless cry—these things will always be the same.

— THOMAS WOLFE, *You Can't Go Home Again*

THE GREAT LAWN

A THUNDERSTORM CHASED US out of the park. The clouds gathered suddenly and were rising over the wall of trees cutting us away from the rest of the city. The stretch of blue over the green where we sat turned orange and then gray into an almost silver. His hair was silver. He had gray wings; that's what I called them.

"You have gray wings," I said, touching his hair, "just over your ears. Has it always been gray?"

"Since I was nineteen. I don't mind it."

"You're a cloud," I said, leaning back on the grass. He leaned over me, his face against the sky. "A little to the left, Cloud. The sun is in my eyes."

It was the delicate cool of an early spring day. The kind that says put your shorts on and ride your bike to the park, because the winter was long and summer might never arrive. And shivering without your jacket, pedaling into the wind, you will the summer forward. It was the end of March, and the sky was blue and uncluttered but for a few bare trees; we were going to play Wiffle ball on Central Park's Great Lawn.

We leaned into the park and laid our bikes at the edge of the green. In the brightest parts of the field, women in bikinis lay sunning themselves, while, nearby, a few men played Frisbee, pausing now and then to look at the girls. We, our limp Wiffle ball league, sat lolling near the edge of the grass, laughing, stealing puffs off a joint we'd rolled at home and sips off the beer warming slowly in our backpacks.

"It's much smaller than I thought it would be," Jacob said, scanning the Great Lawn for a place to set up.

Jacob, my friend from college, had planned the game a week in advance, but then canceled and rescheduled and canceled and rescheduled, as the weather report changed and our faith in meteorology fluctuated. Most of his friends hadn't shown because the weatherman predicted rain finally, though now the sky showed no signs. Sitting Indian style, pulling at the grass, we took out our phones. "I did show," some said or, "I left an hour ago"; "I'll be there in an hour"; "I don't care for Wiffle ball."

We had to modify the game to suit our limited company. With three players per team, we made a line instead of a diamond — first base, a pitcher's mound, home plate and a catcher behind. A batter would race to first only to race right back. The teams were made up of the Doctor, whom Janice was dating; Dave (Jacob's friend from his hometown of Atlanta — "Atlantis," he liked to say, "my lost city" — who was just out of a relationship and taking the game very seriously; he could not afford to lose again, at least not again this week); and me, a little drunk, with pulled grass decorating my hair ("Lady of the Grass," they'd call me later) and coy looks to Philip on the other team. The other team: Philip, my new boyfriend; Janice, my friend from graduate school; and Jacob, perennially unattached.

Jacob served first. The ball cracked soft against my bat and I took off, passing Jacob, nearing Philip, who was crouched low to receive his pass. I ran straight into him, fell on top laughing — a tackle — which informed our revision of the game. "Wiffle Tackle," we called it after that.

"Ooouuut!" Jacob said, and I crawled back to home plate.

"The Doctor," as we called him — because he was one and

this was so funny—Ben, couldn't hit the ball. He was tall, muscular, capable, good with his hands, a surgeon, but he couldn't hit the ball. He kept trying to use one hand—the yellow plastic bat in one hand—and as the game wore on, he was unable to make contact. Everyone began giving him pointers. Even I tried to show him how to hold the bat, but nothing. You could see his self-esteem waning, his giving up with a "whatever" attitude, as Janice struck him out again and again. Poor Janice.

When Philip threw them easy for me, I complained and said I knew what he was doing. "Don't give me special treatment just 'cause I'm your girl." Denying the accusation, he lobbed another slow one, and I ran to first base as if it were the first and last kiss of my life. But the game wasn't high stakes for us really, not like it was for the others. They needed to win, while Philip and I already had it all. At one point he sat comfortable in the outfield looking up at the sky, letting the Doctor take his swings. Philip sipping tepid beer, Philip puffing on a cigarette though he didn't smoke—*why not take up smoking?* He blew a ring.

The day was ending, and the snack vendors were leaving the park. I spotted a silver cart glinting in the sun, as it moved up a distant hill. Hungry, Janice and I chased after it. We ran and I told her, "Quick, he's going that way! Isn't Philip handsome, isn't he the most handsome?" And she said, "Can you believe he couldn't hit the ball, not even once, zero contact!" I said, "He told me he loved me this morning," and she said, "Why wouldn't he use both hands?!"

Then we took our bikes to Sheep Meadow, telling Janice and Ben before we left that we might meet up with them later for dinner. Janice wanted to. "Sure," we said. "Later."

Philip and I took off and found his friends at the other end of the park. They all had bikes, too, and we laid ours among them. We sat far away from each other, our legs outstretched, and drank mango mojitos from an illegal vendor nearby. And then I became the Lady of the Grass veiled by handfuls that rained over me and Philip as I baptized him. Our feet touched while others spoke, and we smiled about what we knew. What did we know?

The storm was coming, but we held out until thunder cracked loud just beyond the trees. The sky changed suddenly. The clouds began rising over the meadow, rising after us, so we took up our bikes and left to race the storm home.

The rain caught us. We rode beneath it to his place on the east side of Tenth Street. Later I would joke that that was the source of all our problems, that we lived on opposite sides of Tenth Street. I rode behind him much of the way, though occasionally I'd speed ahead to show my independence. I would ride without looking back, knowing he was watching.

We rode down Broadway through the traffic, through the flashing lights of Times Square, past red double-decker tour buses and yellow cabs screeching to the curb. Down, down, through the city, the streetlights haloed by rain, painting us yellow, red, and then green. The storm bellowed over us, delivering sharp reproofs, telling us to hurry, that we hadn't much time. A chorus of drops, a splash of wheels, the squeaking of my own bicycle tires as I slowed to an intersection.

Everyone else stopped, but we were suspended in motion — Philip ahead of me, cascading into right and left turns, my legs soaking wet and shining in the new dusk, and the city, so beautiful, because it had to be, because it was for us. We roped east and south and east and south until we arrived at his apartment, and I pushed the wet hair from my face.

We walked upstairs, carrying our bikes the five flights, and then felt bad for Janice and the Doctor because it would all fall apart for them, because it mattered that he couldn't hit the ball, because nothing like that would ever matter for us. We discussed their situation: "I don't think she'll be able to get past this," I said with concern. "I told her he might be good at Frisbee, that she ought to give him another chance."

"A shame," he mimicked my pity, that everyone couldn't have what we had. Then he took me in his arms and kissed me, his face wet against mine, his wet hair falling into my eyes. We peeled off our soaked clothes, ordered sushi from the restaurant downstairs, and lay together huddled under his bed covers.

When the food arrived, we were dry but for our hair. We sat on the couch in our underwear and turned on the TV. We changed the channel a few times before settling on a Christmas movie, speculating at the oddity of a Christmas movie airing in spring.

"Perhaps the guy in charge of programming knows something we don't," Philip said.

"That the world will end in autumn," I answered, "that it's now or never."

We finished eating and finished the movie, and it continued to rain hard, the windowpane banging occasionally from the wind. We laid down before the TV, and Philip pulled me close. Another Christmas movie, followed by another . . .

"I do love you," he said, kissing the back of my neck. His arm around my waist, his breath against my ear. "I do love you," he repeated, as if he knew he never would.

The Great Lawn stretched before us.

Catherine . . . was, after all, a rather mature blossom, such as could be plucked from the stem only by a vigorous jerk.

— HENRY JAMES, *Washington Square*

PHILIP
HAS
A
SMALL
PENIS
BLOG.COM

Monday, 7:30 PM

My boyfriend broke up with me over Instant Messenger. "I don't love you," he typed softly, from his work computer. My mom asked me what happened, so I forwarded her the chat.

He made a list, which should be clear enough. Still, I had to call and explain: "Mom, I'm selfish and fat. I wash my hair only every other day. I make funny faces in the mirror. I'm bad in bed."

It was confusing for her because at Thanksgiving dinner all he could do was sing my praises. "She fucks like a god!" he said, opening the first toast. Everyone thought it was the real thing.

After we broke up, he agreed to come over. On my couch, holding my hand, he said he'd like to take the pain away. He said, "Is there anything I can do?"

"You could buy me a blanket," I answered. I told him that

without him I'd be cold. That winter was starting and I'd have to sleep under my coats.

"No," he said. "You can call me whenever you want to talk though."

"But I don't want to talk. I'm cold. I want a blanket."

"Sometimes talking helps."

The next day I called three times, but he let it go to voice-mail. So I left a message — three of them. The last one said, "Come over and use me for sex. Don't call, just come!"

He called and told me he didn't like the sound of my voice.

On my bed after, on top of my coats, he held on to my hips and raised me in the air high, so that for a while I was like a bird, flying over him, going nowhere. Then he put me down and said he had to go.

I asked him to take the spare condoms with him, told him I didn't need them, that it made me sad to see them.

He shut the door.

When I walked into the bathroom, I found them on the sink.

He came over again the next night. "Leave the condoms!" I announced. "I might need them now that I'm single again."

When I looked in the bathroom after he left, they were gone.

I took my bike to his apartment at 4 AM and knocked on his door until his neighbors asked if I was a criminal. "Yes!" I said. "A rapist and a thief!" Then Philip let me in. He said I looked ugly and drunk and tired. I said he disgusted me the way he was about to have sex with someone so ugly, so drunk, so tired.

"You have no integrity," I said. "I've always hated that about you."

I left him in bed at 8 AM, and he called me an hour later on his way to work. "Did you steal my keys?"

"Why would I steal your keys?"

"They're missing and it seems like something you would do."

"You don't know the first thing about what I would do!" I said, and hung up.

Later I texted him, "Check the freezer. I think I saw them in the ice bucket."

Yesterday my friend Reggie got mad, because I invited him to lunch and then sat under the table crying. "You need to pull yourself together," Reggie said. That's what everyone says.

I IM'ed him as soon as I got home. "philip," I wrote without punctuating, "come over and fuck me"

He said I didn't seem stable the way I used all lowercase letters, that he didn't like it when I cursed. He called me a moment later to say, "I don't like it when you curse."

"I don't give a fuck what the fuck you *like,* fuck fuck fuck!" I said, and then he came over with the special kinds of condoms, a handful in exotic colors from Condomania around the corner. "Special condoms, because I'm special!" I said, standing over him without my underwear.

"They're loosies—like the way you buy cigarettes if you don't want to make a habit of it."

I took off the rest of my clothes and trilled, "I'm beautiful! I'm ten pounds thin!"

He remarked at how my breasts seemed smaller, barely able to hold his cock between them. Then he felt bad and apologized. I told him to stop. I told him his cruelty made me hot. I said, "Sing to me, Philip, the list of all my flaws!"

But he wouldn't. Instead, he wrapped me in his arms. Instead, he said, "Iris, you're so special, you're perfect!" "Iris, oh, Iris," he kept repeating until instead of coming, I cried. And when I reached my arms around him, he came and then receded like an ocean leaving only debris.

Tuesday, 5:45 PM

About this blog:

Caroline said cable helped. When she got dumped, she ordered cable and felt fine.

"I'm not into TV," I told her.

Publishing articles about the size of her ex-boyfriend's penis proved a big help, too. She published two articles in *Playgirl* and suggested I do the same via my blog.

I told Caroline that's not how I operate. I said, "Caroline, what could possibly come from my typing on my blog that PHILIP HAS A SMALL PENIS!"

She agreed and suggested I start a new blog just for that, so here it is.

Thursday, 12:30 AM

Philip, if you are reading this, I hate you.

In other news: I'm thinking about moving, but I don't know to where. I'm too romantic to choose an apartment. What if it's ugly and stupid, but I love it anyway?

My realtor says I should make a list of deal breakers, but everything strikes me as negotiable. Of course I want a sunny apartment with lots of space, but is that even possible? How uncompromising should I be? It will help her to help me, she said, if I give some serious consideration to my list.

I looked at some apartments in Brooklyn today. There's a bike trail outside one of them, and when I looked out the window I thought I saw you riding by. For a second, it was your gray hair catching the light, and your stupid face looking up at me grinning, grinning as if you'd done nothing wrong, as if you had a right to go on living.

The apartment is a bargain because it's on a land lease, which means someone else owns the thing you think you do, and you can be kicked out at any time without warning. I said that didn't seem like the makings of a good deal, and she assured me the technicalities really didn't matter, not unlike your mentioning two months into our relationship that you were not officially divorced, you prick.

I told her I had to think it over, that I still had some questions. Like: Did you sleep with her that weekend in Boston when you went to sign the divorce papers and finally close your joint bank account? And why did I apologize after I asked you this, after I saw the photo of you two kissing that you "accidentally" left out on your coffee table? And why did you answer that I was the most jealous person you'd ever met? Why not the prettiest?

Why do I know what your ex-wife's vagina looks like, the really great style of her pubic hair? Why do I know what you were thinking the first time you two met in college? Why do I know what you said and what she said that day in the library and how it was all so funny? Why do I know what you wore on your wedding day? Why did you wear the same thing to a costume party with me? Why do I know that you tied her up and she liked it? Why do I know what she thinks about my favorite things—*my* books, *my* songs, a movie *we* saw together? Why did I need to know what she would have guessed for five down in that Sunday's crossword puzzle?

Here is a list of things I could drop on you if it *were* you on that bike trail, and some reasons—besides the interesting layout and good light—that I might take the apartment:

It comes with a microwave, which is heavy, and a dishwasher, which would be hard to remove but very effective and not my fault if it accidentally fell from my window and onto your fat head while you were exploring the neighborhood carefree. An iron, hot and terrible, and good for fashioning pleats, might hit you just right. My computer speakers. A mouse-repelling device that plugs into the wall and projects a sound that only mice can hear could pick up enough speed on its way down to knock you unconscious. A lucky horseshoe, which I would have to buy or else break into your apartment and steal the one I gave you. A heart-shaped box of lead. A measles blanket. Dry ice. A Scotch tape dispenser. An American flag might accidentally fall from my window as I was waving It patriotically on the Fourth of July, and smother you while you were launching toward Washington on your bike, ready to protest the cruel ways of our government abroad and also meet girls who are into the same cause, if not on your way to protest loneliness at your favorite bar. A Roach Motel. An orange straw bending at the neck. A bronze bust of Hoover. A live snake. Five of them. Ten of them. The shower curtain rod you said you'd hang for me but never did. My collection of mix tapes given to me by all my ex-boyfriends except you, because you never gave me anything, might fall out my window in a plastic mess just next to you, just below the window of my brand-new apartment with the great light and interesting layout, which you wouldn't know is mine, because you wouldn't know that I moved, because you wouldn't know a thing about me, because I wouldn't tell you, because I hate you.

Friday, 9:30 AM

On Christmas Eve, I rented *The Texas Chainsaw Massacre* and watched it with my parents. I was home visiting.

My mother cried, "Oh, god! How can you watch these atrocities?"

"Shhh!" I silenced her. "You're killing the mood!"

"Horrible! How can you sleep at night? No wonder you can't sleep at night!"

"It takes my mind off things," I whispered, over the whir of the saw.

Saturday, 11:21 AM

Alistair had excellent gift-giving instincts this year. Having waited until the last minute to do his shopping, the only store open on Christmas Eve was Crazy Billy's. So, he gave Teddy a bottle of Scotch, my parents a box of fine liqueurs, and me a basket of wine. He'd filled the basket with shredded green cellophane left over from his Dollar store's Easter inventory—"To my sister, the basket case," the card read.

My mother gave me a robe and slippers, understanding my need the previous morning. I'd come downstairs with my hair matted into a shark-fin-like tuft and ate breakfast in only my underwear.

"Couldn't you get dressed?" she'd said.

"Why bother? I'm just going to have to get undressed again," I said, slurping my coffee.

When I complained of feeling cold later, she wrapped me in paper towels—unconditional love. And when she ran out of Bounty, she used foil. After, in the kitchen while she cooked, I danced the robot and she clapped supportively.

For Christmas I gave everyone I love a copy of *Caddyshack*. *Caddyshack* for Mom, *Caddyshack* for Dad, *Caddyshack* for my brothers.

Mom opened her *Caddyshack*.

Dad opened his *Caddyshack*.

Teddy opened his *Caddyshack*.

Alistair opened his *Caddyshack*.

I opened a bottle of wine and spit out the cork. "What should we toast to?" I said, taking a hit in the face—a Christmas angel had fallen from the top of our tree. Some branches and then my head broke her fall. "Owww," I groaned, then picked her up and searched her eyes: *Was it an accident or did you jump?* Then I tilted her head back and poured in some wine. "To the Merry Gentlemen, god rest 'em!" I heard her slur.

Wednesday, 7:45 PM

I got back to the city just in time for New Year's Eve. It was "an auspicious beginning," to quote Walt Frazier—I'd had to start drinking earlier than I wanted in order to quell my nerves after executing the mouse. Well, disposed of the body, really. I found him already dead, poisoned and motionless in one of my favorite shoes. Murder is a filthy business. I threw out the shoes, both of them, and had a beer.

The Bastard Felix came over, and I asked him to help me decide between two dresses: the beige or the black? Then I went into the bedroom to get dressed, but just lay for a while on my bed instead, rereading parts of the introduction to *In Search of Lost Time,* stopping now and then to stare at the wall and listen as the Bastard danced in the next room to Daft Punk's "One More Time." Whenever Felix comes over, he puts it on repeat, and if I ask him to play something else, he concedes, but then asks, "One more time?"

I decided on the black dress, which would later rip open in the brief slit at the back. It would rip with my first step out of my apartment, my steps too long, too "auspicious."

Walt Frazier once got on the treadmill next to Martin—my ex-ex-boyfriend—at the gym, so Walt became one of our celebrities. We had celebrities the way other couples have songs and got sentimental whenever Walt commented on the game—according to him, many began "auspiciously." We also saw Kirstie Alley at a restaurant in Positano once, which made us romantic whenever she appeared in Weight Watchers commercials screaming about fettucine.

The Bastard wore a brown suit and said between sips of his second tallboy, "I'm gonna pace myself tonight."

"I wish I could do that," I said. "Remind me, would you?"

Felix said he couldn't do that, said he couldn't accept that kind of responsibility. "Okay," I said, knowing it wouldn't make a difference anyway. Whenever I'm told not to do something, I just end up plotting how to do it more. I cemented my smoking habit that way. Martin mentioned he hated smoking, and despite the fact that I hated smoking too, I felt after that a compulsion to smoke all the time.

"It's the New Year and I'm single," I told the Bastard. No Martin. No Philip. "I can do whatever I want!" I was tempted to do nothing.

We went out. I sipped my drinks, while posing ladylike in the costume jewelry my grandmother gave me and black fishnet wrist gloves. I sat up tall and stiff and looked at the cigarette decorating my hand.

I got drunk. I started talking to some guy, then another guy, then another until it was midnight and everyone began counting the wrong way. And then it was the New Year, and I was still talking to some guy. I am always talking to some guy it seems. Everyone around us kissed, so I put my hands on some guy's face, pulled him in close, and laid one on him hard. Pulling back, his head between my hands, I said, "I know it was you, Fredo. You broke my heart."

Then I found Reggie at the drinks table and told him he had to choose between Philip and me. Then I said I was just kidding. Then I said I wasn't kidding. Then I said I was. Then he said he and Felix and Philip had gone out together a few nights ago. They'd gone out for drinks, but he didn't like it because Philip is so boring.

"That's like saying you didn't inhale," I snapped.

I moved away and began dancing with some guy. Bumping into me, he spilled my drink. "Someone bumped me from behind," he said instead of apologizing. Then he began spinning me.

We went to the kitchen after to refill our drinks. Felix went to the bathroom to vomit. "Should have paced myself," he said, shaking his head on the way out.

I was sitting, balanced delicately on the arm of a long sofa. My dress was covered in crackers, and I had my arm dug deep into an open bag, as I complained how I couldn't find a decent cracker, how all the crackers were "broken." I removed a handful, showed them to everyone, and angrily shoved them in my mouth. "Whoops," I said, almost losing my balance, before regaining it just in time. I sat completely still for a whole minute, then dropped onto the floor.

The Bastard pointed and laughed.

"The rotation of the earth," I explained, looking up. I'd said this before, but I went on saying it again, as if I'd only just thought of it, as if the new year were any newer. "It caught me off-guard." And then, feeling the world still moving beneath me, I laughed and tried to move with it.

Thursday, 2:31 AM

Rejection casts me in a fine light, as evidenced by my datebook, which has never been so full. The dark circles under my eyes from all the crying, the hair locked in knots from too much time in bed, the waist tiny from not eating; I'm irresistible. Wherever I go, men turn up with soft shoulders. Passing right over Janice —energized from spin class and screaming with confidence— they stand before me, offering tissues and eye contact.

"Since when is weeping a good pickup line?" Janice snapped.

"I'm not trying to pick anyone up," I told her, sniffling, "though the attention *is* very good for my self-esteem."

But with my self-esteem waxing, I worry about my sex appeal

waning. My appetite has started to come back, though I try hard to suppress it. I've begun washing my hair again, though I finish by teasing it. And on Saturday nights, just before I go out, I look at myself in the mirror and say, "You, you're nothing much." And then, the way men do push-ups before heading out the door, I force myself to cry and rub my eyes till I look like a prize, elusive, lost, stuck at the bottom of a claw machine.

"You're beautiful," men say, surprised to find me alone, "Where's your boyfriend?"

I blink pathetically, suppressing tears, as I tell them we broke up, tell them that I'm a mess, tell them to wait while I get out my datebook.

Wednesday, 11:31 AM

Gregory asked how to dim the lamp.

"There's a trick. It's slightly broken," I said. "Look, you hold it this way."

Jeff asked how to get at the cold water.

"They're mislabeled," I said, turning the knob labeled "hot."

Craig asked how to turn the lights on in the bathroom.

"No, not that one. It's out. Try the one over the mirror."

Clagmore apologized when the shower curtain fell down.

"It's not your fault. The screws are loose. I used nails 'cause I didn't have a drill. Angle it this way, until it's wedged good into the walls."

Jonathan asked about the overwhelming heat while trying to adjust the knobs on my radiator.

"Oh, no," I laughed. "Nothing can be done about that. You can open this window, though, if you wish it to be cooler."

Charles asked me about the draft, too.

"The windows are all cracked," I said, closing a shattered pane. I shrugged. "That's why I'm wearing my jacket."

Lawrence asked about the broken record player.

"The speakers are a little off, but"—I fiddled with the balance—"you get used to the heavy bass after a while, and you can still hear the song if you stand close to the speakers."

Nathan asked about the hole in the couch upholstery.

"Put a pillow over it. Yes, that one. That's what it's for."

Reggie asked about the missing piece in the backgammon set.

"Soda cap," I said, offering a replacement. I turned it over and read the inscription aloud. "'Drink Coke, Play Again.'"

"And what about this?" B whispered, before laying a curious hand over my chest.

"Everything in my apartment is half-broken," I confessed. I held my hand over his. "Turn the heart like this."

Monday, 6:20 PM

I am dating a man named B. The other night he gave me his address and told me to meet him at his place.

"Apartment 1B," he said, "as in B."

The letter comes up in a variety of words, and I find myself often thinking of him. I called the super yesterday about a gas leak. "Where do you live?" he asked. "Which apartment?"

"3D," I said, "as in Dog."

"3B," he said, "as in Bog?"

"No, Dog. Dog," I said.

I watched *Wheel of Fortune* with my mother last weekend. Among the many prizes was a brand new Saab. I bought no vowels, but one of the contestants requested a "B." Vanna turned a single letter. *There is only one B.*

I gave B three belated Christmas gifts. Just some things I picked up at my brother's Dollar store—a laser pointer, a bow and arrow with suction cups, and a T-shirt on which I'd ironed the letter "B." I wrapped each gift separately and put the stickers on that come preset, saying "To:" and then "From:"

"To: B or not," "To: B or not," "To: B or not," I wrote Shakespearean. "Read the cards!" I said excitedly.

When we stop seeing each other—if we start to more often and then stop—will all those B's start to bother me? Will my Birthday hurt? Will I use the word "Yet"? Will I explain away our end by saying, "He liked me [yet] not enough."

And when I visit home and watch Pat and Vanna, dressed up before the studio audience, will I be so distracted with grief that when it's time to solve the puzzle, I'll fail to venture a guess. Will I lose the Saab? Will my mother say insensitively, "Better luck next time?"

How much will I cry?

ReBound. ReBound. ReBound.

Begin again.

My advice to all who have the time or inclination to concern themselves with the international language movement would be: "Back Esperanto loyally."

— J.R.R. TOLKIEN

PHILADELPHIA

HE WASN'T EXACTLY TOOTHLESS. He was only missing the one, but it was a good one, right in the front. He sucked at the gap then looked toward the street. "*I astynomía,* bah!" he said, referring to the cop who'd tried earlier to give him a speeding ticket.

Greeks regard the law as a style more than a rule. He had his own style and gave the cop what for, he explained to the gathered company, before sitting back in his chair. Then, lighting a cigarette and exhaling from his nostrils in two powerful streams, he turned his head and gave me a wink.

He did this often. He'd suck at the gap to accentuate a point, show he was serious, suggest that someone he was arguing with wasn't, or indicate with a nod that the waiter bring round another beer. It was very sexy, as if in calling attention to that rotted empty space, he were calling attention to all that was lacking in the world. He'd throw a hand, make that sucking sound, then look up from under his heavily flexed brow, hinting at the kind of wisdom that can only be earned from loss. *"The only teeth are teeth lost," Proust would say.*

He chain-smoked and rode a motorcycle and had greasy hair like a teenage villain from out of a YA novel, though when we met, he was well into his twenties. He worked on cars at an auto shop in nearby Volos and at the end of the day, would take his motorcycle from the garage and drive down into the seaside villages nearby, happy to have a cold beer and a laugh. His hands were rough, his fingernails permanently blackened, and we started seeing each other one summer when I was nineteen or thirty.

We'd meet at this beachfront café, go for a walk, smoke some of the pot he'd brought down from the city, and look around skittishly. Unlike the other laws, those governing drugs were non-negotiable. Marijuana was whispered about in hushed tones. He'd never smoked with a girl before; good Greek girls didn't smoke, he told me or tried to. "They think is bad," he said, motioning to his head to suggest such girls had nothing in theirs, before returning his attention to the giant spliff he was preparing on his lap.

Occasionally he'd pause between his perusal of the street and his perusal of his work, in order to peruse me; he'd flash his special smile. Then we'd get high and kiss in the dark on the beach. I barely spoke Greek and he, almost no English, which made our conversations that much more interesting. If we had nothing particular to say, we had at least a very particular way to say it. We'd make our faces telling, our hands expressive, perforating the language barrier with excited jabs. Sometimes we'd bring a still-tangled string of words back to the café, where, over a lavish ice cream sundae, we'd ask our waiter friend to translate.

I was most likely nineteen, according to my work with a calculator just now. I was nineteen when my waiter friend asked about our unlikely romance. "How do you talk to each other?"

"We speak the language of love." I explained, "It's a lot like Esperanto."

He translated his name for me. The first time we met, in a thick accent he said, "I am Bob."

"Bob," I repeated slowly, wondering at the oddity of his stilted American name.

The waiter hit him on the shoulder. "His name is Vagelis," he intervened. "He thought you wouldn't understand."

The practice of name translation has always struck me as odd. The notion that they need translating, I mean. As if Bob were a universal concept applicable in every language. As if we all have tables, and we all have Bobs. Tables have four legs and a flat surface; Bob has two and is down one tooth.

"Bobocles," I christened him. "It's your ancient Greek name," I said, laughing and poking him in the chest, as we stood facing each other under the dock. He laughed in kind, not having a clue what I was saying, before applying his sloppy kiss.

Bobocles' best friend was also missing a tooth. The same tooth, so they called each other twins. They were like blood brothers but with teeth, tooth brothers or rotted gap brothers —it was sort of black where the tooth was supposed to be, from plaque and cigarette tar, I guess.

"Philadelphia," Bobocles said, pointing back and forth between himself and his toothless twin. They were good friends, he was trying to tell me by way of introduction, "Philadelphia" stemming from the Greek phrase meaning "brotherly love."

Every night, we'd have beers at our standby café, and Bobocles and his twin would reprise their long-running joke: They'd take their cigarettes and wedge them into the gaps where their teeth weren't. Then they'd bring the plastic ashtrays close to their faces and point to the gap in the ashtray lip where you rest a cigarette when you're not smoking it, before pointing back to their respective smiles, with the cigarette stuck in usefully.

I didn't smoke myself at that time, but I admired Bobocles'

ingenuity and how like Shakespeare's hunchbacked Richard the Third, he'd turned "disadvantage into commodity." Smitten, I got on the back of his motorcycle, and he drove slowly through the mountains.

Eventually, he took me to meet his parents. His extended family was camping on a nearby beach for the summer and that night were having a party. He made sure I had a clean aluminum cup to drink from and then sat opposite me between his mother and father, glowing drunk in the firelight.

His parents tried their best at English, and I worked my best Greek, offering English words with Greek roots, the way Bobocles had offered "Philadelphia." But it wasn't too hard to understand them anyway, for they said essentially the same things Bobocles said—how pretty I was (his mother pointed at me, then motioned to her face and hair), what a good girl I seemed to be (his father pointed to me and then to his heart). . . . They suggested their son was a good boy, too, before his uncle messed up his hair good-naturedly and helped himself to more retsina.

Looking shyly over the kerosene lamps, at the faces of his parents and then at mine, Bobocles blushed. It was extremely unattractive. So much better when his hand was up my shirt at the bottom of the dock, so much better when he was groping me crazily without feeling. I was bringing out his good side. A calamity, for I wanted to be bad.

After that night, my attention drifted, and when he asked me to go for walks with him under the dock, I only agreed if he had weed and then, spurning his kisses, attempted to improve my Greek, not bothering anymore to speak the language of love, understanding instinctively why Esperanto never caught on.

When I returned the next summer, I saw Bobocles again. I

was exiting the market across the street from our old café, when our waiter friend caught my arm. "Vagelis wants to see you," he said with some urgency. "Come tomorrow night."

When the sun fell, I went as planned, ordered a beer with my waiter friend, and chatted with him at a table in the back.

Bobocles turned up on his motorcycle some minutes later, slowing to a stop on the street before the café. He parked and hopped off, swaggered over with nervous confidence. Then, kissing me on both cheeks, he stepped back and smiled broadly. I was happy to see him, but whatever it was I'd loved had somehow gone out of it. Or into it. *"So we beat on, boats against the current, borne back ceaselessly into next summer,"* Fitzgerald *would say.* "You got a tooth!" I exclaimed.

He looked at me quizzically, asked our friend to translate. "It's okay," I interrupted, and pointed back and forth between my tooth and his new one—perfect, white, gleaming porcelain. He grinned, proud, lacking nothing. I noticed, too, his hair was neatly combed, still wet, his shirt buttoned to the top; he had dressed for me. At the table we looked at each other, then with little left to say, looked around.

He bought me a beer and drank his own with great solemnity before motioning to offer me another. "No." I waved my hand, wanting to end the awkwardness even more than I wanted a refill. He finished his quickly and quietly and then, as before, asked me to go for a walk. I said I had to get going, had to meet my cousin at the other end of town. Then, with darting eyes, he drew his hand to his lips, showing he meant to smoke. I considered the detour, but at last declined and left.

Later that night, as I was walking home, he spotted me from

a bench facing the sea. He rose, came toward me, and opened his mouth to speak. Swallowing air a few times first, finally, he got out, "I love you. You love I?"

I reached into the shallow well of my limited Greek; the language of love had no words for "I like you as a friend." So I kissed him on both cheeks, took his hands and looked into his eyes. "Bobocles," I said, "Philadelphia, I'm sorry."

YOU DON'T LOOK HAPPY. WE CAN HELP!

Tired of posing for selfies alone in your apartment? Are you a lone Jones with no hope of keeping up with the Joneses? Then book a photo session with Insta-Life!

Shot on iPhone 6 with a carefully planned upload schedule designed to mimic the unfolding of "real-life events," our photo packages enable you

to exhibit the glamorous, fulfilling life you've always wanted and know you'll never have.

Curate an online photo album filled with exotic vacation surroundings, fun friends, a loving family, gracious home, and a life partner that will make your ex consider suicide.

Enhance just one area of your life, or sign up for Insta-Life Complete!

A LA CARTE MENU

FUN WITH FRIENDS

SELFIE

SEXY TIME

TOUCHING MOMENT

OFFICE PARTY

INSTA-LIFE COMPLETE
includes everything on the a la carte menu, plus:

WHO'S THE BOSS?
Daily photos of your morning macchiato that let everyone know you're in charge.

NEWBORN HI-JINX
Select your offspring from a vast catalog of races and ethnicities.

ON THE TOWN
Beautifully plated gourmet dinners, nights at the opera, and invitation-only gala events. With our team of makeup artists and stylists, you'll be the belle of every imaginary ball.

CASUAL NIGHTS IN
With a loved one, your jammies, and a crackling fire, because sometimes even the life-of-the-party needs a good rest.

FUN IN THE KITCHEN
The baked goods and home-cooked meals you've always dreamed of preparing.

#NOFILTER #NOMAKEUP
There's no better way to showcase your natural beauty than to have all of your flaws removed in Photoshop by a professional.

CHECK OUT OUR CATALOG ON INSTAGRAM AND SCHEDULE YOUR FREE CONSULTATION TODAY!

Are you a genius? Take this quiz and find out!

1. Which one of the five is least like the other four?
a) orange   b) globe   c) ball   d) corpse   e) moon

2. If Edvard is 6 when Torvald is born, how old is Edvard when Torvald dies in a blizzard at 13?

3. Fish is to water as cow is to
a) lobster   b) jail   c) pandemic   d) supermarket   e) land

4. If you rearrange the letters lbeao, you would have the name of a
a) fruit   b) domesticated animal   c) fatal disease
d) color   e) family gaming center

5. There are 11 gum drops on the table. You took 7. How many do you have?

ANSWERS: 1.D, 2.19, 3.E, 4.C, 5.7

If you answered all five questions correctly, congratulations! Your critical thinking ability far exceeds that of most people.

But then, you already knew that, didn't you? Moreover, your score on this test renders you eligible to join the *Genius Guild of America*, an exclusive organization made up of highly intelligent members like you who find themselves a bit bored by conversation with those of average intellect. Founded in Cambridge in 1979, the GGA is dedicated to identifying and bringing together America's most exceptional minds and invites you to register your score with us and receive official certification through our board. To join, simply enclose your scored quiz along with a $29.99 processing fee and within two weeks you'll receive a GGA diploma certifying your membership and genius status.

Please send my Genius Guild of America Member Certificate to:
Name.............................. Address...
City..State............................

Send this coupon along with the $29.99 processing fee to:
GGA, 8765 Tory Ave., 3rd Floor, Cambridge, MA.

The Sky! The Sky! The Sky!

— STÉPHANE MALLARMÉ, "The Azure"

PHATSO

THE ACE OF SPADES SHOWS a naked woman on a desk with her legs opening upward, as if to embrace the sky. In her right hand, she holds a book—*The Collected Poems of Mallarmé,* I imagine, for the title is out of focus. With her left, she adjusts her reading glasses. All this to say, she's "bookish."

Years ago, growing bored of bottle caps and pencil erasers, I started collecting pornography. Since then I've amassed a book of 3D nudes, *The Collected Tijuana Bibles,* a few instruction manuals with illustrations—*Total Sexual Fitness for Women!* features exercises I can practice by myself—two fetish DVDs with lots of spanking but no sex at all, and five sets of dirty playing cards ranging in theme from "Ancient Greek Lovers" to the more contemporary "Poke-her," from which I've pulled the ace.

It's natural to identify with the characters in books and movies, and so I identify with the figures in porn. Because I'm not sure what "type" of woman I am, I end up identifying with all of them. As a child I related to Cinderella, for example, though clearly she and I had little in common. She was an underprivileged blonde left to tend the hearth; I was a suburban brunette accustomed to central heating. Still, knowing I wasn't right for the part, I cast myself in the role anyway.

My new boyfriend Max says he's into bookish women, but I think he just likes librarian-themed pornography. "You're exactly my type," he told me on our first date. I'd worn a sweater vest, dressing for the role. Having met him at a bookstore, I assumed he was bookish, too, and decided to play up that aspect of my character. I'd imagined a brilliant first date conversation in which we'd debate the finer points of Henry James's later work and had even prepared an off-color joke about the master's testicular injuries, which I planned to trot out over dessert to show my lighter side.

Alas, my prepping was in vain, as Max, it turned out, had wandered into the bookstore only to buy coffee and had little to no appetite for the books themselves. This was a disappointment. Though it did little to lessen my attraction to him, as I noticed he had a remarkably hairy chest. A veritable beast he was, judging from the wild tangle that sprang ferociously from the top of his V-neck. It thrilled me to imagine myself Boof to his Teen Wolf, while he busily imagined me teacher to his student. "Is that wool?" he whispered, touching my thick, scratchy vest with trembling hand. And then, a few dates later, we adopted two new roles: a young man and a young woman at the start of a great romance.

I didn't mind being reduced to a "type." That he managed to boil down my whole personality in order to meet the demands of his fetish was actually exciting; I belonged to a category and also to him. I've always enjoyed being objectified, if I'm being honest, to be called by pet diminutives like "baby" or "doll." It can't be so uncommon, this desire to become small, to be furnished with sensible handles by which one might more easily be held.

I told Max he was my type, too. Bringing the back of his furry hand to my cheek, I told him I loved his flaxen knuckle curls and began waxing bookish about his type's recurrence in the novels of H. G. Wells. I described how I imagined him long before we met, naked, running through a forest shrouded in dense fog, pursued by trappers, nearly escaping. Then a tangle of nets! And another! Now a cage! Inside of which he was delivered to civilization, to a secret lab just outside of London, where an evil genius performed ungodly experiments on him, injecting him daily with a mysterious serum that would bestow upon beast humanoid characteristics, giving him some, but not all, of man's higher brain functions. "And with the injection of this daily serum," I went on breathlessly, "your body was transformed into the human shape that sits before me. Max!" I cried. "Your hands are a vestige of the savage beast within you, the beast which I adore!"

Max asked what "serum" meant and then, pulling his hand away, asked me to stop making fun of him. Reluctantly, I released his paw and took out my stopwatch to time his beard growth while we waited for appetizers.

I don't actually have a "type" myself, but have over the years cast a variety of men in the role of prince. To me, this is proof of my being open-minded. To my friends, it's indicative of a vast collection of fetishes. My dating a man of forty-two when I was only eighteen was proof, they asserted, of an "avuncular fetish." And my dating a carnie one summer on Coney Island made apparent, they said, my "toothless fetish." And then, when in college a rash of boyfriends were overweight, I was dubbed "chubby-chaser."

One ex was so fat, when he lay on top of me I feared being crushed, snapped in two, like a twig on the forest floor in Fenimore Cooper's *Leatherstocking Tales*. After our first night together, he pulled me close. "See how I mold so perfectly to your body? If I were thin, there would be all this space between us. I don't want there to be any space between us."

I was touched by his logic and could genuinely appreciate the way his flab curved into the small of my back. It was like being encased in bubble wrap. I felt very secure. Like a very delicate plate being transported overseas via superior postage.

I quickly came to enjoy the look of him, too. How he was planet-like, I'd think, as he exhaled rings of marijuana smoke that wreathed him like Saturn. And there I was next to him in the kitchen, barefoot and so tiny by comparison, his little moon. I began to think of physical attraction in a whole new way. He was a large physical mass with its own powerful gravitational pull, making it quite natural, quite inevitable really, that I should fall for or into him.

Phatso and I had fun all the time. No one had ever made me laugh the way that he did, and his were the most skillful penis puppet shows I've seen. And I've seen a lot. I don't know if this is something most couples share, or if there is something unique to my "type" that inspires a man to give his penis a stage name, but nearly all of my boyfriends have erected such presentations. It would never do to ask if this is their first time reading for the part of *Mame* or if there were girlfriends before with whom they'd rehearsed. "But that," as Rudyard Kipling would say, "is another story."

Phatso had always wanted to be a filmmaker before he decided one winter—the one of our discontent—that he really wanted to act. Returning from his agent's office one gray afternoon, he told me what his agent had just told him: As he looked presently, he'd be too difficult to cast. He'd need to either gain or lose weight to fit "a type." Did he want to be a character actor or compete for leading man roles?

Fatter sounded good to me and I told him. "Roles are rolls,"

I said, my hand drifting unconsciously toward his gut, where it stuck against his shirt, like an ecstatic ten-year-old pasted to the wall of a Gravitron ride. I gave him a squeeze, raised an eyebrow, and nodded toward the bedroom.

He didn't see himself that way, he answered. He wanted to be a leading man and took off for the kitchen to continue the conversation over soda and Hot Pockets. He took off and, without noticing, released my hand back into space like a bottle of Coca-Cola Classic in that commercial from 1985. I caught up to him by the microwave, where he was already punching in numbers. After a moment, he turned around and looked at me with tears in his eyes. The timer beeped, like "Taps."

Later that afternoon we rented *Fatso* with Dom DeLuise. We sat on the couch, and I stroked his hair and fed him Devil Dogs while he cried. He began his diet and exercise regimen the next day, and a month later he was muscular and thin. He took to eating soy, got his hair spiked at the salon and, I don't know, it seemed as if his whole personality were disappearing with his chins. The man I loved had been pissed away in water weight.

After that I found someone fatter. Really fat. His body was a true extravagance. Breaking up is always hard, but perhaps he, with all his padding, might make for a softer rebound. My friends nicknamed Phatso's sequel "Type 2," short for "Type 2 Diabetes." More romantically I nicknamed him "the Love Barge." And whether by his side or taken up into the berth of his great arms, like a dinghy attached to a monstrous ocean vessel, when I was with him I felt so marvelously small.

It was at a bar where all my friends drank regularly, that he kissed me for the first time. We'd been flirting all night when, instead of flashing the bewitching smile I'd meant to, I accidentally threw up a shot of Jägermeister. (Later I found out he had a fetish for young alcoholics.) Mortified, I covered my mouth.

And so I ran, like Cinderella at midnight, while he, obese prince, panted after me down the steps and into the men's urinal where, letting my upchuck burst into full flower, I had just enough time to rinse my mouth out in the sink.

A moment later, Type 2 caught up to me. Wheezing at my back, he spun me around and took me in his arms. His hair! His eyes! The jack of hearts! — he kissed me.

Dr. Sheila Werther-Marxen

It's been said that shopping is more effective than therapy. The buzz when you enter the store and see so many beautiful things, all so artfully arranged. The way the real world and all your dissatisfactions with it fall away when you slip on that perfect dress, the one that costs more than anything you could ever afford, a dress you have no occasion to wear, but if you bought it, if you put it on your credit card, you might. The way, looking into the mirror, at your bare, regal shoulders—really the shoulders of someone important—you're transported to that occasion, that gala evening in the life you've always dreamed of but long ago gave up on, until now, until this dress reignites in you that life-giving spark, hope!

He'll see you from across the room. You'll be adjusting your shawl of the most delicate pale organza as the waiter offers you a glass of champagne, as you smile shyly and bring it to your lips. "Who is that?" the highly eligible oil tycoon will ask his associate. "I must meet her, I must know her, I must marry her!" "He wants to marry me!" you tell the mirror, who reminds you that your credit card is already maxed. "But there is another card, I can put it on that one," you answer. For what is more worthy of your money than hope? "I can still have that life! This dress is the beginning!" "Welcome," your reflection responds. "Welcome, my dear, to your new life!"

While shopping may be better than therapy, what's not better are the prices, especially when your problems run toward designer. Uninsured shopping therapy can really add up, compounding your previous issues with anxiety and debt. That's why I opened my practice in 1992. I'm a licensed therapist selling designer clothes at prices your insurance company can afford. I accept Medicare, Emblem, Blue Cross/Blue Shield, but not Metro-Plus.

• • •

Patients are invited to browse our Upper East Side Treatment Center for one hour each week (stock varies weekly). You'll be amazed at how much better you feel after you purchase a $350 pair of Jimmy Choo shoes for a manageable co-pay of just $30. (Note: Deductible must be spent in our store in order for patients to qualify for treatment. Therapy is a process, and we encourage regular visits.)

Make an appointment with one of our board-certified stylists or, depending on your condition, meet with our fully accredited in-store psychiatrist and pharmacist, who can assess, prescribe, and administer the right psycho-pharmacological therapy while you shop.

Dr. Sheila Werther-Marxen and Associates
1090 North 91st Street, Suite 2E
New York, NY 10024

This is the best thing to wear for today, you understand. Because I don't like women in skirts and the best thing is to wear panty-hose or some pants under a short skirt, I think. Then you have the pants under the skirt and then you can pull the stockings up over the pants underneath the skirt. And you can always take off the skirt and use it as a cape. So I think this is the best costume for today.

— EDITH BOUVIER BEALE, *Grey Gardens*

THE FAMILY POLITIC

MY FAMILY IS DOWNSTAIRS YELLING. They're not arguing, that's just how they talk. It's a Greek thing. That's what we say, but the truth is when we visit Greece, people remark on how loud we are. We respond, "It's an American thing."

I'm in my old room at my parents' house because I just got into a fight with my brother Teddy. He was going on about the Internet spelling the end of physical books. Lowering his voice to just a yell, he said, "In the future, no one's going to want your precious little books, Iris. The book will be obsolete!" I told him he was wrong, that people will always want books. Then he said, "Nah, nah, nah, nah, nah," and I lost it and ran upstairs.

So now I'm up here, digging out old swimming trophies and dance costumes from under my bed. I have a trophy from 1992 that says "Highest Achiever." I dust it off and think about bringing it back to my apartment in Manhattan. Maybe I could turn it into a cigarette holder or something.

I try on a blue ballet costume and am excited to find it still fits. I look at myself in the mirror and think about Zelda Fitzgerald. She was about my age when she took up ballet. Taking stock of my reflection, I understand, for the first time, her insanity. I turn in my tutu and notice my thighs are thicker than they used to be. I'm an oversize child, a monster of wilted potential. I put on my pointe shoes and attempt a few poses in front of the mirror.

After a while, I change back into my regular clothes and head downstairs. Everyone is standing around the kitchen table, yelling at the top of their lungs, agreeing that Bush has betrayed the party. I hold up a hanger with the tutu on it and ask my mom, "What's the best way to remove wrinkles from tulle?"

"What do you want with that old thing now? Throw it out."

"No way!" I say. "I can't believe you had it all scrunched up in a bag. I could use it for a Halloween costume, or my author photo—a web magazine is going to publish one of my stories this spring!"

"Oh, god!" she says, giving up. "Steam it, maybe. Hang it in the shower."

I pull at the blue tulle, worry a loose sequin, then sit at the end of the table and listen. I don't know how to talk to them. All they ever talk about is politics, which I've given up, having decided long ago that cultivating opinions about politics is against my better interests. I lean right economically, which, as a writer, would put me at odds with the artistic and academic communities in which I work.

I recognize my views are somewhat paradoxical. For example, idealistically speaking, I'm a "rugged individualist." "The government is a necessary evil," I like to say, "like boyfriends." But practically speaking, were it not for my parents, I would need government handouts more than anyone. I'm prime welfare material. In fact, trying to assuage my father's disappointment in the McCain candidacy last election, my mother told him, "On the bright side, if Obama is elected, the government will help us support Iris."

It's pretty well understood in my family that I can't take care of myself, which is why "family values" are so important to me. It's paramount that I marry so as to preserve my identity as a rugged individualist. If my parents ever cut me loose and I were forced to rely on the state for support, my whole ideology would crumble. "I don't approve of social programs! FDR ruined this country with his pinko rescue plan! Let those in need pull up their socks!" I say, all while dreaming of the day that my parents' burden (me) might be transferred to a rich husband, and I might continue to cultivate my pioneer spirit in safety.

My brother Teddy, a computer programmer, is exactly my opposite—he's a great success. He is a programming savant and his skills are much in demand. If the movie *The Terminator* were to come true, I often think, Teddy would side with the machines. He's the villain. Sometimes, when I'm home for the holidays, I pretend I'm a visitor from the future and that my assignment is to change the fate of mankind by changing my brother's mind, by appealing to his heart before he destroys civilization as we know it. Teddy thinks I'm an idiot.

Teddy spends most of his time staring into his computer and swears by the *Drudge Report,* which keeps him pretty well informed. He used to be Libertarian, but is getting into anarcho-capitalism now, and says that all social security is a form of corruption: "I was standing on line at McDonald's yesterday, and the family in front of me paid with food stamps! Why am I paying for their chicken nuggets?" He reads everything online but my writing—which would be, I admit, a waste of his time. What would he learn from my column? How his prodigal sister spends his parents' money, how she calls it "free time"? It angers him enough that I was born at all. He still hasn't forgiven me for "invading the nest."

"If we were birds, you'd have been pushed out," he says sometimes, and I imagine myself quivering and featherless on the tile floor of our mother's kitchen. I laugh because he's joking, but feel bad, because it's true. He calls the financial help my parents give me I-fare, "like welfare but for Iris." He says, "Why should she be rewarded for her failure, and I get nothing for my success?" "Bureaucrats!" my brother calls my parents. The whole family believes in small government.

My other brother, Alistair, owns and manages a Dollar store, works seven days a week and very hard. He's our own "Joe the Plumber." He has the hots for Ann Coulter and is the most conservative one in the house, though recently we got him to move more center when we convinced him that there was in fact a moon landing. He'd been insisting for months that the photos were made with tiny astronaut figurines and a Styrofoam moon like the ones we made in elementary school when Pluto was still a planet. He pointed to astronaut ice cream as proof. "Like a grown man's gonna eat that shit!"

My parents have cut McCain out of the campaign photo of Palin and McCain that they got after donating money. Now there's just a picture of Sarah Palin propped up next to a picture of me in my tap shoes and sequins costume from a dance recital when I was ten. They say she energized the campaign. That's why they're all trying to destroy her still, even after the election. "It's because she's special," my father says. I can relate. For years I've been trying to destroy myself for the same reason, I think, feeling hung-over, remembering some of the more idiotic things I said last night at a holiday party.

My family suspects me of being a closet Democrat. They think I'm a spy. It's because I live in New York City, am an "artist," and work occasionally in academia. Also, the magazine in which I was last published included poems by Amiri Baraka and a cover announcing an essay called "Why I Am a Socialist."

Teddy smirks and asks, "So, who'd you vote for, Iris?" Everyone waits. *Will she finally come out?* I deal with this the way I deal with almost everything. I make a joke, usually one that no one but me seems to get. I say, "I didn't vote. I couldn't see my way clear to allow for a black man, a woman, or a senior citizen in the White House. I'm just too racist, chauvinist, and ageist for these progressive times!"

Neither Democrat nor Republican, my parents think. *What we have is an idiot.* No one says anything except for Teddy, who begins interrogating me, trying to catch me in a contradiction and expose my dirty, bleeding heart.

I cut him off and continue, "Further, as the leader of the Women's Anti-Suffrage Party, I will not rest until a woman's right to vote has been repealed!" I bang the table and stand up. "Of course, getting such legislation passed is tricky as my constituency refuses to speak until spoken to. Naturally we can't vote for it ourselves. My only hope is to persuade the voting male toward my way of thinking. Which is why I date."

My parents look horrified. I sit down and eat my baklava, happy to have weighed in during our political congress. "What time's dinner, Mom?" I say loudly. "Do I have time to go upstairs and type up some pamphlets? I have this idea for a 'good society' that I might write about in my next column. Teddy, do you ever read my blog?"

Before dinner my dad fetches a bottle of Wild Turkey. He doesn't drink much but has it around because he's been using it to self-treat a toothache. My father hates doctors and believes everything can be cured with either peroxide or a T-shirt. The Wild Turkey is a new addition to his medicine chest; it's to ameliorate the pain. "Wild Turkey for Turkey Day!" he announces festively, and we all have a few fingers' full.

I don't usually like to drink with the family, because I can't drink as much as I want. But since I'm still hurting from last night and worried, too, that last night's whiskey is emanating from my pores, I decide to have just one drink as camouflage. "A little hair of the wolf that mauled me," I say, pouring myself after everyone else.

My mom eyes me, checking the level on my glass. "She drinks like a Kennedy!" she sighs.

"The swimmer!" I answer, and gesture toward the photo of me in a bathing suit at one of my high school meets, which they've framed and arranged next to a pastoral of the Reagan ranch.

"That's not funny," my mother says. "That poor girl died under that bridge. You see what happens when you drink?" she warns, referring to the Chappaquiddick scandal, about which I wrote an in-depth report for my seventh-grade social studies class.

My mother declines a glass herself, and my dad repeats an old joke about my mom getting drunk and dancing on the table at the Ground Round when we were kids.

"I never did that," she says soberly.

My dad laughs. "You ever wonder why we stopped going there?"

"Stop slandering me now. The kids think you're serious," she says, before Alistair emerges from his middle-child cloak of invisibility and offers, "You know, Rosie O'Donnell used to perform there." My mother tells me to set the table.

During dinner the topic shifts to television, to politics, to prices, and then to pain. Neck pain, joint pain, headaches, the works. My mother mentions a lower back pain she had three days ago, and my father explains how he had her roll up a T-shirt and position it beneath the affected area as she slept. "I'm all better!" she says.

"And so's the pain in my ass," my dad jibes, throwing a quick eye to my mother, whose shoulder he rubs affectionately.

My mother groans with annoyance, fatigue, and then delight.

I laugh and then sneeze, and my dad suggests I cover my head before I catch cold. Leaving the room, he returns with a T-shirt, which he instructs me to wrap around my head like a turban.

Finishing my one glass of wine, I make a big show of refilling the glass with apple cider.

"Good. Stop drinking now!" my mother says.

"I only had one glass and now I'm having cider!"

"You smell like a hobo," she says.

"It's from before. I got a paper cut and Dad poured some Wild Turkey on it." I lift my hand and flare my bandaged, whiskey-soaked finger. "You're the wino, Mom. You're the one not allowed back at Ground Round!"

"Rosie O'Donnell used to perform there," Alistair pipes in.

"You see what you did, Dad!" my mother says, shooting him a look.

Teddy chews in silence, plotting the rise of the machines.

After dinner my mother shows me a dress she's bought for my older cousin's daughter, then looks at me as if to say, *When are you going to get married?* "Isn't it beautiful?" she says, holding it against her.

"Beautiful, but a bit small for you, no?"

I return with her to the den, where as a family we've begun watching a heartwarming film about Italian immigrants.

"I know it was you, Fredo. You broke my heart," Al Pacino says, just as I walk in with the bottle of Wild Turkey. I pour both my brothers and father a glass, but don't pour one for myself, carefully displaying my self-control.

An hour later *The Godfather Part II* is over, and my family is yelling at the TV, which they've tuned back to Fox News.

"How 'bout we watch this?" I introduce a DVD: *Grey Gardens*. "It's a documentary about Jackie Kennedy's crazy cousins, a mother and daughter, Bouvier Beale, aristocratic beauties living in squalor in an East Hampton mansion. It was made into a Broadway musical," I say, trying to persuade them. "Like *Xanadu*."

I pop in the movie. Annoyed, my brothers head to the basement to watch C-SPAN, leaving my parents and I alone to watch two aging women eat cat food in the corner of a dilapidated mansion. The film opens with a shot of the daughter, Little Edie, fifty years old but strangely childlike, as she stands in an overgrown garden. With something wrapped around her head, she looks almost chic, but finally just crazy.

"What's she got around her head now?" my mother says in the next scene.

"It looks like a sweater pinned with a brooch," I say. We continue watching in silence as Little Edie recites Robert Frost poems from memory, as she makes allusions to Hawthorne's *The Marble Faun,* as she dances around the house, telling of how she could have been a great dancer, of all the men she might have married but didn't. The mother, Big Edie, speaks glowingly of Little Edie's poetry, for which she won high school awards. What potential! I squirm in my seat and try not to look at my parents. The rest of the movie passes in a delicate silence.

When it's over, my parents say nothing. I want to say, "That's not me. I'm fine! I'm not going to end up eating cat food and dancing around with a sweater on my head, past my prime and full of regrets about never having married!" But I can't. I can't. Because I don't know how to talk to them. I want to reassure them, give them proof that I'm going places, give them evidence that my career is finally taking off. I tell them about a short story I have coming out in a literary magazine this spring—"No, it doesn't pay anything, but it's a very important magazine!"

And then I switch tacks. With the T-shirt still wrapped around my head, I jump down from the couch. And standing before them, I offer to show them my Tarantella. *A joke,* I think. *I'm hilarious!* But you can't laugh at your own joke—another catch-22, like my not being able to vote for the repeal of women's suffrage. So with a straight face, I begin bouncing and twirling around the room, waiting for them to get it, waiting for them to laugh, to join me on the other side of the joke. But my parents' faces remain frozen in horror. Staring up from the couch, as I hop and spin ecstatically, their worst fears are confirmed—the Democrats have gotten to me.

In the afternoon they came unto a land
In which it seemed always afternoon

— ALFRED, LORD TENNYSON, "The Lotos-Eaters"

MENU

YOU NEVER EXPECT A ZOMBIE to lean over and bite you, so you won't really notice until it's too late and the zombie apocalypse has already begun. If you noticed, you could easily outwalk one. Just pick up your pace a little, and you'd be fine. The problem is you're not thinking about zombies. The problem is, some guy shuffles over and you think, *Oh, he's going to ask for directions.* He mumbles something, and you think, *Oh, he's probably French.* Then he leans in and you lean in to better hear him and maybe take a look at his subway map, and the next thing you know he's taken a chunk out of your shoulder. That's how they get you.

With the fast ones, you have a better chance, because if someone starts chasing you, you'll naturally start to run away. Still, zombies, fast or slow, are determined, and once they see you, that's it. Nothing stops them. Not fire. Not gunshots (unless you shoot the brain). You *could* climb up a ladder. Zombies can't climb ladders. But what happens—movies never address this—when there are no people left? Will the zombies starve? Have a seat? Begin to think perhaps they acted rashly? Become university chairs? Occupy tollbooths?

I went to my aunt Kathryn's funeral yesterday.

It was agreed I'd take an early train to Long Island and then drive with my parents to the funeral home in New Jersey. Since I had to wake up early, I didn't go out the night before. It was

Friday though, so I drank a six-pack of tallboys in my apartment, after I finished some wine and reread some poems and stories from my favorite books. I like to read the same ones over and over, even though I've a pile of library books still to get to.

I often forget to return them on time and end up selling the books I own in order to pay the late fees on what I borrow. I underline phrases in the borrowed ones, too, clues for the person who will find them next on the circulation cart. They will notice what's important, how "it doesn't matter that six is not seven," how a cab can "yawn to the curb," how "it is possible to be happy even in a palace."

At ten, I ordered out for Chinese. I almost never order out; I don't like strangers knowing where I live and what I eat. But I was tired so I picked up a menu from the pile of menus blocking the front door. When I'm home during the day, I can hear the menus being wedged into the slit between the door and the door frame. I figure I'll pick them up when they stop coming, but then they never stop coming, so it's hard to open the door now.

At Penn Station the next day, they charged me too much for a Diet Coke. "Two dollars!" I exclaimed, wiping sleep from my eyes. I paid it anyway. Once they get you underground, they can do whatever they want to you.

On the train, I read three Barthelme stories from a book I haven't sold yet. My hands were shaking and my heart was racing from the recession of last night's six-pack, the wine, the 40 oz. I picked up from the deli after that, and a week of so much smiling and laughing.

"Let's get drunk, let's get really drunk!" I'd announced to friends on Monday, Tuesday, Wednesday, Thursday . . . each time saying it as if it were a completely novel idea. *I can't go on like this,* I thought, looking out the train window, and my heart jumped with the idea that I might be killing myself.

I closed my eyes and reminded myself to breathe. Sometimes I forget to breathe. When I remember I gasp, but sometimes I worry I'm too late and feel like I'm suffocating. I looked out the train window and gasped. It's hard to sleep because of this. Because when I do, after just a few minutes, I wake up with a violent shake and gasp, as if I hadn't breathed in a very long time, as if it were possible, probable, to die of forgetting.

In the car on the way out to New Jersey, I tell my parents about all the good things that are happening to me, because I don't want them to worry. There are never very many good things, so I repeat myself, "Yeah, great news!" worried we'll run out of conversation.

I read more Barthelme stories in the back seat next to my brother Teddy, who has things to say. I read three or four, and think about the rain and the sky. There is one story about zombies who will weep on you if they catch you. Teddy says that Internet dating is not so bad! Teddy says his company is taking off! Teddy says loudly that the weather is fine!

We talk about politics, but I have nothing to add. Instead, I interject with a passage from my Barthelme book. I read aloud from a story about capitalism: "'The first thing I did was make a mistake. I thought I had understood capitalism, but what I had done was assume an attitude—melancholy sadness—toward it. This attitude is not correct. Fortunately your letter came, at that instant. "Dear Rupert, I love you every day. You are the world, which is life. I love you I adore you I am crazy about you.

Love, Marta." Reading between the lines, I understood your critique of my attitude toward capitalism.'"

The car is silent.

"Socialism is all about the benevolent dictator," my dad says.

Cousin Thalia and her son Lincoln greet us at the funeral home. Then Aunt Kathryn's friend Helen arrives and compliments Aunt Kathryn on her dress.

Aunt Kathryn is wearing a pink cardigan with a white scalloped collar. Her skirt is blocked by the closed bottom half of the casket. Her face is still. Her eyelids are still. Her hands don't fidget. She does not shake.

At Thanksgiving dinner when I was a kid, I could never look at her because her hands shook terribly, and when she'd bring the food to her mouth, her head would shake in the opposite direction. If I'd look, I'd laugh, so I didn't look.

I hate this room. I hate its flowers. I hate the chairs in small neat rows. I hate looking at someone who doesn't know they're being watched. I look at her after trying not to for a long time and see her sitting up suddenly, not shaking at all. Her eyes are wide and she is a zombie who will weep on me.

Thalia's son Lincoln is five. He smiles and I smile, while Kathryn's friend Helen takes pictures of the casket. It's the second funeral for her that day. She gets a close-up. Then she asks us all to pose. "Good, good, a group photo." We're all wearing black, and the rooms are covered in dust.

I read two days ago that dust is 90 percent dead skin. I am afraid to sit down here. There is something horrible about the cushions. Helen snaps another of Kathryn in profile, then another straight on. When does she take these pictures out? Does she keep them in her wallet next to photos of grandchildren? Mount them on slides, bring them out over coffee?

The sound of the camera being wound. The flash across my father's crying face behind the podium, next to Kathryn laid down. She taught him to swim, he says. He was afraid, but she took him out deep, and he was never afraid again. The camera flashes. The priest blinks.

Kathryn took pictures at her husband Manish's funeral two years ago. Helen wheeled her around to get his face at different angles. "Here, let's have another one gathered round the body!" My father stops speaking and stands still for a very long time. He looks down, chin shaking, and I don't know where to look.

After, we went to Friendly's for dinner and ice cream. We, Helen and Thalia and my parents and us kids, hadn't seen one another since the last funeral, so it was sort of a special occasion.

I tutored Lincoln in the eating of sundaes and asked if he was worried about having caterpillars instead of eyebrows. I explained about caterpillars cocooning and becoming butterflies. I told him to be careful, that one morning he might wake up and find nothing between his forehead and eyes, but look around the room and see two fluttery things chasing each other in the air. He said it wasn't true. I advised him just the same, "You should probably sleep with your hands over your forehead. Just in case."

Lincoln told me secrets, then told me to tell my mother, who sat next to me. "I can't!" I said, after he finished whispering in my ear. "Then it won't be a secret!"

He told me that had nothing to do with it.

"The secret is," I began repeating, "that Lincoln has knuckles on his head, and an apple in his brain, and when he went swimming yesterday, he left his teeth in the pool."

He laughed and said, "Nooo!" That was no longer the secret. "Nooo, now there is a new one."

"Tell me!" I insisted, but I had to guess, he said, if I wanted to know.

I fell asleep during the two-hour drive home. It was raining and dark, and Teddy went in the other car; Lincoln needed help with a puzzle. It was decided as we said goodbye that we ought to have Thanksgiving all together this year. "That's a wonderful idea!" everyone agreed, before making their respective excuses. Helen had another funeral tomorrow. Lincoln and Thalia had to get back to California.

"The pictures!" my mother gasped. "Really!" she said in the car.

"Your mother is becoming such a gossip," my father said, as I drifted into sleep along the New Jersey Turnpike.

"And Lincoln . . . and Thalia . . . and that Helen with her hair!"

I took the train home that same night and finished reading the Barthelme story about the zombies. I looked away from people when they looked at me, then out the window and then back. I took out my phone, reread a text from a man I dated a year ago. We'd gone to see a horror movie, and then I told him I didn't love him. I told him over and over again with him beneath me.

I wrote him a message on the train. "I'm on a train nearing New York City. Reading Barthelme stories and looking out the window. One story is about zombies who will weep on you if they catch you. What are you doing? Are you standing under an awning? Has the rain made your pizza wet?"

I got drenched on the walk from the subway to my building. Inside, my apartment was as messy as I'd left it. Dust everywhere. Mine. Ninety percent dead. Living alone is not so easy sometimes, coming home to a room where nothing has changed and everything belongs to you. Sometimes I hide things then put them out of my mind. When I find the stapler behind the couch a month from now, I'll be surprised and feel less lonely.

I got into bed. The rain beat hard at the windows, now and then crashing the screen into its frame, waking me. I gasped. I had forgotten to breathe again.

I dreamed of zombies. They were chasing me, and I couldn't close the door fast enough. I couldn't get my hands on the doorknob in time, because my hands were shaking terribly. If you can just close the door, they can't get you. Zombies can't open doors. They chased me around the house; it was the house I grew up in, where, for Christmas, I was given a plastic turtle on wheels, a slow thing on a string that I raced through the rooms, past Grandma and Cousin Thalia and Uncle Manish and Aunt Kathryn, who yelled at me to stop as I whizzed by. In my dream, I got so tired and the zombies were so fast. They were small, too, the size of children, but fast. I ran and ran until I was too tired to run anymore. And then I stopped, held out my hand to one, and offered him a bite.

Finally, Someone in Your Corner

Are you an only child who's always dreamed of having a sibling that by order of blood has to be friends with you? Or, do you perhaps have two brothers already and that's the problem; they gang up on you?

It's time someone took your side for a change, and we're here to provide you with just that person. Visit us at mailorderbrother.com and browse our online catalog of middle-aged Eastern European men who are looking for an American sibling that could be you.

Does your family make you feel small? Do they deny you the respect you know you deserve? Not anymore. Thanksgiving dinner's going to look mighty different when you bring your new brother home. And no need to go to that singles bar alone anymore either, not when you've got your brother acting as wingman. Pick-up basketball games on city courts intimidate you? Pass the ball to your brother. Uh-oh! Looks like your brother needs to borrow money again. Loan him some quick cash like you would any other no-account family member, knowing full well you'll never see a dime in return, because that's what family's about. Yeah, your brother maybe be a screw-up, but guess what? That means you're the successful one.

In your 40s, you say? Married to a shrew who never lets you have anything of your own? That's OK. Your mail-order brother doesn't even have to live with you—most don't—though they are contractually obligated to take you out for birthday drinks.

Get started by filling out our online questionnaire engineered to help us broker the kind of sibling bond* best suited to your lifestyle and needs, then choose from a selection of hundreds of eager former communist bloc defectors looking to move to America and form a familial connection of lasting import.

TRUE FRIENDSHIP MAY BE A GIFT FROM GOD, BUT BROTHERLY LOVE IS A GIFT FROM US.

Are you looking to be a mail-order brother? Fill out our online application and we'll add you to our database free of charge.

MAILORDERBROTHER.COM

*Search our sister sites for mail-order sisters, aunts, uncles, nieces, nephews, and cousins.

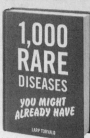

BOOKS XVII–XXIV

What do you want to add?
Value [or] Time[?]

— MTA METRO CARD VENDING MACHINE

TALKING

"I WAS HIT IN THE head with a bat," I told Glen. I'm an excellent conversationalist. "It was an accident when I was five. A neighbor was trying to teach me baseball. I have this small scar under my left eye, see?"

"I can't see it."

"Look," I said, pointing. "It becomes more pronounced if I've been crying."

"Then I hope I never see it," he said, surprising me with a smile.

That was about a month ago, when Glen and I were still getting to know each other and talking a lot, very carefully passing over conversational lulls, as if silence were a dangerous moat surrounding the relationship castle.

Martin, my ex-ex-boyfriend, used to complain that I talked too much. I complained that he didn't talk enough. He said it was because I didn't give him a chance to talk. I said I spoke a lot because he wasn't speaking and someone had to and, anyway, "I make suggestive pauses, which are cues for you to enter the conversation." Then I made a suggestive pause. He didn't say anything, and shortly after that we broke up.

"I'm testing out my Roomba," I told Glen an hour after our first kiss. He'd called me as soon as he got home. "I can't stop thinking about you. Did I wake you? Is it too late to call? What are you doing?" he asked. And then, "What's a Roomba?"

"It's a robot vacuum. It vacuums all by itself. My parents gave it to me for Christmas. What are *you* doing?" I returned.

"Listening to music. Thinking about you. Wondering what you're doing. Calling you to find out."

"It's an amazing device," I said, sitting down, watching the Roomba spin through the room. "I'm going to decorate it with rhinestones, and then I'm going to name it. Do you have any pets?"

"Not since I was a kid. You?"

"I have a ficus named Epstein and a stuffed animal, a golden Labrador, named Herbert. Also a stapler with a lot of personality. It's white and from the side looks like Moby Dick. I feed it staples when it gets hungry. But I haven't given it a name."

"I can't wait to meet them," Glen said, yawning. "I used to have a pencil that looked like Captain Ahab."

"Really?"

"No, it looked like Serge Gainsbourg." He paused. "So what kind of music do you like?"

Brilliant people talk about ideas. Average people talk about events. And stupid people talk about other people. Eleanor Roosevelt said that. What kind of people talk about nothing?

"I've decided to name my Roomba 'Oedi.'"

"King Edward!" Glen sang in a magisterial voice.

"No, Oedi, as in King Oedipus, because he blindly roams my apartment like Oedipus blindly roams the earth in self-imposed exile after he kills his father and marries his mother. Though my Roomba has no eyes, he has acquired 'insight,' for how else would he be able to navigate my living room and pick up the dust so effectively."

"I like to read, too. I just reread *Reclaiming Your Life*. It's seminal. The word comes from semen, but I don't mean it that way. It's totally helped me heal the wounds of my childhood."

"I love self-help! Did you know the self-help movement actually started with AA during the Great Depression? It has its roots in a very American, pre-FDR, ruggedly individualistic, let's-pull-ourselves-up-by-our-bootstraps idea of things, which is so different from the kind of New Age narcissism surrounding the self-help industry today."

"Alice Miller's pretty much my favorite author."

"I found this great book on the dollar rack the other day: *How to Get the Upper Hand*. It's about getting the upper hand. Also, I found this weird pamphlet at the checkout aisle at the A&P called *Why Am I Dancing Alone?* It's about being single and has all these wonderful nineteenth-century illustrations of women in long, lacy frocks looking unbearably lonely on the dance floor. Now I'm reading *Hot Monogamy: How to Get the Sizzle Back*."

"*The Drama of the Gifted Child* is also very good. It's my emotional toolbox."

"What I love is the calm, firm tone of self-help. The writing is so persuasive. I always end up thinking I have whatever problem I'm reading about. Like the other day I was reading this book about how to cope with erectile dysfunction, called *Coping with Premature Ejaculation: How to Overcome PE, Please Your Partner and Have Great Sex*."

"I don't know it."

"It was so well-written that for a while I really believed the author was talking about me. And then I remembered I don't have a penis. I don't know. It's just nice to feel you belong every once in a while even if you don't have a penis. And then, also, I think it's good to be reminded that the feeling of belonging or not is pretty much an illusion, that life is 99 percent sales, 99 percent seduction."

"What kind of pornography do you like?"

I wasn't always so easy to talk to. As a child, for about seven years, I hardly spoke at all. I went to ballet school five days a week and never said a word the whole time I was there. If anyone asked me a question, I'd just nod or make a face as if I could communicate in no other way. My classmates and teachers assumed I was mute.

In the beginning, I was just shy. Later, I wanted to talk but didn't know what to say. And then after that, once I'd gotten in the habit of not talking, it was too difficult to start. What would I say first? When you think about it — and you think about it a lot when you're not speaking — how much of what is said really needs to be? Trapped within the ice I'd failed to break, I'd watch my peers chat boisterously as we changed into our pointe shoes. I wanted to talk to them, lots of things would cross my mind, but then, why say one thing and not another? And then, why say anything at all?

My silence became so loud that to speak, I felt, would require my screaming over it. It was June when I stood in the wings in my tutu. It was the end-of-the-year recital, and I was waiting beside a classmate, who, nervous for our upcoming performance, was pacing back and forth. "Oh my god, I'm freaking out! Oh my god, my heart is racing!" she said over and over.

I commiserated by stretching my mouth into a friendly line.

"That's it. I've officially lost my mind; I'm actually talking to a person who can't even speak!" she said finally, looking at me, as if I were not really there, as if the whole time she'd been talking, she'd been talking only to herself.

"I can speak!" I blurted out, just to prove my existence. Then on cue, Tchaikovsky—eight counts—the two of us fluttering onto the stage like interrupted moths.

I think that's why today I talk so much. I'm afraid that if I stop, I might not be able to start again.

If you date at all often, you can't help but develop a talking routine. The same questions come up again and again—about childhood pets, about your family, about your education—and having responded the same way so many times, you begin to refine your answers.

"I had a pet peacock when I was twelve. He emerged from the woods behind our house one day and stayed. We named him Dan, Dapper Dan," I told Glen on our second date.

"I had a rock," he answered. "His name was Stony. Tony for short."

For a while I worried that something about me was silencing men, because all my former boyfriends had started out talkative, but then eventually, after we'd been sleeping together awhile, just sort of clammed up. But now I think they were never very talkative, that they only talked in the beginning as a means of seduction, so that once our relationship was settled, there was nothing left to say—so they chewed.

"Martin!" I'd say, two years into our relationship, interrupting

another of his long swampy silences. "Martin!" I'd repeat, thinking perhaps he hadn't heard me when I asked what he thought
of the low-pressure system expected to move into our area from
the south. After only the scarcest reply, he'd stare off at the ex-
posed brick decorating our favorite restaurant. "What are you
thinking?" I'd finally ask.

He said such questions—what are you thinking?—put too
much pressure on him, that if I gave him time to think, he'd introduce a topic on his own. "Okay," I said, sitting back silently,
watching him chew while I waited, indefinitely.

The same way some anecdotes are regularly trotted out on
first dates, others come up frequently on or near the last ones.
My telling of the chicken story, for example, is something of a
breakup harbinger. "So I picked up the chicken and started waving it. 'You see this chicken!' I said. 'You see it . . .'" With fervor,
I'll be relating the situation, when a sense of doom begins to
wash over me.

Back in college, I told the chicken story to Jed after we'd
been seeing each other for about a month. He capped my tale
with "I'm tired of *The Iris Show*!"

"Pathetic!" my friend Caroline said on the phone later that
night. "He's just jealous because his show isn't as good as yours."

"You think so?" I sniffled. "I feel like my show's been canceled
and taken off the air."

"It may not be popular, but it's a favorite with the critics," she
said supportively.

My new boyfriend Glen calls all the time just to talk, which
I'm not used to. The phone rings and he says, "What's up?" and

then waits for my answer. My first impulse is to say, "Nothing. Nothing's up," but then I worry he'll find me boring, so instead I struggle for something interesting. "Well, before you called I was thinking: you can't undo popular linguistic errors and shouldn't try. There is no going back from 'irregardless,' for example. The only way is forward. For that reason, I'm trying to popularize the word 'dis-irregardless.' This way, the two prefixes will cancel each other out, bringing us closer to the original, correct 'regardless.'"

"What's wrong with 'irregardless'?"

I'm tired of *The Iris Show* and don't want to have to explain, so I lie and say, "I'm in the middle of feeding my stapler. Can I call you back in twenty minutes?" Then I text him instead of calling and type that I'm about to take a nap, that I'll talk to him tomorrow. Not wanting to hurt his feelings, I add an emoticon suggesting how my breasts look in profile.))

Glen is starting to get on my nerves. It's the things he says when we talk. Like when he wondered aloud about how many bones make up the tongue bone. I told him there are no bones, that the tongue is a muscle, but he kept insisting he could feel them. I tried to change the subject and asked him how his day had been, but instead of answering, he began counting the bones. Finally, I lost my patience and hung up. A minute later, I called back and apologized. I felt so bad. I told him thirty sounded about right. "Thirty bones, Glen," I said dejectedly.

I've begun to really dread our conversations and so, in the interest of preserving our relationship, I've started to avoid him. I won't answer the phone when he calls. Or else, I try to call him when I know he'll be unavailable, or when I'm about to get on a train, forcing me to end the call quickly. "We're going into a tunnel!" I suggest movie dates over dinner dates so that we won't have a chance to talk, and I make our plans over the phone in loud places—under elevated subway trains, near construction sites.

And then, when finally we do get to talking, I ignore him. I pretend I'm listening and then just think about other things. *What shall I name my Roomba? Clothilde? Mr. Fitzsimmons? I should send out a Christmas card next year with a photograph of me and my Roomba and my plant and my stuffed animal. I could write on the bottom: "Happy Holidays from Iris, Epstein, Herbert, and whatever I decide to call the vacuum cleaner." Should I include the stapler?* "What are you thinking?" Glen asks, interrupting my thoughts.

When Glen came over yesterday, not wanting to bicker as we've begun to so often, I suggested we write a script for our conversation, "like a game." My idea was that we'd write the dialogue down and then just act it out instead of talking off-the-cuff as we normally do. Glen's an actor and immediately thrilled to the idea.

I'd wanted us to write a pre-sex scene dialogue, but then Glen's writing was such a turnoff. We fought for a while over edits, before, acquiescing, I fed him my line.

"Cut!" he said—all actors want to direct. "Let's go back and try it again. This time with feeling!"

"I'm *so* happy to see you," I repeated, looking up from our script.

My friend Janice wants to talk all the time, too. She's always calling, asking me to spill the details about my current relationship. Feeling obliged to hold up my end of the conversation, I tell her about my most recent fight with Glen. I tell her what I said and then what he said and then what I said and ask her what she thinks. Then she tells me what someone told her about something she said to her own boyfriend, well, ex-boyfriend now, and how that helped and maybe could help me, too.

"I told him the chicken story," I confessed to Janice yesterday. "About the lady not packing it separately from my other groceries."

"How did he respond?"

"He laughed and told me a story about an eye of round."

"So what's the problem?"

I told her that I don't like his laugh. That it gets on my nerves. That the chicken story is not even very funny, I've begun to realize. That I don't know why I've been telling it all these years, and then I decided right then that I would stop. "Janice? Are you still there?"

Luckily, Janice is an excellent conversationalist, too, and so she's unfazed when I go on for too long, knowing instinctively to just use that time to think about what to say next.

"My lips are chapped. Um, yeah, I'm still here."

I'm starting to think I might actually hate talking. There's a lot that I *could* say, I often think, recognizing Glen's suggestive pauses, but—when I look at my ringing phone and see it's Janice on the line; or blink at Caroline, who's waiting for my response; or am out at a party where everyone's yelling over the music, leaning in close, trying really hard to be heard—there's nothing much I want to.

Lately, I find myself thinking a lot about Dan. Peacocks don't make very affectionate pets, and Dan was no exception. Dan would perch at the edge of our wooden deck, stately, aloof, content to ignore me but for the leftovers I brought him every day for supper. Growing up, I didn't have any close friends in whom I could confide, but every day, for a while, I'd go outside and sit with Dan. The two of us, separated by silence and a distance of at least six feet, would gaze out into my father's yard, a patch of grass bordered by a deep stretch of woods. Eventually, I'd start to tell him about my day, about everything that happened, about some things that didn't, about what I was thinking.

And then one day Dan left. Celebrating my graduation from elementary school, we had a party in the backyard to which I invited all my classmates. Everyone was talking and carrying on, dancing to Z-100, and singing along to Paula Abdul. Dan said nothing. He just turned and walked back into the woods from which he came. I never saw him again.

For the rest of the summer, I wandered the woods, looking for some trace of him, but found nothing. "Dan!" I'd call, cupping my hands around my mouth. But there was no response.

My father said Dan probably left because of the noise, and then, after that, maybe he just couldn't find his way home. I find myself thinking about him pretty frequently these days. While other people talk to me, I think of conversations I used to have with Dan. I think: *Perhaps I should have listened more.*

Two is company, four is a party, three is a crowd.
One is a wanderer.

— JAMES THURBER, "One Is a Wanderer"

THE FRIEND REGISTRY

I'VE BEEN POKED, bitten by a vampire, nominated coolest person, and knighted all in the last week without ever having to leave my apartment. Such are the advantages of social media and yet, still, I find myself alone at dinnertime. According to my online profile, I have over nine hundred friends. So why when my free time kicks in, do I find myself with no one I want to see and nothing I want to do? Wanting to get out of my apartment, sometimes I go and stand around in public places.

My phone rarely rings anymore. It used to ring at all hours, but since I no longer answer, most of my friends have stopped calling. Instead, I receive invitations by email, which is good, as it affords me time I need to compose my refusal. My friend Janice might write and ask me out for dinner, and what I'll do is write back that I'm way too busy this weekend, how about next month? I'll spend the week this way, fielding invitations, worried always about my schedule being overwhelmed, about the unbearable weight of too many social obligations. I knock each invitation back defensively, as if I were playing tennis. No No No. And then the weekend arrives and I find myself with nothing to do, wondering why it's my lot to always be alone.

Shall I read some Yeats? I wonder, pulling a volume of poetry down from the bookshelf, as I prepare for a quiet Friday at home. And then, no. I put it back, unable to commit to a night of my own company either. Instead, I get dressed and quit my apartment for the streets.

Union Square is nice for standing. Also, some bookstores downtown. I don't like to sit. It's too much of a commitment. As soon as I sit, I immediately start thinking: *Now what?* By standing, particularly at intersections — I like the L transfer at Fourteenth Street, and some parts of Penn and Grand Central — I remain always in transit, which I find comforting and, lately, the only tolerable way to pass an evening. I dislike restaurants, feeling hemmed in and at the mercy of wait staff who might ask how I am tonight. I prefer to make my own dinner or, better, pick up a hot dog and eat while I walk. I like eating things that are perfectly consumable. I like there to be nothing left when I'm finished, no proof of my having been anywhere, no residue. I want to eat carnival food all year round. I want always to be strolling.

When my phone does ring I look at it suspiciously, waiting until it stops before I'll even go near it. My ringtone is eerie, as if a ghost had just entered the room in a scary movie. Which is fitting as it's been so long since I've seen most of my friends.

I stopped answering the phone about a year ago and stopped calling people back, too. Or else, in order not to be impolite, I'll call back in a month or three, depending on the urgency suggested in the voicemail. I make an exception for men with whom I'm considering sex. With them, I'll text or else call from a very loud place so as to be able to say, "I'm sorry, I can't hear you. The elevated train is coming. Let's just meet at your place at eight," and end the call quickly.

Incidentally, I have an iPhone — the best call-screening technology money can buy. I write down the calls I owe to friends on my To Do list under things like laundry and taxes. Laundry and taxes eventually get crossed off, while the ink used to write "Call

May" or "Call Henry" fades like a tattoo on the arm of an aging hipster.

I try to call at hours when I think it unlikely my friends will be available. After leaving a message, I am free of my friendship duties, until they get back to me. Hopefully, they won't get back to me too quickly—some of them do, and this causes me a lot of pain. When they do call back, I wait patiently. Then, once the phone's stopped ringing, I get out my To Do list and write their name under "clean toilet" or "pay Con Ed."

What I hate is when they get back to me right after I call them, within minutes or seconds, so that I'm forced to answer. I can't be there one moment and absent the next; I don't want to insult them. They are my friends after all. So I pick up, unhappily.

At this point, I do my best to get off the phone quickly by making false promises to get together soon. If I'm unlucky, my friend will suggest a specific day later that week, and I'll begin to panic, feeling again that my schedule is being overwhelmed. I'll say I'm not sure I can do this or next week but definitely soon. "Next month is better. I'm just so busy right now," I'll say, highlighter poised over my *TV Guide*. "We'll figure it out." Then, having bought myself another month before another call is due, I feel relieved. Next month I repeat the pattern, and the next and the next, for as long as possible.

Mostly I find once you've declared your desire to get together, there is little to no need to actually get together. Isn't it with friendship, after all, that it's the thought that counts? About once a year or so, sometimes less, sometimes more, my friends and I *will* get together, but only once it becomes impossible to put it off any longer. Every friendship is tied by an invisible elastic band, I've found. You can stretch your friendship a pretty long distance, but stretch it too far, go too long without checking in, and your friendship will snap. And it's important to have friends after all. So now and then, I arrange to meet mine.

Unfortunately, when I haven't seen friends in a long time, they want to "catch up." They want to get together just the two of us over dinner and say things like, "So how are you?" A question that has always stumped me.

The short answer is "fine." It's short because it stops conversation dead. Then you have to think of something else to say. The long answer is "miserable." It's long because they'll want to know why and then you have to tell them. The medium answer is "Good. What's new with you?"

These evenings of catching up are the social equivalent of being audited. There you are, forced to account for all the time since you last "checked in." Though, having put it off for so long, the eventual get-together is at least festive, like the main branch of the Post Office on April 15th — Tax Day — when there are long winding lines and local vendors giving out free orange juice and tiny hamburgers. "Let's share an appetizer!" you say.

What I would like to do is go to a loud party where talking is impossible, or else see a movie — though in truth these are also things I'd enjoy more alone. But my friends, whom I haven't seen in a while, they don't want to do that. They don't want to go somewhere loud. They don't want to go to a movie. They want to go somewhere quiet where the two of us can talk, and so, there we are, quietly fishing through our purses for the social receipts of last year.

"I was with someone. Then we broke up." This is what you say to the "How are you really?" follow-up to "How are you?"

"How are you really?" they say, as if asking after the condition of your soul, which, like money, should never be spoken about.

You can always avoid soulful discussions and try, as I do, to keep things light, speaking only of the concrete and mundane. "I got a new job." "For my New Year's resolution, I've taken to drinking eight glasses of water a day. My skin looks great, but I constantly have to piss. I have time for little else. Which is why we haven't seen each other in so long. Between the new job and the pissing, I'm swamped. What's new with you?"

The whole enterprise is exhausting. It's only natural I should want to avoid it. What with work and love and staying optimally hydrated, who has time for the additional obligations friends bring with them? And yet, one needs friends. No man is an island, I'm told.

If exhausted after these get-togethers, I also feel great, the way one feels great after having accomplished something one has been putting off for a very long time. I'm free, I think, mailing my tax return, that is until next year's tax season approaches and, like every year before, I begin the ritual of filing for an automatic delay.

The great thing about close friends is that you can go for a very long time without having to hear from or see that person. For a good while, they will still consider you a dear friend. Every friendship has a different degree of elasticity, however, and in the last couple of years, I have stretched most of mine too far.

Recently, I've seen one of them snap. I feel quite bad about it. For months now, it's been on my To Do list to win this person back, but I've not yet gotten around to it. My friend Katie, with whom I went to college, with whom I made "the grand tour," called and emailed a number of times without reply before she finally stopped. Even the IRS will not let you defer forever. This makes me sad. If only there were some way—besides calling or writing or seeing her face-to-face—to communicate to her that I think of her often, to tell her that, indeed, her friendship means the world to me.

A year and a half ago she was married. Unfortunately, I was unable to attend the wedding due to work obligations. I was unemployed at the time, but she didn't know that and so it seemed a good enough excuse. Still, I clicked onto her wedding website —they all have them now—and found her registry. She was registered at Crate and Barrel and also with this new honeymoon fund. Friends and family could put money toward airfare to Aruba among other honeymoon incidentals.

Feeling guilty that I couldn't attend the wedding, I bought the couple two gifts: wineglasses and the scuba diving lessons listed on their Aruba fund. I just clicked on the two items they'd listed, punched in my credit card info, and, *bam,* my friendship obligation was fulfilled. Automatically, a warmly worded response email was generated from their service, thanking me on the couple's behalf. It was such a simple exchange, and I felt very good about it. By purchasing their wedding gift, I had successfully renewed our friendship for at least another year.

To celebrate, I put my pants and shoes on and decided to go stand around on the corner of Sixth Avenue and Houston, where the cars come in from the highway and swirl around before splitting up into smaller streets, where those huge vaulted signs instruct drivers how to exit the city. Standing at the corner of WALK and DON'T WALK, my hands stuffed in my pockets, I thought warmly of my friend Katie and her husband, and of another friend of mine I hadn't seen or spoken to in a long time who, according to Facebook, had just gotten engaged. I felt my-self a rich woman to have a life filled with so many good friends, and then wondered what I might have for dinner that night.

If I walked over to MacDougal, I could get a falafel for fifty cents cheaper than most other places in the city. The saved fifty cents would be helpful, I considered, as I could put the money toward the upcoming wedding gift. At least I wouldn't have to go to the trouble of picking something out. My friend assured me, via email, that a wedding website was on the way.

For a while people really disliked the whole idea of wedding registries, arguing that they made gift-giving impersonal and obligatory, going against the very spirit of the thing. On the other hand, people argue, it simplifies matters for both gift-giver and gift-receiver. Gifts are not duplicated, and each gift is exactly what was wanted. No returns! It took a little while before reg-istries caught on, but now pretty much every couple has one. If only we could have this for friends, too.

If only there were a friend registry, something like Face-book but reserved for people with whom one is actually friends. Friendships after all are worth only as much as one invests in them. One cannot *really* be friends with nine hundred people, because it's the giving that connects us, the mutual obligations that make a friend more than just another casual acquaintance.

The friend registry would simplify our social lives once and for all, making it easy and convenient to maintain our most cherished relationships with none of the bother of face-to-face meetings. Instead, if we wish to continue our friendship with Bob or Jenn, we just sign up for the automatic payment plan. Wouldn't it be lovely if we could sign an agreement stating that every year on some prescribed date, April 15th, say, a fee of some amount — $20 for distant friends, $30 for close ones — would be automatically debited from our account, like our electricity bill? And if Bob or Jenn are our true friends, they will not simply take the money, but reciprocate with their own deposit, so that no money is ever lost between us.

Friendship is the perfection of give-and-take, after all, and this way we could keep track of ours online by perusing our account balance. And if our balance ever dipped too low, and we found ourselves unexpectedly in debt, then we'd know, with certainty, what it is to feel lonely.

ADVERTISEMENTS FOR MY POSTHUMOUS PAPERS

THE AUTHOR OF *Excavating Kafka* claims that the pornography collection Kafka kept hidden in a locked drawer in his parents' home is essential reading for anyone seeking an in-depth understanding of the master's work. Fearing that the publication of Kafka's bestiality plates might damage the author's legacy, a few scholars moved to suppress them before they were finally published in 2008.

In early 2009, only four years after her death, the first volume of Susan Sontag's diaries was published. More volumes have followed. *Reborn* is a chronicle of the author's youth and includes reading lists, ruminations on her burgeoning sexuality, and reflections on what it means to be an intellectual. Should a reader feel squeamish about accessing her intimate papers, David Rieff, her son and the editor of this volume, suggests in his introduction that the eventual publication of her personal notebooks was always very clearly his mother's intention.

All this raises the question: What should be done with my own papers?

I've kept a journal for as long as I can remember and undertook the project with the expectation that it be published after my death. I informed my father thusly when he asked on my fifth birthday could he read it? "When I'm gone," I said, turning the tiny key in my diary's heart-shaped lock. But with the publishing industry imperiled as it is today, I'm fearful. What if, upon my death, I am unable to secure a publisher? Will all my labor have been for naught?

To get a book out these days, one really needs to sell hard. With publishing houses purchasing fewer and fewer titles, it's not an easy time to be a writer, alive or dead — neither the Sontag nor Kafka book sold particularly well — which is why I've decided to publish some excerpts from my journal now, while I'm still alive. By slipping a few pages in here, I'm hoping to drum up some buzz for when I'm gone.

It's become industry standard to coordinate the launch of a book with an author blog or YouTube video — anything to capture the interest of a world turning steadily away from the printed word, which is why I'm arranging for the posthumous release of a sex tape. When the time comes, my publisher can market these items together: *"The Annotated Notebooks of Iris Smyles* . . . and this free DVD of her taking it hard in the New York Public Library."* I plan to film it in the stacks against the books of my favorite authors as a way of suggesting my rightful place in the canon.

The following selection of meditations, story ideas, and aphorisms should prove an invaluable resource for future scholars seeking greater insight into my oeuvre and a remunerative storehouse for the savvy publisher invested in its legacy.

IRIS SMYLES: SELECTED NOTEBOOKS

Watched Perfect Strangers *last night: the episode where Balki and Cousin Larry get snowed in at the ski lodge. Bronson Pinchot is a virtuoso. And while I've been a devoted Pinchot follower since the show's inception, more and more I find myself excited by the actor playing Larry. Neither of them appeal to me sexually, however, and I've begun to wonder if I might be lesbian. I've begun experimenting with* Kate and Allie *and* Murphy Brown, *watching as many as four episodes in the last month. But on a physical level, I remain unmoved. I must confess to becoming excited when I happen upon Alf. The alien is coarse, distinctly anti-intellectual, and yet something about him thrills me. Third grade, I trust, will resolve these ambiguities.*

I had that nightmare again, the one in which I am a single thirty-year-old woman waiting in line to see "the summer's hottest movie" starring four sexy singles who live in Manhattan and "have it all." Woke up screaming, "Fabulous!" Mother is baffled by my anxiety and by my insistence on calling her "Mother." "Call me 'Mom,'" she says, but I feel it's too familiar; I've known her only nine years. Maybe when I'm ten. When I told her I was afraid to go back to sleep, Mother submitted that I try to "think happy thoughts." "Think about Minnie Mouse," she said. Then I dreamed that Minnie and I were both thirty and single and sharing a "fabulous" apartment in New York City.

OPENING FOR A SHORT STORY

It was a dark and stormy night with a 60 percent chance of precipitation and temperatures hovering in the mid- to lower fifties though the wind-chill factor made it feel more like forty.

TO DO

- Try to work the term "hand gig" into conversation. Whereas "hand job" denotes steady work, perhaps with a boyfriend, "hand gig" has freelance connotations.
- Start a book club called "Club Foot" in which members read only novels featuring characters with clubbed feet. *Of Human Bondage, Madame Bovary,* etc.
- Continue work on novelization of *Weekend at Bernie's II.* Play around more with the POV.
  "As the weekend drew to a close and the sun came up over Bernie's decomposing body, his face looked ashen, yet there was still something in his sunglasses that suggested life. I looked out to sea, put my arm around Bernie, and said, 'Friend, there are more adventures in store for us yet.'"

INVENTIONS

- The Roominator
  A refrigerator that keeps things at room temperature.
  Ad copy: Few things other than revenge are best served cold. In fact, many foods taste best at room temperature! The Roominator utilizes special technology (cardboard) to store those foods at room temperature for up to three or four hours prior to serving.
- Stuffed Plants
  For children who feel they're not ready for the responsibility of caring for a stuffed animal.
- Septuagenarian Dolls or Stuffed Curmudgeons

A refreshing alternative to the traditional baby doll, these small, wrinkly old things need a child and/or hospice nurse's love and care. With Septuagenarians, instead of pretending to be a mother taking care of a baby, children can pretend to be an estranged middle-aged son or daughter taking care of an elderly, ailing parent. Some Septuagenarians will have a string you can pull to make them say grouchy things like "You're a disappointment!" and "Hand me my cigarettes!" Others wet themselves. (Depends sold separately as are calcium pills.) Just as the popular Cabbage Patch Kids came with their own birth certificate, each Septuagenarian comes with its own last will and testament.

The difference between an "alcoholic" and "alcoholist" is that the alcoholic drinks because he can't help it, while the alcoholist, like the feminist or Marxist, drinks as a matter of ideology.

A fast-food restaurant called Burger Viscount that serves only the lower nobles.

IDEA FOR REALITY SHOW:
AMERICA'S NEXT JOHN SMITH

Thirty men named John Smith gather from all over the country to compete for the title of "Best John Smith" and a cash prize. Identity crisis meets game show meets reality television . . .

FOUR NEW QUESTIONS
FOR PASSOVER SEDER

1. Why are men with eye patches considered sexy? What does the one eye have that the one leg doesn't?

2. Why are all porn actors called "porn stars" no matter what level they've reached in their career?
3. Aren't muffins just cupcakes without icing?
4. An alien killing machine with acid for blood, yes. But is Ridley Scott's *Alien* happy?

INVENTIONS

- Baby Botox
  Who wants a wrinkly old baby?
- Indoor Hats
  For the bald gentleman who dislikes a cold head, but is too polite to wear his hat indoors. Similar to the toupee, but without the stigma, the indoor hat looks just like real hair.
- Festive Penis Calendar
  Each month a photo of a penis dressed variously in bullfighter outfits, Three Musketeers costumes, as Scarlett O'Hara, etc.
- Designer Colostomy Bags
  Partner with Louis Vuitton, Gucci, and Chanel.

SHORT STORY IDEA

About a courtroom artist and the difficulties he faces as his style evolves toward Conceptualism.

Went to the movies and saw Last Chance Harvey, *a love story between two middle-aged adults starring Dustin Hoffman and Emma Thompson. I was the only person in the theater under sixty and enjoyed the feeling of civilization among the elderly. The theater was perfectly quiet. Too quiet. After a while, I started to worry that one of the seniors might die and no one would know until the movie was over. I couldn't concentrate on the film, feeling compelled to look around every once in a while, just to make sure everyone was still breathing. I wonder how long it takes a body to smell; people say the dead start to smell much quicker than you'd expect. When the movie was over, I made sure I was the last to leave so I could notify the usher should anybody have been left behind.*

TO DO

- Rent soul to Devil.
- Bring maxi pads back in style, the way I did leg warmers.
- Study plants and save money by learning to photosynthesize my own food.
- Laundry.

I think I'm having a midlife crisis, which is annoying because I haven't resolved my quarter-life one yet, but also encouraging, as I've got the jump on all my friends. Finally, I'm precocious. I've started reading self-help books about the trials of dating in the second half of your life, and yesterday I saw a program on PBS about Baby Boomer dating called Life (Part 2). *The older women had short spiky hair; it's easier to manage. And their breasts were huge. Are my breasts going to get that big? Will my hair, so lush and unruly now, one day prove so manageable?*

TO DO

- Try to popularize saying: "I smoke like a fish that smokes a lot."
- Introduce upside-down question mark from Spanish to English and use at the end of sentences to connote irony.
- Write screenplay about a contemporary Virgin Mary in New York. Replace Immaculate Conception with Immaculate VD for a modern twist.

Consumed by thoughts of death. Was reading some essays by Joseph Epstein last night; he talks a lot about accepting death as if it were just the next stop on the train. I couldn't sleep. Maybe it's harder for me to come to terms with death, since I haven't yet come to terms with life. I'm worried I'm running out of time.

PR IDEA

Write blurbs for my first book inside new books by authors I admire. Cover blurb with Post-it note and hit up crowded book signings where authors are appearing. Ask them to sign beneath my blurb and then use signed blurbs on future book jackets.

"Like Proust but less effeminate."

— Milan Kundera

"Ms. Smyles writes like Norman Mailer might have were he not such a pussy."

— Salman Rushdie

"Not since Salman Rushdie has any writer so deserved a fatwa against them."

— Ira Glass

"What Proust did for naps, Smyles does for the alcoholic blackout!"

— Frederic Tuten

"Iris Smyles writes like Updike practiced infidelity — exuberantly!"

— James Wood

"I laughed, I cried, I brutally murdered a homeless drifter whom no one will ever look for. You will love this book."

— Francine Prose

"My favorite writer."

— Tom McCarthy

I think I might have empty nest syndrome. I wandered into Pier 1 yesterday and considered buying a hand-painted toilet scrubber—anything to fill the void. Been feeling pretty bad lately, like I betrayed my parents by growing up. Like families don't work unless there are babies to take care of. On visits home, everything's terrible. We're all so tall, my brothers and I, which makes us seem even more single. We're three tall adults with nothing in common, three overgrown children hanging around the kitchen drinking coffee. We talk so loud, like babies wailing to be picked up. I think my parents are shrinking. Sometimes they remind me of key chain ornaments.

IDEA FOR A BOARD GAME

The Game of Death! Combine elements of the Game of Life and Monopoly to make a new game of "far-out funereal fun!" Compete against other players who are also trying to get their affairs in order before it's too late. Challenges include making out a will for surviving players! Outsmarting the government of its inheritance tax! Setting aside money for a good headstone!

A special "writers edition" can include the challenge "Selling your papers to a university library!" Sontag is at UCLA. Robert Frost is at NYU. Is Harvard's library in the cards for you, or will it be a shelf near the men's room at Nassau Community?

Pick a card: "There are only a few coveted plots available at Père Lachaise. Roll the dice to see if you will spend eternity there next to Colette, be buried in unconsecrated ground like the fifteenth-century French actors who refused to renounce their profession before dying, or just disappear among the dead in Hart Island like Dawn Powell, whose executrix refused to claim her remains."

Being my own Boswell has not been easy. Indeed, sometimes I wonder what I might have accomplished had I put a fraction of the energy into my life, as I have into my plans for literary immortality. But only some times. Other times I think about crafting the perfect epitaph:

"Fine, How Are You?" would look good on a marble slab. And when mourners pass my plot on their way to someone else's, they won't think me rude.

"Hope I didn't leave the stove on" is honest, but lacks solemnity.

Or perhaps in granite, I'll tell it straight:

IRIS SMYLES
February 28, 1978–
Even Then She Knew

Exit, pursued by a bear.

—WILLIAM SHAKESPEARE, *A Winter's Tale*

LIONS AND WOLVES

THE SMALL LITERARY MAGAZINE I'd founded was in its second year when, instead of publishing another print issue, I decided to put on a show. Closing my eyes, I could already see Philip Roth performing a ventriloquism act, John Updike playing the water glasses, and Joan Didion in a tap-dancing battle with my friend Reggie. There'd be a tweed-clad kick line made up of tenured professors: "Ladies and Gentlemen," I'd announce in my blue tutu from the side of the stage, "I give you the Tenurettes!" And then Harold Bloom, Judith Butler, and Henry Louis Gates would hustle out arm in arm, kicking in unison, the audience exploding in mad applause.

Excited and in need of a few supporting acts, I placed an ad in *Backstage*:

Acclaimed literary magazine seeks unpaid, non-union actors for its upcoming vaudeville debut! Seeking singers, dancers, comedians, magicians, harpists, water glass players, contortionists, ventriloquists, puppeteers—shadow and corporeal—balloon animalists, burlesque dancers, and any other acts of note. (BA required, PhD preferred.) Mail headshots and résumés to: 689 West 10th Street, Suite 3D, New York, NY 10019.

Becoming more ambitious, I decided to film the audition and make a documentary of the making of the show. I had no budget, however, so I had to pull the whole thing off on favors, which is why nearly everyone involved I had either dated, was dating, or "might consider dating once production wrapped," I told Jerry, after he returned with our third round. Preparatory meetings at my apartment were a minefield of sexual tension and resentment.

The audition was on a Saturday in the basement of Union Square's Vineyard Theatre—a guy I kissed at a New Year's Eve party loaned me the space. I'd assembled a three-camera film crew, a panel of six judges, a few stagehands, and a guy in a gorilla suit just in case. Vlad showed up near the end of the day and took his place on a small platform.

I asked him to state his name for the camera.

"Vlad."

Vlad told a few jokes in a corny Catskill-style routine and then improvised a song with our accompanist, Jack, whom I kissed once while drunk and then pretended later, when he tried to bring it up, that I didn't remember. Then I asked Vlad to try his hand at the water glasses and, after that, to give a go at making "Shakespearean balloon animals." A few balloons burst before he was able to make a snake and, finally, a pirate hat, which he placed on my head.

He was handsome and had great stage presence, I noted in a conversation with the panel after he'd left the room. Jack, the accompanist, said he was pitchy.

That was almost a year ago. Production on the film has since stalled. I have twenty hours of gold, but it needs to be edited. For a while I had this guy Roger editing, but then he got a girlfriend, so I had to find someone new, which ended up being quite hard as I wasn't dating very much at the time. Figuring I should finish the movie before mounting the show, I ended up not contacting Vlad for callbacks, and then eventually the show itself fell away.

After that, every once in a while I'd recognize Vlad on television. In various TV commercials, he'd been cast in the role of regular guy/husband/father. In one public service announcement, he played a clean-cut businessman who reluctantly agrees to have happy hour drinks with some colleagues. One of them says, "Come on, just one drink!" and Vlad finally relents. "Just one drink," he says, as they pat him on the back, before he winds up in a crack house alone later that night, and then in the hospital the next morning after having accidentally overdosed on speedballs. Cut to his pregnant wife driving him home in silence, before she parks their SUV in the driveway of a large suburban house. The babysitter opens a heavy oak door to greet them, and a little girl runs out smiling. "Daddy!" she says. And Vlad booms, "There's my girl!" and picks her up lovingly. Then a voiceover says: "Sometimes even one drink is one too many. Know your limits. Other lives depend on it!" Then the camera closes in on Vlad's bloodshot eyes next to the fine blonde hair on the back of the head of the little girl he's still hugging. He looked really handsome, I thought, and I was touched by his rapport with the kid playing his daughter; I couldn't help but think he'd make a great father. I liked this best of all his commercials, much more than the one where he eats fiber-enriched cereal and discusses it with a neighbor.

And then eight or nine months after the audition, I ran into him in the men's department at Macy's. I was trying on an orange cable-knit sweater over my clothes, when I spotted Vlad wandering in the aisle separating gloves and sweaters. My first instinct was to hide. That's what I usually do when I run into people I know during daylight hours. But then five minutes later he wandered by again in the other direction and caught me staring at him. I turned away quickly but then thought, *Well, why not say hello?*

"Vlad?" I said, approaching tentatively.

He seemed not to recognize me, so I launched into a brief summary of how we met.

"That was a strange afternoon," he replied with a smile.

"Yes," I said, sweating beneath the orange sweater. I pulled it over my head. "I'm not gonna get this, I don't think," I stammered, laying it on a pile of similar sweaters.

He looked at me curiously.

"It's big."

"Hmmm."

"So," I said, looking out over the department store with feigned nonchalance — I'm very shy when not unconscious. I passed a hand over the nearby cashmere to calm my nerves. "I come in here sometimes to blow off steam," I said, feeling the need to explain myself. "What've you been up to, Vlad?"

He looked at me for a moment longer. He had piercing blue eyes, strangely shaped, and long eyelashes that made him look like a cartoon wolf, a friendly one, like a wolf in a Disney movie that's been orphaned and raised by hedgehogs who like to sweep the forest with little hedgehog-size brooms. "Call me Billy. Vlad's my stage name."

"Billy."

"I mean it's my real name, well, Vladimir is, but I don't use it in real life. Everyone calls me Billy, which is the English equivalent of Vladimir. Well, 'Universal Ruler' is, but it's a bit awkward to ask people to call you that, so everyone just calls me Billy."

"Okay, Billy." I smiled and caressed an embroidered whale.

We talked for a few more minutes and then he left. I tried on the orange sweater once more, and then brought it to the register.

About a week later, I saw Vlad — Billy — again. I'd been sitting on a couch in the living room section of the furniture showroom at Kmart in Cooper Square and reading my horoscope in the *Village Voice* ("You're in an excellent position to slip away from certain illusions that enslave the people around you, Pisces. You have an enormous power to rapidly understand new information and acquire new skills."), when Billy appeared beside me.

"Whatcha doin'?"

"Hi," I said, surprised. I stood up quickly.

"Can I sit down?" he asked, motioning to the futon.

"Of course," I said, and then we both sat down. "I'm not going to get this," I explained, running a nervous hand over the back of the cushion. "It's a futon . . ." I trailed off.

Billy was looking for a Swiffer. "I hear they're very good on dust," he said. "What do you use?"

"I don't clean. When my apartment gets too dirty I just move." He watched me for a while and then smiled.

We talked for another half hour after that. I asked him about life as a stand-up comedian. He told me a few stories. And then he pretended he was my husband and that Kmart was our house. He put his feet up on the coffee table in front of us and, holding an imaginary remote, pretended to change the channel on the cardboard cutout of a TV—"a flat screen," he called it —set up inside the pressed wood entertainment center across from us. "Would you get me a beer, hon?" he asked, rubbing his belly. He sniffed, "It's been a long day."

He wrote down my number before he left.

I hailed a sales associate and asked about delivery.

A few days later, he called midafternoon. "It's Billy," he said. "What are you up to?"

I told him I was at Bed Bath and Beyond on Sixth Avenue and Sixteenth Street, testing the massage chairs. "Don't move! I'm right around the corner," he said. Twenty minutes later, he walked in smiling and out of breath. "Oh, good, I'm glad you didn't leave. I was at home," he confessed. "I live in China-town," he said, catching his breath. "But I wanted to see you." He took off his jacket and sat in the chair next to mine.

"What setting is yours on?" he asked, fiddling with his re-mote. "Mine's on Knead."

"Full Back."

"I'm gonna try Full Back, then. I want to feel what you're feel-ing," he said, before resting his head against the chair. I leaned back, too, and looked out over the pots and pans suspended in the kitchen department across from us. "Oh, these are for you," he said as an afterthought, producing two brightly colored flow-ers from out of his jacket.

A few days after that, we had our first date. We were at a Jap-anese restaurant and he was perusing the sake menu when he asked me what I'd have to drink.

"Water is fine."

"You don't drink?"

"No," I said, smiling too much. It was the first time I'd said it out loud. I blushed and looked down, worried I might cry.

"Me neither," he said. "I'm not an alcoholic or anything—I just made this bet with my brother to see who could stay off the sauce the longest. I have amazing willpower," he said, and flexed his bicep for me. "Go ahead, see for yourself."

"Yes," I said, squeezing his arm. "It's true."

The discovery that we'd both forgone booze for a while— him "just temporarily," and me, "Oh, I don't know, maybe I'll start drinking again when I'm fifty, like Rocky in *Rocky VI*, AKA *Rocky Balboa*, when he gets back in the ring one last time and embarrasses his family . . . or maybe never"—forged an immediate bond between us. We traded stories from our new sober lives and conspicuously downplayed what had led to the decision. It was just something to do, like you might try hang-gliding were it an activity featured in your resort package, or Ritalin if your college roommate had a learning disability. No big deal.

We talked about our former drinking selves gently, like these great guys we used to know, like dear friends you haven't seen in a while because their behavior has started to embarrass you, old friends about whom you don't want to say anything bad, so you glide over criticism and just call them "characters." "Iris is such a character. She passed out in her hallway and her neighbors found her." That sort of thing. Of course, I didn't report that or any other detail. Instead, I blushed. "I'm actually somewhat wild," I said tentatively, trying to confess.

He smiled. "I'm sure you're a party animal."

"No, really," I said, reddening more.

He paused and looked at me like I was some strange, delightful creature he'd found at a pet store in Chinatown in 1985, like I was Gizmo at the beginning of *Gremlins,* like he was certain I'd never change.

"What?"

"You're so cute," he said.

Our first official date had gone very well.

It was unseasonably warm for March so, after, we walked around awhile. He offered to escort me home, and on the way, we decided we should stop for ice cream. Outside the Continental Bar on St. Mark's Place, he asked a pair of punkish teenagers if they knew of any ice cream shops nearby. "Sorry, man," one of them said. "Could I bum a cigarette though?"

Billy joked about what they thought of us, boring adults looking for ice cream instead of heroin. We passed a couple of drunk girls outside Nevada Smiths, a big NYU hangout on Third Avenue. In my freshman year of college, I'd gone there with my friend Katie two weekends in a row — we spun each other around to "Dancing Queen" and threw back the shots of Jägermeister some ROTC boys had bought for us — and then never again.

One of the girls sat down on the curb out front and began throwing up on her shoes. "Sweetie, sweetie," her friend said as she pulled her hair back. Billy made a joke about her being allergic to shellfish, then added, "Seriously, though. Drunk women are so unattractive."

"Yeah," I said, watching her as we walked by. "Poor thing," I said, as if it were her that I was pitying.

• • •

The truth is when I stopped drinking, there was nothing casual about it. And when Billy and I ran into each other that first time at Macy's, it had been months since I'd spoken to anyone. Outside of the two classes I taught at a local college, and the occasional phone call with my parents, the only time I heard my own voice was at checkout counters when I'd buy something, or when the cable guy came over to install my new box.

Cutting alcohol out of my life left a giant hole in its center. In an effort to replace drinking with other activities, I began watching TV and shopping obsessively. All the money I'd previously spent on booze, I now spent on cable and in shops all over Manhattan, buying things I hadn't realized I needed until I set foot in the store. I bought a curling iron (still in its box), though I have naturally curly hair. *But what if I want to augment the diameter of my curls?* I thought one afternoon, weighing the pros and cons in a brightly lit aisle three.

My apartment, cluttered with gleaming new things, had become a storage unit. There I sat among my acquisitions, like a bored pasha still unsatisfied. It was so crowded, I couldn't stand it. So I'd go out again. Wander the streets. But since it was winter and too cold to spend much real time outdoors, too cold to sit in the city parks and daydream, I found myself visiting the shops again, just to see people, just for the view.

The larger department stores are best. Some of the best views in the city are from inside the big stores. The view from Filene's Basement, located unexpectedly on the fifth floor of a building overlooking Union Square, is beautiful at night. Macy's has the loveliest escalators—wooden, antique, from some other New York that existed before I was born. I'd go to the Brooks Brothers flagship store on Madison, whose fitting rooms made me feel like I was in a country club, visit the sweaters, run a hand over the cable knits, which calmed me down, then head over to the fourth-floor windows to take in the view.

I hadn't isolated myself on purpose. In the beginning, I tried to be social. But the situations I'd once reveled in — house parties with nothing but beer to qualify them as parties — without alcohol had no savor. Clear-eyed, chatting with someone I'd never see again, someone I never wanted to see again, I'd wonder: *What am I doing here? Is this fun?*

How had I ever managed to make a game out of a roll of Scotch tape? I thought, when Felix handed me the dispenser and tagged me "it." How had I ever managed to fall in love, and with such frequency? Love is blind, I thought, only when you're blacking out.

I stopped going to parties, stopped seeing friends, stopped dating. I began reading more. In quiet crisis, I dug up my college copy of *The Myth of Sisyphus*; I struggled to imagine Sisyphus happy. I took long walks along the cold Hudson until I couldn't feel my hands in my pockets, hung out in the reading rooms of public libraries, rented French films, saw the whole of the New Wave. I looked up at the sliver of sky between buildings, watched the clouds pass quickly, and felt the world really large. I wondered of my place in it. I ate dinner alone and cried into my single slice of pizza, thinking of Epicurus's axiom, which I'd read earlier in one of the thirty library books on rotation in my apartment — thirty was the limit one person could have out at a time — "Before you eat or drink anything, consider carefully who you eat or drink with . . . for feeding without a friend is the life of a lion or a wolf." I chewed silently and wondered if I was a wolf.

I stopped answering my phone, which had previously rung at

all hours, as anyone who needed a drinking partner always knew to call me. I put off returning calls until I stopped bothering to return them at all, not wanting to see or speak to anyone. What was there to say? Having spent the last ten years in a manic state of celebration — every day was a holiday, every hour a cause to corral friends, chat up strangers, dance, drink . . . — the change was confusing. I was a party girl, a people person, a person with a social circle so large I could endeavor to make a feature film on the basis of favors. And yet, here I was presenting a definite misanthropic streak. A streak so wide and long, it covered my whole body.

Sober, I was impossibly critical. A tense double of the girl so eager to find common ground with everyone — a taxi driver who stopped the meter and took me for a joy ride round the city and later sent me letters; a homeless wino I met on Phatso's stoop with whom I chatted and drank for two hours, making me late for my date; the daytime drunks in a dive bar behind Port Authority, one of whom stole my wallet but then kindly mailed it to me afterward, having removed only the cash; a pimp; his brother the thief; a semi-homeless coke dealer named Carl; a slew of Russian mobsters in Brighton Beach one June just after graduation; a 1980s roller-skating champion who'd fallen on hard times . . . And as for love, if I couldn't find someone to inspire it, I'd go to work transforming them through my special art. Like a painter creating beauty through his depiction of the mundane, the swallow was my brushstroke; I'd drink until a man's eyes twinkled like Van Gogh's stars. Sometimes this required a lot of drinking, and here I'd demonstrate my romantic pragmatism, my dedication to things fine. Nobly, for art's sake, I'd drink until I passed out.

But that was then. Now, I stayed home watching TV for the first time in years, missing the company of others, desperate to avoid them, recognizing Billy.

Our second date was a little more choppy, though Billy seemed not to notice. At Sammy's Noodle Shop on Seventh, he slurped his noodles happily, then suggested we head over to the theater; we had plans to see a movie called *Bicycling with Molière*. "Something you should know about me is that I love movies," he told me before we walked in, as if this were a hang-up peculiar to him and not the focal point of a major industry based in California. "Consider me warned," I said, as if our date were occurring on a sitcom. Canned laughter. *Why am I so critical?*

We took seats in the middle of the middle row, in accordance with his system. I didn't care where we sat. I was distracted with wondering when he was going to kiss me. If he would do it at the end of the evening when we said good night, if I'd be expected to kiss him, or how exactly the whole thing worked. I'd kissed plenty of men, but when I thought about it, after high school there were very few first kisses I actually remembered. What I remembered instead were nights of heavy drinking, waking up next to a date, our heads already close on the pillow. We'd kiss very probably because we'd kissed already.

But how do you go from talking at a polite distance to kissing, I wondered. I'd wondered the same thing as a teenager, but couldn't remember arriving at any solution. How could I be so old and still not have that figured out?

Billy asked if anything was wrong.

"Me? No," I said. "I'm just, umm, hot," I added, and proceeded to take off my jacket. "Can I put this on the chair next to you?" I said, and leaned over him to lay my jacket down on his side.

"What?" I asked, in reply to his stare, my face still in front of his, which is when he started to lean toward me. Naturally, I moved back, thinking I was in his way. But he followed, leaning forward still more. So, I continued leaning back, and he, farther forward, and so on until my back was pinned to the chair and his mouth was against mine. Frozen, I tried to make sense of the situation. After a second, he sat back again in his own chair. "That was even better than I imagined it," he mumbled.

"Oh. Were you trying to kiss me?" I asked.

"Yeah," he said, shaking his head.

"I'm sorry. I didn't understand. I have very bad reflexes, and by the time I realized it was happening, you'd stopped." I sat still for a moment and then said, "If you want to do it again, I'll be ready this time." And so he did it again and I was ready and then the movie started.

On our next date, conversation was stiff. Again Billy seemed oblivious, which was, in a way, comforting. He studied the menu carefully, as if it weren't the same menu as last week. We'd gone to Sammy's Noodles again, this time in their East Village location. I worked hard trying to think up things to talk about. I mentioned a book I'd just started reading. "*Adrift: Seventy-Six Days Lost at Sea*. It's a true story," I said.

"That would suck," Billy said. Then, closing his menu, he looked up. "You look so pretty today."

I blushed.

We talked until the food arrived but were unable to hit on any good conversation. I wished we could just kiss so that we wouldn't have to talk. I wished we could just skip over the whole getting-to-know-you part. I wished . . .

"Did you know that there are one million bricks in the Empire State Building?" he asked. "I picked up that fun fact from a box of Cracker Jacks. I should warn you, I love Cracker Jacks and fun facts."

I decided I needed to sleep with Billy immediately. Quickly, before he said anything else. Quickly, before I got to dislike him. Quickly, before I didn't want to sleep with him anymore. Quickly, before I never slept with anyone ever again. Billy went on about the fruit shakes he'd been making lately, to which he'd recently introduced papaya, and for a moment I considered thanking him and saying good night. But then, did it make sense to cut it off now? And do what? Go home? Alone?

"Billy," I said playfully, "make a muscle and let me feel it."

"Wow," I said, reaching across the table. "The fruit shakes are really working! Your willpower is astounding."

A few hours later, in his apartment, on a mattress on the floor, under his covers, without our clothes, Billy curled up behind me like a frightened chipmunk, or an injured cocker spaniel, or an affectionate monkey on my back. Something like that. He held me tightly long into the night, occasionally nuzzling his face into the nape of my neck.

I couldn't sleep.

Who is Billy? I began to wonder, adjusting his arm still draped over me. *And who does he think I am that he is holding me so tightly? What am I doing lying here next to a relative stranger? But then, we just had sex. Are we still strangers? How much closer can two people get?*

My mind raced. I wanted to get out of bed and reread Camus, practice happy thoughts about Sisyphus and his rock and his hill, as I'd gotten in the habit lately when I couldn't fall asleep—another side effect of sobriety, not being able to pass out. But I was afraid to move, so I just lay there, thinking: *Imagine Sisyphus naked. Imagine Sisyphus having sex after the third date. "I've got to get up early for work," imagine Sisyphus saying, motioning out a girl's apartment window to a hill in the distance. "That stone's not going to roll itself." Imagine Sisyphus lying next to me on a mattress in Chinatown. What if Billy thinks this is as weird as I do? What if he wants me to leave as much as I want to leave? Do I want to leave?*

Suddenly everything struck me as completely out of order. My being sober again as if I'd never been drunk. My feeling like I was sixteen but also feeling like I was running out of time. I felt young and old and excited and terrified and attracted to Billy and repulsed by him, and I didn't know which feelings to throw myself at, what feeling to run toward, whose eyes to paint, if I wanted to be blind again, if it was necessary. What was I doing here in this stranger's arms? What was I doing anywhere at all?

"Billy," I whispered. "Are you asleep?"

He didn't say anything the first few times I asked, so I repeated it louder and nudged him until he woke up. "Billy?" I asked, feeling even his name strange in my mouth. I asked him if he thought it at all odd that we should be lying here like this in each other's arms. "It's warmer that way," he said, as if we were lost skiers trapped on a snowy mountainside waiting for rescue and, having come upon a dry cave, had decided to camp there before deducing our best chance at survival meant sharing body heat. "But I mean . . ." and I tried to explain what I meant.

Billy said nothing, but listened. After another moment of holding me in silence, he said, "Fine. You're right," and unfastened his arm. Freeing me, he turned to the opposite wall. His back lightly touched mine. I could feel it expand as he breathed.

I tried to move away so we weren't touching, but the bed was so narrow there was nowhere to go. Blinking in the dark, feeling the room shrink back to its real size, feeling the borders of my body complete against his, I pulled at the covers. After a minute, I said his name again.

"Billy?"

"Yes," he said immediately.

"I'm sorry," I said, and waited. "Did I hurt your feelings?"

"Yes," he said.

I turned over and put my arm around his waist the way his had been around mine. I let my face fall into the back of his neck. I hugged him tightly. We'd have to stay close if we were going to make it out of this cave alive.

We were beating out to New York from Gibraltar, and I dreamt I was standing on the bridge in mid-Atlantic and looking northward. It was a simple dream. I seemed to vow to myself that some day I would go to the region of ice and snow and go on and on till I came to one of the poles of the earth, the end of the axis upon which this great round ball turns.

— ERNEST SHACKLETON

DONNER, PARTY OF TWO

BILLY AND I HAVE BEEN dating for over a month, and I practically love him. This, despite the fact that he is a little bit stupid, not great-looking per se, that his body has problem areas. Despite his vanity, his too-frequent checkups in shop windows when we walk, in mirrored walls at pizza places, before the medicine cabinet when we shower together, in the sides of Coca-Cola cans purchased from street vendors before he takes a sip. Despite his poor table manners, his chewing with his mouth open and talking with his mouth full. Despite the fact that for the most part I can't stand him and that frequently on our dates, while he speaks, I find myself fantasizing about dying alone, about freezing in a snowy glen somewhere miles from civilization, my body becoming rigid as I lay motionless and the indifferent snow whirls all around me—I open my mouth and let some flakes disintegrate on my tongue because I'm thirsty, because I haven't eaten or drunk anything for days, because I took a shortcut on my way to California with a band of settlers hoping for a better life out west. Looking up from where I lay freezing, I blink into the terrifying vast, into the violent white consuming the trees, the mountains, all and everything, until my mind also goes white, and I become more and more tired, drifting slowly into the final sleep. Then, interrupting my thoughts, Billy will say with his mouth full, "You mind if I steal a few fries?"

For his part, Billy doesn't seem to like me either. He thinks

I'm uptight and fussy, a humorless downer who won't just join in the fun and hazard a guess as to what he's been eating based on the crunching sounds he makes when chewing into the phone.

Since we don't get along very well, we watch a lot of movies. I prefer to stay home and rent, remaining close to the bed, where we get along best. But Billy's romantic and doesn't like sex without a preamble. He requires romance, "closeness and intimacy," he says. So I do my best to fake it for him.

When he does think I'm using him for sex, he gets testy and wills his erection away. Like the other night, when I tried to roll a condom onto his half-hard penis, and he just stared out the window, refusing to become erect until I agreed to a conversation about our relationship.

I'm romantic, too, which is why I try to keep him from speaking, worried whatever he'll say might break the delicate spell of our love. My ideal date with Billy goes like this: He comes to my place, where I've already prepared a large dinner and so am able to keep his mouth occupied with food. After we finish dinner, but before he's finished chewing, I steer him toward the bedroom, where we watch a movie of my choosing. I press Play just as he swallows, thereby shutting the window for all possible conversation. If he begins to speak anyway, I'll hand him a beverage.

I prefer long movies; multi-episode PBS documentaries are great for the soporific effect they have upon Billy, who, already full from a big meal, is now silently devouring the large serving of ice cream I've just handed him. Should one episode end before Billy feels ready to retire, I can just pop in a second or ninth part of a Ken Burns series, however many it takes. Then, when the moment is ripe and he begins to yawn, I nudge him over to the bed and crawl in beside him. "Would you mind turning out the light?" I'll ask. Then Billy will lean over the nightstand and discover the condom I've placed there strategically, which gives him an idea. Turning off the light, Billy takes me in his arms.

The other night we watched a documentary on the Donner Party expedition that I'd borrowed from the library. I'm particularly fond of survival stories that end in cannibalism. It's because I identify so keenly with desperation. While most people become desperate over time or due to a particularly harrowing set of circumstances, I was born this way. I think it's part of my genetic makeup, the way others are born gay or straight, except that instead of preferring men or women, my desperate gene predisposes me to sexual partners who are just not that great.

The way I first consented to have sex with Billy, for example, I imagine to be quite similar to that moment when, stranded on a mountainside beside their wrecked plane, one of the survivors in *Alive* — based on a true story — tentatively took a bite from his dead friend's behind. The shame and horror that must accompany such an act I've often felt during and after sex with Billy. And yet, I press on, viewing my debasement not as a failure of will but the final measure in a heroic tale of survival. Sex with Billy is a triumph of the human spirit.

Alive, The Donner Party, Arctic Passage, In the Heart of the Sea: The Tragedy of the Whaleship Essex . . . I've seen and read them all. Always the hit at parties, I've fashioned a number of games inspired by these plights. A nice alternative to the popular "I'd Rather," which asks of each player, "With whom would you rather go to bed" if you were forced to go to bed with either Dan Quayle or Patti LuPone, one of my games asks whom would you rather eat if your plane crashed in the Andes, as did the aircraft of that unfortunate Uruguayan rugby team, and cannibalizing the dead were your only means of survival. It's a great recourse for when conversation goes stale and your hostess seems not to know what to do. "Let's draw straws!" I'll announce enthusiastically, and then begin explaining the rules by way of summarizing the traumatic events that befell a crew of Arctic explorers, or nineteenth-century whalers, or those eighty-seven American settlers caught up in the "westering fever" and looking for a short pass to California in 1846.

At Wyoming's Little Sandy River, the eighty-seven members of the Donner Party diverged from the well-traveled California trail to follow Hastings Cutoff, a new shortcut named for its founder, Lansford Hastings, who advertised the route without ever having traveled it. The "short pass" proved more difficult than the long way though, setting the group back a crucial three weeks, so that when at last they did reach the Sierra Nevada, a snowstorm blocked their passage.

An impassible winter upon them, the travelers were stranded. One by one, they died of starvation and exposure while the survivors, eventually, began cannibalizing the dead.

"Even the wind seemed to hold its breath as the suggestion was made that were one to die, the rest might live," says an actress in voiceover, reading the journal of Eliza Donner.

All PBS documentaries are structured similarly. A narrator guides us through the artifacts—black-and-white photos, journal entries and letters, testimony from survivors if there were any, remarks from members of the rescue party, commentary from historians looking back.

"Then the suggestion was made that lots be cast and whoever drew the longest slip should be the sacrifice."

Of the original eighty-seven members of the Donner Party, only forty-six made it out alive.

1

It was on one of our first dates, when we were deciding what to order, that I asked Billy if he liked shrimp dumplings. "Oh, yeah, I love shrimp," he said. But then when the shrimp dumplings arrived, he didn't have any, and when I asked him why he wasn't eating, he told me he never ate shrimp, that he hated shrimp.

"Then why did you tell me you loved shrimp when we were deciding what to order?"

"I was kidding," Billy answered. Then, taking my hand, he told me it was okay that I didn't understand humor. "A lot of people don't. That's one of the hardest parts of working in comedy today, dealing with audiences that don't know when to laugh. You wouldn't believe how many times I've performed before a silent room." Billy patted my hand. "Let's just leave the laughing to the professionals."

"Okay." I smiled, blushing from his touch, laughing when he told me a few minutes later about his inner child, which he'd named "Velvet."

"You're so funny, Billy," I said, happy because the date was going so well. He looked so handsome.

He was wearing a modest blue button-down shirt with crisp khaki pants, having come straight from an audition. I didn't know he was in costume.

I think of that moment often now. I think: how often the effort of knowing someone is undermined by one's wish to. I mean, it can be quite hard to see or hear a person amid the bright bellowing of one's own projections. The world is a nego-tiation of wishes after all, and where desire is strongest, so are illusions.

I was counting the silver grommets on his embroidered shirt a few dates later—"finally you get to see me in my real clothes!" he said—when he got to talking about politics. He considered himself a Libertarian, he explained.

Brightening, I encouraged him to tell me more. *So what if his shirt has a little too much fringe? He and my dad might get along great!* (I can't help it. I'm always thinking about the men I date meeting my parents. I'm old-fashioned—romantic—and the idea of one day getting married and not having to work for the rest of my life is never far from my mind.)

I gazed at Billy dreamily, as he told me the war in Iraq was all about oil. Oil was important, he explained, and control of oil is a good reason to go to war, which is precisely why our government had to fly those planes into the World Trade Center on Septem-ber 11th.

"Come again?" I said, nearly choking on my Diet Coke, be-fore I smiled. "You're kidding again, aren't you?"

"Of course not," he went on, eyes aflame. "You can't possibly believe that a plane was flown into the Pentagon and there are no pictures?" He shook his head and sniffed.

I laughed lightly then looked around, half believing I was the subject of a hidden camera program.

Billy went on and I thought hard. I thought about how far we'd come already, how seeing things through had to be easier than turning around, how he looked quite handsome, how on the bright side his eyes showed bluer when they got that crazy gleam. Focusing on the blue, I took a deep breath and said, "Let's not talk about politics."

He was pretty worked up though and didn't want to let it drop, so I did what anyone would do. I began perusing the dessert menu and suggested he order the peach cobbler. "I'm going to have a banana split!" I said ecstatically.

The next morning, Billy wanted to remain in bed in order that we might hold each other long into the day. I was dozing in his arms when he began whispering about "Velvet." And then, something called "Reversion Therapy," and then "the Linguistics Institute," where he'd taken classes last winter.

He'd mentioned the institute on our first date, I recalled. I'd responded enthusiastically, telling him I was an avid reader of Chomsky, too, that I found the idea of a generative grammar impossibly exciting. We had so much in common, I remembered thinking. I couldn't believe my luck.

Billy continued to describe his work at the institute, explaining how through "behavioral linguistics," he'd finally begun to heal the wounds from his childhood.

"I'm sorry," I said, jumping out of bed, "but I can't lie here all day."

Billy followed me into the kitchen to tell me more about Velvet while I made breakfast. I led him back to the bedroom and pressed Play on a documentary about the whaleship *Essex*.

2

On November 20, 1820, two thousand miles west of South America, the *Essex* was struck twice, seemingly on purpose, by a sperm whale it had been hunting. The ship sank, leaving twenty-one sailors to decamp quickly to three small whaleboats. Eventually, they landed on the uninhabited Henderson Island. After only one week, they exhausted the island's resources, and all but three, who opted to remain on the island, got back into their whaleboats to take their chances at sea.

The three boats were soon separated. "Malnutrition led to diarrhea, blackouts, enfeeblement, boils, edema, and magnesium deficiency, which caused bizarre and violent behavior. As conditions worsened, the sailors resorted to drinking their own urine."

The first to die were sewn into their clothes and buried at sea according to custom. But eventually the starving men took to consuming the corpses. When all but bones were left, another measure was suggested; they decided to draw lots.

"Owen Coffin, Captain Pollard's young cousin, whom he had sworn to protect, drew the black spot. Lots were drawn again to determine who would be Coffin's executioner. This time his friend Charles Ramsdell drew the black spot. Ramsdell shot Coffin, and his remains were consumed by Pollard, Barzillai Ray, and Charles Ramsdell. Later Ray also died, and they consumed him, too." In the second boat, Benjamin Lawrence and Thomas Nickerson had survived through similarly desperate measures.

Ninety-three days after the *Essex* sank, the British merchantman brig *Indian* came upon the survivors, nearly dead. The three men who'd remained on Henderson were rescued shortly after, while the third boat was never found. Of the original twenty-one sailors, eight survived. Seven were eaten.

It was ninety-five days after the sinking of the *Essex*, when the whaleship *Dauphin* came upon the small whaleboat carrying Pollard and Ramsdell. Still gnawing on the bones of Coffin and Ray, the two were so delirious, they didn't even notice the great ship as it came up alongside them.

3

"Whatcha thinking?" Billy asks before, during, and after sex, and also sometimes over the phone. He'll call me in the middle of the day, demanding to know what I was thinking before he called. Finally, at a restaurant a few nights ago, I told him:

"I'm thinking that instead of us asking each other all the time what the other person is thinking, we just volunteer our thoughts as we have them." I picked up this way of speaking from Billy. It's part of his self-help argot. He's always saying "we" when he really means "you."

"Okay," he said, and then looked at me for a while, back and forth from my right eye to my left eye. "Is there anything on your mind?"

I stopped fiddling with my spinach and began telling him about my idea for a fictional sequel to the Donner Party documentary called "The Donner Party in Manhattan."

"Exterior: Night. It's snowing in lower Manhattan as a small band of revelers leave a nightclub and head home. There are no cabs. It's blocks between bodegas. It's been hours since their last meal and, in desperation, they draw straws."

"That's crazy. There's a bodega on every block."

"I know. It's a joke."

"It's really insensitive to the survivors to make light of it that way."

"But you're a comedian!"

"Exactly," he said. "That's in really poor taste, Iris."

We were both silent. Then he told me about the mistakes his parents made in raising him and how that led to him becoming a hoarder. How when he was eighteen, just after his first summer of doing stand-up, he found himself crying in the shower one morning and didn't know why, which is why he took a four-year hiatus from comedy, needing, he felt, to embark on a search inward, which he did while selling Mizu Salon coupons to tourists in Times Square, until he was able to come to grips with this twisted impulse to make people laugh, which really, he now understands, comes from a place of deep hurt; his inner child and what his parents did to it.

"What did they do?"

"They raised me in Westchester."

"Only in the last year have I come to grips with myself as a comedian and learned to accept it as my particular cross to bear," he continued, on the street, after we'd left the restaurant.

"My god. I had no idea comedy was so little fun."

"It's a nightmare."

The walk home seemed an eternity. When we arrived, I popped in a PBS documentary: *Shackleton's Voyage of Endurance*.

4

Sir Ernest Shackleton's Imperial Trans-Antarctic Expedition would be the last major quest in what scholars now call "the Heroic Age of Antarctic Exploration." Its mission: to cross the

Antarctic continent from sea to sea. While the expedition itself would fail, the story of the crew's three-year survival would make history.

Setting out from Buenos Aires, the *Endurance* would sail the Weddell Sea and land near Vahsel Bay. The crew would then walk across the South Pole to the Ross Sea. Because Shackleton's group would not be able to carry enough provisions, however, they'd have to access a series of supply depots laid out across the Ross Ice Shelf on their way to the Beardmore Glacier, which would be deposited by the Ross Sea party, who'd travel to the opposite side of the continent in their own ship, the *Aurora*, before establishing camp in McMurdo Sound.

But the *Endurance* never reached Vahsel Bay. Caught in the pack ice before it even got close, it drifted north for the rest of the winter. When spring finally arrived in September, the breaking of the ice put pressure on the ship's hull and water began pouring in. On November 21, 1915, nearly sixteen months after the ship set out, the *Endurance* sank.

For almost two months, Shackleton and his party camped on a large ice floe, hoping that it would drift toward Paulet Island, 250 miles away, where stores were cached. It didn't. After a few failed attempts to march across the ice, Shackleton decided to set up camp on another floe, praying that the ice would drift toward a safe landing. But on April 9, that ice floe broke in two. Back in the lifeboats, the crew headed again for land. After five more days, they reached Elephant Island and set foot on solid ground for the first time in 497 days.

Elephant Island, however, was far from any shipping routes, so, as long as they stayed, there would be no hope of rescue. Thus Shackleton decided to risk an 800-mile journey to the

South Georgia whaling stations. For fifteen days, they sailed the waters of the southern ocean amid stormy seas and hurricane-force winds, until they landed on South Georgia's unoccupied southern shore.

There, after a brief rest, Shackleton began to cross the island on foot. Leaving three behind, he and two others traveled thirty-two miles over mountainous terrain and eventually reached the whaling station at Stromness. Immediately, a rescue mission was dispatched to pick up the remaining men on the other side of South Georgia, those who had stayed on Elephant Island, as well as the surviving members of the Ross Sea party.

All survived.

When the film was over, Billy said he was glad to finally see a movie in which no one had been eaten. "But maybe next time we could watch, like, a comedy or something?" He hugged me tight, like a stuffed animal that's lost its shape, and told me he was starting to feel really close to me. He suggested he might pick the movie on our next date. Perhaps *Beethoven* with Charles Grodin, he said, and then began to laugh as he remembered a scene. "It's hilarious . . . about this family and their dog, who gets into all this trouble."

5

Last week, we almost broke up. We met in the late afternoon for coffee, after he called and told me he was just around the corner: "Come out!"

Twenty minutes later, the espresso machine was screaming, the barista was banging some jar, and because the shop was so quaint, it was all very loud. Billy and I had to yell just to hear each other, which prompted annoyed looks from neighboring patrons, students typing quietly into their laptops, unbothered by the ruckus but clearly by us.

The conversation was about manners, how I thought they were important. Billy disagreed and thought I was being critical of him because he chews with his mouth open on account of his deviated septum. I could stand to be a little more understanding, considering he'd had to have an operation because of it (his nose job in high school, actors . . .), and he walked out, making a scene, leaving me all alone among the patrons who hated us.

Embarrassed, I collected my purse and left right after.

I walked around the block and felt really bad: It was finally over. And now I wouldn't be able to have sex with him anymore. And now my number of sexual partners was higher. And now I was single and would have to work after all . . . I cried as I made my way through the curvier streets of the West Village, nearly getting lost on my way to the Hudson River.

When I reached the river though, the wind rose and an unexpected sense of relief blew through me: yes, it was over, over at last!

Then my phone rang. "What are you thinking?" was the first thing Billy said.

I explained that after he left, I'd assumed we were through. He asked why I would think that. He said, "Of course it's not over," and asked me where I was. "Stay there!"

I was standing at the end of the Christopher Street Pier, staring at New Jersey, when he arrived. I told him I was tired of arguing, that it seemed like he was tired, too.

Billy admonished me for wanting to quit. "Relationships are about work, Iris!"

"But we've only been on five dates!" I said in a moment of rare clarity. Indeed, it had been only five Friday nights, with countless phone calls in between and a few daytime meet cutes. It just felt like much longer.

"We've been seeing each other for over a month!" he countered, which was also true. "I've been *inside* you! How can you say that?" he asked, his voice cracking with emotion. "Can you just stop this breakup talk, please? Our relationship is never going to get stronger if you keep talking about breaking up all the time!"

We walked for a while inland, before he stopped and pulled me close. The wind came up again, catching my hair and blowing it around. "Iris," he said, sweeping it from my face, which he held, tightly, between his hands. "Iris," he said again before he kissed me. Then, pulling back, searching my eyes: "What are you thinking?"

I began to cry. "I recently read an article about how people who have sex regularly tend to live longer. Billy," I told him, "I want to live!"

Billy took my hand and we walked for a while in silence, ignoring the cold Hudson as it rushed alongside us.

6

After sex, when we lie together, when I look into his eyes, I feel so warm and happy. "What are you thinking, Iris?" Billy will say then. Maybe he'll begin to stroke my hair. And I'll say, "Billy, I adore you," and wonder if he'll run away; he's never said he adores me. His eyes will widen before he averts them, and I will become excited by this idea of his running from me, excited and afraid that I might finally be rid of him.

7

Billy calls me every day. I hate talking on the phone but feel bad if I don't answer, so I answer reluctantly. "Hello?"

For a moment all I hear is chewing. Then, "Hey, it's Billy," followed by more chewing.

"What the fuck, Billy?!" I yell. I never used to curse. "You can't fucking finish fucking eating *before* you fucking call me?"

"You should take it as a compliment," Billy says calmly, still chewing. "I couldn't wait to hear your voice."

"What!"

He can't just apologize and say he won't do it again. No! That would be too easy. Instead, he has to tell me, still chewing, that I'm the one who's wrong, that if anyone should apologize, it should be me, because I hurt his feelings. Then he says I should be happy about his chewing, because it means he feels comfortable enough not to pretend to be someone he's not. "Please pretend!" I beg. And he laughs, thinking I'm kidding. Then, after he asks what I'm thinking a few times—"I read somewhere that there's a chemical in women's bodies released after sex that fosters feelings of attachment to one's sexual partners"—he asks me out for the weekend.

Last Friday I cooked dinner and rented a documentary on the Franklin Expedition. Billy brought over his worn copy of *Ishtar*, which I consented to watch after—*Ishtar* being one of my favorite movies, too. I took the DVD from him and laid it on top of the TV, then sat down beside him, curling into his embrace.

8

In 1845 the Franklin Expedition set out among the uncharted, icy waters of the Arctic in search of the Northwest Passage, an invaluable if fabled trade route that might link, crucially, the Atlantic to the Pacific.

For centuries, explorers had ventured north in pursuit. Unlike previous efforts, however, Franklin's ship was equipped with every advantage of the modern age. His voyage would be easy, it was supposed, their mission to be completed within one year of their departure. But just in case, they brought enough canned food — a modern innovation — to ensure survival for many years. Among the cans, they stocked lemon juice too, to stave off scurvy, which had crippled previous missions. Their ship, large and imposing, had everything, even a library, so that, in the event of having to winter over, the crew might read and also stave off boredom. An undernourished mind, it was understood, was as great a threat as a malnourished body.

Bad luck found them early. Near Beechy Island, their ship got trapped in the ice, and there they remained for five winters. Patiently, the crew waited, expecting that eventually a path would clear. But unlikely weather conditions worked against them, and on those particular summers, the ice never thawed.

According to the logbooks, the crew managed well at first. Ironically, it turned out, the seed of their doom had been planted in their sustenance; the cans containing their food had been made with lead. Aside from fatigue and a blackening of the skin, one of the chief symptoms of lead poisoning is paranoia and dementia.

After they consumed the last of the poisoned food, hungry, sick, and unable to think clearly, the men turned on one another. Some resorted to cannibalism. Others, in a last-ditch attempt at survival, took to the land, packing up a smaller boat filled with personal items, which they then dragged for miles across the snow.

Not one of Franklin's men survived.

9

"Iris, you make me crazy," Billy moaned.

I popped my head up from what I was doing. "Like lead?" I asked, examining his face.

We were in bed after having watched the documentary on the Franklin Expedition when, with Billy's penis in my mouth, it dawned on me: perhaps sex had made us irrational the way lead had Franklin's men. For the sex renews us, spurs us on, but to what?

"Remind me to get vaccinated."

"The flu vaccine is a tool for mind control."

"How's that?"

"If I have to explain it to you, then you're more brainwashed than I thought."

" . . . He had all these unresolved issues from childhood and ended up giving himself cancer."

"You can't give yourself cancer, Billy."

"Well, that's just the fluoride talking."

"The pyramids weren't tombs like they want you to believe but early nuclear power plants. If you look at all those small tunnels, for example, what were they for?"

"For the thieves to get in and out."

"It's amazing how much more advanced than us they were. I mean, we still don't know how they built them!"

"You say that as if today's developers all want to build pyramids but have to settle for glass high-rises. We're pretty advanced, too."

"That's what they want you to think."

Whenever I try to end things with Billy, he says he doesn't think breaking up would be good for the long-term health of our relationship. And though this doesn't make sense, sense has ceased to matter. *Yes, Billy. Onward! Into the ice! Into the blinding white!*

No one knows exactly what happened to Franklin's crew. Their story has been pieced together from the recovered logs of crew members, from bodies exhumed from icy graves, and from secondhand accounts of the local Inuit population who'd briefly come into contact with the group.

The strangest thing about Franklin's story is that while he and his men struggled to survive, while their plight grew worse and more harrowing by the day, the Inuit people living alongside them were thriving.

We meet regularly now in public places, at the movies, on busy sidewalks, and at restaurants surrounded by happy couples. Every date with Billy offers some new horror; he's taken to wearing a shark-tooth necklace. But rather than despair of these developments, I've taken to viewing them as but one more test of our endurance.

"Relationships take work," Billy says, and I nod. But at what point does perseverance become insanity? How much more *should* we endure?

The Franklin party would not give up their boat; when it would no longer carry them, they carried it, dragging it through the ice for miles.

"What are you thinking?" Billy repeats.

I am thinking that if a PBS documentary were made about our relationship, complete with voiceovers, photos, and accounts from our journals giving detail of each terrible date, among the assorted artifacts would be testimonials from the patrons who sat beside us at the restaurants where we were last seen as a couple.

"Yeah, we saw 'em," one of them might say. "No, I don't know what happened, why they didn't make it. After a while, they just stopped coming in." And when asked if they could recall anything else, anything that might help historians piece together what happened to those two who ventured out, so confidently at first, on their first date, the man would shrug and put his arm around his wife. "No, not really. Just that they looked hungry."

Next to the writer of real estate advertisements, the autobiographer is the most suspect of prose artists.

— DONAL HENAHAN

MY REAL ESTATE
AGENT'S BEARD

ANY REAL ESTATE AGENT will tell you, if you don't sell within the first few weeks, you'll not only have to lower your asking price, but must seriously consider throwing in a washer and dryer. That's just the market.

I'm on the marriage market, my parents recently reminded me. And because I've been on sale a little too long now, they decided to throw in a condo.

We closed on June 4th, and the days leading up to it were a whirlwind of negotiations: transfer taxes, inspections, contracts brokered by The Corcoran Group, promises of quiet and parking spaces, Facebook friendship requests, and long looks between me and my real estate agent.

Should I tell you next about my great apartment in Brooklyn, about the ample square footage, the wonderful water pressure? Or should I tell you more about my real estate agent's beard?

He has this long full beard that makes him look like one of those aliens on that old TV show *Lost in Space*. One of those aliens the main characters find living alone on an otherwise uninhabited planet. An alien that starts out very nice—he may even offer you alien cake—though the visitor's suspicions build with every forkful.

"What a shady business, selling!" I told Lawrence, as we

looked over at Manhattan, on what would soon be my balcony. "One rung up from a used car salesman," he said. Dating a real estate agent is the adult equivalent of dating a boy who smokes cigarettes and works at a bike shop. "My high school sweetheart smoked cigarettes and worked at a bike shop," I told him. "He's a real estate agent, too."

It had been a long time since I'd been alone with a man, and there we were, all alone, on the final walk-through to check the faucets and light switches. Lawrence had just finished remarking on the spectacular city views as described in his *New York Times* listing, when he asked me, "Are you going to write about this?"

"Write about what?"

"Me and my beard," he smiled.

"What is there to say about you and your beard?"

We stepped back inside, and I asked if the windows would be washed before I moved in, what kind of tiles would be installed on the terrace, and if the banister on the stairway would be varnished. Then I said, "Actually, I might write about this in a few years; it takes me time to figure out what I think. If I do, I'll tell you and point out which character you are [*this is you, Lawrence, I am writing about you now*], otherwise you might not recognize yourself, and the events, too, might seem different from how you remember them. You may recall a different apartment, for example, an entirely different view; you may even think you're me."

"Have you seen *Lost in Space*?" I asked, before leaning over to test a light switch directly behind him. "No," he said, and his Corcoran Group cologne swirled all around me. "Should I see it?" he asked, his face close to mine. "No," I said, smiling, as if that were my answer to everything.

"Besides actors, real estate agents are the only professionals who use headshots for their work," he noted. We were standing on the roof.

Accompanying each of his emails is a photograph of Lawrence, licensed real estate agent. In the photo he is clean-shaven and angular, though the first time I met him, he was hidden behind a thick tangle of brown hair.

"Did you grow a beard because you were worried you were too handsome?"

"I'm not handsome," he said.

"I think beards are an act of aggression against women. They're unattractive. They say, 'It will be up to you to figure out how to like me.'"

"Really?" Lawrence asked.

"Really."

I tested the doorknobs, and Lawrence told me a little bit about himself. "My parents are wealthy, too, you know. I grew up on a large farm in Australia."

"I see a problem," I announced, emerging from the bathroom, before asking him to step inside. Standing beside him, I pointed at the wall. "There is no towel rack or toilet paper holder!"

"It's easy to install. I can help you with that."

"You personally?"

"Me, personally," he confirmed, two inches from my face. "I help a lot of my clients after their purchase."

I turned and walked ahead. Lawrence followed at a polite distance. I looked in the bedroom closets, while Lawrence surveyed the view—a large picture window next to where my bed would be, opening onto a panorama of the many smaller buildings surrounding mine, my neighbors' windows and their neighbors' windows, above which loomed the Manhattan skyline — "Such a great view," he repeated.

I turned from the closet. "Yes," I said. "It reminds me of *Rear Window*, which won awards for its set design. I love most if not all of Hitchcock's window treatments."

We made our way to the front balcony, to a large glass door, which he opened before stepping out. I stepped out after, but carefully, for the landing was narrow. "I'm afraid of heights," I said, holding on to the railing. "Me too," he said, putting his hand beside mine. He looked at me. I squinted. "So why are we out here?"

Lawrence met my parents at the closing. They spent the day together. I was at work, speaking at a literary conference, talking about the difference between fiction and nonfiction, and trying to conceal the fact that I hadn't published much of either.

"Such a nice young man," my father said later that night. "He takes very good care of his beard."

"He says he shampoos it," my mother added.

Such a nice old-fashioned way to meet a man, I thought, him knowing my parents, my income, my marriageability.

"That makes you a very good catch," Lawrence said, referring to my parents' upcoming fortieth anniversary. We stepped off the balcony. "My parents would still be married had my mother not died. I don't hold with divorce," he said sternly.

I'd seen the apartment online and wrote him an email. I wrote that my parents were prepared to pay cash, then faxed him a statement from their accountant testifying how much. He called almost immediately after I pressed Send.

"He thinks I'm rich and lonely, but I'm much more than that," I told a friend, laughing. "I'm also single and unhappy."

I'm not in the habit of visiting salons, but I got my nails done before I met him at the apartment one last time, this time to test the soundproof windows during rush hour—"I require great quiet," I said, gazing down at my polished nails (mauve). And then again just before we closed, to check the electrical sockets—I flicked a few switches (French this time). And then again (lavender), before we met at a neighborhood bar where I'd agreed to pick up my keys after he'd spent the day with my parents. It was a hot June night, and I was perspiring—I fanned myself with a wad of bills.

My apartment is modern, airy, and light. It's so spacious, so well appointed, that I've little desire to venture out anymore, though when I do, I feel different. More powerful, more confident, like the casual cruelties of the world can no longer touch me.

"I have superpowers," I told a friend after my first night in the new place, "a fortress of solitude!" "They won't have Dick Nixon to kick around anymore," I added over coffee.

"An apartment can be transformative," another friend told me, noting my changed disposition only a week in. Quoting Dostoyevsky, he said, "In a young man's life, three thousand rubles can make all the difference."

I nodded from where I sat on the other side of that three thousand.

Lawrence came over twice after the closing. The first time he brought me breakfast—bagels with cream cheese—and a wrench; and the second, a bouquet of yellow daisies and a screwdriver. He used the wrench to assemble my new desk and the screwdriver, the dining room table, on which, after, we sat side by side.

The room was filled with boxes, too many to count, so we sat on the only free space just above them, a privileged view overlooking all that I owned, my riches, my palatial estate. I swung my legs back and forth to test his work, and when it wobbled I complained of the shoddy job.

That's when Lawrence told me his girlfriend was out of town and that I had nice legs. He placed his hand on one of them. "Girlfriend?" I asked. "These old things?" He traced his hand up my leg and asked if I thought he should leave. I said, "Yes, you should leave." Then I took his hand in mine, pulled it toward me, and then released him.

A few nights later, Lawrence invited me to a party. I accepted and then considered canceling one hour before. *I'll go, but I won't let him kiss me,* I told the mirror. Maybe he has a nice friend who is not a real estate agent, a nice friend who does not have a beard or a girlfriend.

At another new condo on the other side of town, I found myself in a room full of strangers. Lawrence was one of them. The host was Lawrence's former roommate. A thick, gay black man in a denim jumpsuit and big sunglasses. I told him he looked like a Charlie's Angel, and he fixed me a drink of seltzer and lime. "I don't drink either," Lawrence told me, opening the near beer he'd brought with him. The party was mostly populated by gay men, though there were a few women, too, girlfriends of the few straight men they'd accompanied.

It was the kind of party that makes you think about stealing;

if a heart's not locked up, if you find it on the floor somewhere, is that theft? The kind of party that makes you wonder if you're capable of such parties. After an hour on the balcony talking to a guy called Nico about the genesis of his name — it was Nicholas, then he spent a semester in Paris — I excused myself to the bathroom.

The door was locked and stayed that way for ten minutes before two men emerged amorously, offering assurances that they weren't having sex. "It's not what you think," they told me. I blushed not knowing what I thought. I'd been watching Lawrence across the room.

When I returned, Lawrence said things like "fuck that shit" and spoke about abuses of police power and tax preparation specialists. I told him primly I didn't care for such language, and then he stood very close, apologized, and asked what I did care for. His Corcoran Group cologne swirled all around me.

Was I having a good time? Did I want another piece of cake? Did I need my drink refreshed? Yes, I kept saying, yes, yes, and before I knew it, it was as if it were my answer to everything.

"How do you know Lawrence?" another guest asked me. "He's my real estate agent," I said haughtily. "Lawrence, do you mind if I refer to you that way? May I add you to my staff?" He moved close, as someone made his way through the crowd behind him. "Not at all. You know," Lawrence said, "Iris has one of the most beautiful apartments in Brooklyn. She got a great deal. And you should see her view!"

We stood on the balcony bursting with people, and I told him his beard made him look like a conqueror. "What makes me look like a conqueror?" "The way you stand. The way you look. The way you conquer." I imitated Garibaldi drawing his sword. Lawrence looked out over the railing. "It's as if you were made of marble and standing on a pedestal in a public park."

He suggested we leave and, taking my elbow, led me downstairs. He hailed a taxi and gave the driver my new address.

We sat on my couch, recently freed from a mountain of boxes. The rest of the room was still stacked high. He swept my legs up onto his lap. Caressing them, he told me he despised liars and cheats. He told me honor was all that mattered in this world. He told me what might happen if he stayed a moment longer. "I will lie beside you and hold you, my face will fall into the back of your neck; I will want to kiss you, to take off your clothes . . . I will want to hold you all night."

I asked him about his girlfriend. He sighed and said he despised cheaters. "And thieves," I added. "Me too." We held hands and felt small and lonely in our moral universe. He raised my hand to his face. I said, "Break up with your girlfriend, then call me and ask me for a date." He said that made sense and opened my palm, which he kissed. "Then it's settled," I said, and motioned to the front door.

When it was over, we lay naked in the dark, side by side, staring out the large picture window next to my bed, at the lights of Manhattan glittering across the river. He remarked on the color of the sky, the faint outline of clouds, the spectacular city views as described in his *New York Times* listing. "Yes, it's a great view," I whispered. "Your description really captured it." Then he said he had to go.

"You're not staying?"

"I'm afraid I won't be able to sleep if I do."

"Oh," I said, looking down. "I was kidding when I called you a conqueror."

"Do you know how beautiful you are?"

"No."

"I'm sure people tell you you're beautiful all the time."

"That wasn't your question."

"In this light"—he traced my breasts—"you look magical."

"You should see me in the kitchen. Also hallway fluorescents do something marvelous to my veins." I showed him the inside of my wrist. "Look how blue." Then, "You have a great body," I lied. He was much thinner than in his Facebook photos.

Lawrence put his pants on, and I walked him to the door, worrying over my tears, hoping he couldn't see them or if he could, that they looked large and diamond-like, rich.

"Will I see you again?" I asked.

He shrugged. "Will I see you?"

It was a long walk back to the bedroom—the apartment is so large, so many square feet of luxury condo living—where I slept alone in the swirl of his Corcoran Group cologne. The light from the view, too bright without blinds, kept me awake.

I woke a little before noon and lay in bed, staring up at my twelve-foot ceiling. "You look nothing like your Corcoran Group photograph," I'd said before he left.

I went to the kitchen, to my pristine Kohler appliances, poured myself a fresh glass of water, and checked my phone. I found a text from Lawrence sent just after he'd left. I hadn't heard it beep all the way in the next room, not over the great steady hum of central air.

"Thank you," it said, the way it does on receipts.

I went back to bed and curled up on my side.

"A guy has to wonder," he'd asked from under my desk, "why's a smart beautiful woman like you still single?"

"It's my sense of humor. And my vagina."

"What's wrong with your vagina?"

"It's too cheerful. Men prefer one that broods."

"You're kidding," he verified. He stared up into the corner of the desk and twisted a screw. "But don't you get lonely?"

"Not as lonely as when I'm with someone I don't love."

I got dressed. Would it be rude if I didn't return his text? I imagined him opening his phone and reading "You're welcome."

"Manners are important to me," I had told him at the party. "What kind of world is it where men sit while a woman stands on the subway?"

I picked up my phone and typed: "Never call me again!" I pressed Delete.

I grabbed my keys and went out.

Twenty minutes later, I ate a bagel and drank coffee from a paper cup while sitting on top of my wobbly table. I thought, *Why end things now when I could keep him on staff, use him for sex, have him install my shower door?*

"Thank you for taking me to the party," I typed into the phone. "You have a great body," I added. I smiled and pressed Send. His body was nothing much.

An hour later, the phone beeped and I ran downstairs—a duplex, *plenty of room for a home office or second bedroom*—to find his message: "It was nice to see you."

I stared at the words until they became blurry, and then I stared out over the room.

I opened boxes for the rest of the afternoon, the whole time imagining what I'd say if I ever ran into him. "You, you salesman!"

Or would I be nice? Ask him to come over and tighten the screws on my bedside tables — he'd promised to bring me an Allen wrench — and then change my mind once he arrived. Very coolly, I'd say, "What does your girlfriend think of your Allen wrench?"

I opened more boxes, an odd mix of items — hats, books, a clock radio, pillows, and a long, red wool scarf I should have just thrown out.

The boxes were everywhere, crowding my fortress of solitude. "Like my apartment, Superman's Fortress of Solitude was built by a crystal bestowed on him from his parents, who sent him to Earth just before his home planet was destroyed," I'd told my friend earlier that week.

"The last of his kind, Superman can hang out there and watch HDTV when he's feeling sad, which is often, for Superman is alone in the world, will always be alone, which gives him the blues. Though he may possess the strength of ten men and can defeat evildoers with one sizzling look, he can never overcome his loneliness." Who can?

It was getting dark. The lights from my spectacular view were coming up. The bridge across the way was beginning to twinkle and, sitting there among my boxes, my great wealth, my vast estate, my floor-to-ceiling windows, my high ceilings, my perfect white walls, the central air humming, I used a corner of my red cape — the scarf I should have thrown out — to wipe away a diamond tear. They were much higher-quality tears than I'd cried in the old place, I thought. Things were certainly going to be different.

TAXONOMY OF EXES

JED'S EX WAS MARLA, a vegetarian, which was something he disliked about her. He told me so after I ordered a steak on our second date. He said, "I like that you ordered steak; Marla never ordered steak." They dated for ten years. They liked the beat poets and tried swinging with another couple with whom they went to high school in Brooklyn.

Martin's ex was Meghan, whose father was a writer who'd won the Pulitzer. We ran into her after a weeklong drive from San Francisco to LA. We argued the whole drive down the Pacific Coast Highway and stopped only briefly after he saw her outside a restaurant called Brooklyn Diner. She'd gone out there to act, she said. We all ordered pastrami.

Jess's ex was Lauren. They lived together two years, but he wasn't ready to marry. He left her and is not over her and doesn't know yet if he ever will be, which is why he wasn't ready for a relationship, but thought I should sleep over anyway.

Jack had been married; his ex left him for her graduate school professor, and his eyes become glassy at the mention of "wine and cheese."

Max's ex was Linda. They dated for two years. He told me one day he just knew; they were floating side by side in the Atlantic, looking at their feet sticking out of the gray-green brine, and he just knew that she was the one.

Philip's ex was Katherine. They were together for ten years, married for two, and separated for one and a half, but he was over her. In bed one night, after we'd had sex—after we'd broken up and got back together and broke up and got back together —Philip told me he'd had a breakthrough in therapy earlier that day. "I'm still in love with Katherine."

Glen's ex was Heide. She was from Poland and needed a green card. Glen sometimes thinks he should have married Heide, even though he didn't want to and unquestionably did the right thing by not. He wonders what she's doing now. If she had to return to Poland or if she married someone else.

Billy's ex was Lindsey. He got her pregnant and took her to a clinic for the procedure.

Kevin's ex was Lara, an artist in upstate New York. Her last project involved a personal ad inviting men to be photographed next to her on her couch. They dated long-distance for a full year, and when they broke up, she attempted suicide. She called him from the sanatorium where they were holding her and asked what she should say to get the doctors to release her; Kevin is an emergency room psychiatrist, so she knew he'd know. He kissed me and told me it was the least he could do.

BRILLIG

1

YESTERDAY WHEN SAM KISSED ME, I remembered where I left my keys. They'd been missing a few days — I'd had to call a locksmith — when, with Sam's lips touching mine, I had a revelation and cried out, "Eureka!"

I don't know where I got the word "eureka" from. I'd never said "eureka" before, but there it tumbled out, as if it were the most natural thing. Sam thought I was calling him "Eureka" and said he preferred some of the names I'd given him previously. "I like 'Conan the Librarian' better," he said, before kissing me again.

I'm absent-minded and more than once have tried to fit a metro card in the front door, swiped my lip gloss at the subway turnstile, and brought keys to my lips when looking in the bathroom mirror, which is, I guess, how they ended up in the medicine cabinet. But who knows? I've a terrible memory. Just like my dad.

"I remember what's-his-name" is the setup of my dad's favorite joke. He'll say the line as if about to begin a story and then stop; the setup is also the punch line. He repeats this joke fairly often, every time as if it were the first time, and I laugh every time, too, though sometimes I can't remember why it's funny.

If I can't remember some things, others I can't forget: Running on the beach with my father when I was six. We were going so fast; I was afraid my legs weren't long or quick enough, that I'd fall, and I remember looking up at him, as he laughed and pulled my hand and said faster and we were flying and my feet, I swear, were barely touching the ground.

I also forget words. Last summer I was helping my father in the garden, and I wanted to say, "Hand me the hose," but couldn't remember the word for "hose," so I stood there stammering, until finally I gave up and pointed toward "the snake that spits water."

He immediately understood, as we share the same affliction. He's asked me numerous times for a "writing stick" when he wanted a pencil and sometimes asks for "brown champagne" when the Coca-Cola is on the other end of a lunch table. People, places, and things—it's nouns that give us the most trouble. Grasping at metaphors when our memories fail, sometimes our conversations become inadvertently poetic: "Dad," I'll say entering the living room where he's watching CNN, "Mom says 'the night fuel' is ready."

My mother, forgetful in her own way, replaces most of her nouns with the phrase "the thing." "Pass me the thing." Or, "We're going to the thing." Recently she advanced to replacing verbs as well, so that sometimes whole sentences will consist of nothing but "the thing." "The thing the thing in the thing," she'll say to my father, who will know exactly what she means: "Bring the groceries in from the garage." Forty years of marriage is its own language.

Ironically, my mother is named Calliope, after the muse that inspired Homer. Each of the nine muses was assigned to a different art, and my mother's namesake worked with words. "Sing in me, Muse," Homer says at the beginning of *The Odyssey,* for the Greeks believed inspiration was mostly listening. The writer, a conduit, did not invent but record whatever the muse told him. To imagine, in ancient Greece, was really to recall.

In fact, memory gave birth to imagination rather literally, as the muses were the daughters of Mnemosyne, the goddess of memory, whose name was also given to a river in Hades — Lethe's rumored counterpart. While dead souls drank from Lethe to forget their lives, one might alternately drink from Mnemosyne and remember everything.

In Greek, the word *lethe* means "forgetfulness." It is the root word of *aletheia,* meaning "truth," which translates to "unforgetfulness," suggesting that knowledge, even self-knowledge, exists someplace outside of oneself, and so could be misplaced, like keys. Thus, the common phrase "finding oneself" tells of a deep, perhaps unconscious belief that we do not become but uncover who we are, that the future is pursued nostalgically.

Another myth, not exclusively Greek, offers that every child upon his birth holds within him all the wisdom of the world, until an angel visits and, pressing a finger to the child's lips, impels him to keep it all secret. "Shhhhh," the angel says, and like that the child forgets. That place in the middle of our upper lip that dips down is the scar and symbol of what we've forgotten, reminding us that wisdom is not acquired but recalled.

The Greeks felt that spot, the philtrum, to be the body's most erogenous zone, so they called it *philein,* meaning "to love." In countless stories since, love and truth are thus entwined. Only a kiss can restore the frog to his true form of prince. Forget the eyes, forget the soul; the lips are the door to memory, which can be unlocked or sealed, as they say, with a kiss.

2

In *De Oratore,* Cicero describes a mnemonic device called "the Memory Palace," which requires you to imagine a physical space, a great house with many rooms, in which each of your memories can be stored. To retrieve a particular memory, you've only to enter that room and go to that place where you've left it.

This device, used by memory champions, is a bulwark against a basic tenet of physics, which states that entropy is ever increasing. Our minds, like our homes, become messy over time; the Memory Palace untended becomes a house filled with lost things.

If you stay up late, you'll see plenty of infomercials selling kits to improve your memory. My father, plagued by insomnia, is a connoisseur of self-improvement. Having already purchased *Teach Yourself Greek!,* Tony Robbins's *Unleash the Power Within,* and a Total Gym that folds away to fit neatly under the bed — where it stays — he's bought a few memory kits, too. Unfortunately, he forgets to use them; the trap of the bad memory is forgetting one's mission to ameliorate it.

The trouble with all of these systems is that they can only improve one's deliberate memory, so that you have first to say to yourself, "I want to remember this," and then perform the suggested exercise upon the thing you want to remember. This method won't help with remembering things already forgotten or remembering things one isn't anticipating forgetting. The exercises must be employed preemptively, so that one must begin by remembering not to forget. They do nothing to solve the real problem, which is forgetting to remember in the first place.

The trickiest thing about a bad memory is that one doesn't remember forgetting. To even know one's forgotten requires first remembering what's forgotten. And how can you know you've forgotten anything until by some accident you're reminded? Until a person from out of your past appears before you at a party, on the sidewalk, at a restaurant, in the elevator at your new office, and says, "You look familiar," and cocks his head and asks where you're from, then squints and says, "Eureka!" Until he reminds you that you were inseparable in second grade—"Don't you remember?"—and goes on reminding you of a field trip your class took on a fishing boat off Sheepshead Bay, how the two of you got in trouble with the teacher, "Mrs. What's-her-name, remember her?" for spitting over the side.

And you don't remember, but then you start to. "Oh, yes," you say, after more details jog your memory. "My god, what are the chances?" And then, looking around you on the street later that day, at the faces of so many strangers, you wonder again what are the chances and are struck by an uncanny feeling—every person you see looks suddenly familiar, as if at some time long ago forgotten, you might have known them all.

Each of my dad's mnemonic kits offers variations on a few classic memory exercises. The basic strategy is to strengthen memories through association. If you meet someone at a cocktail party, for example, and you want to remember his name, try to pick out one specific thing about him. If he is wearing a red tie, say to yourself, *red tie—Donald, red tie—Donald, red tie—Donald . . .*

In college, I had a big crush on a Donald whose memory was great. We were in the dining hall when I confessed mine wasn't. He insisted my memory could be great, too; it was only a matter of strategy. Eager to prove his point, he climbed on top of his chair and instructed me to memorize what he was about to say. The unusual circumstances under which I was receiving the information, he explained after, would make a lasting impression, making it impossible to forget.

When he quizzed me after ten minutes, however, I remembered nothing of what he'd said, only the way he looked when he said it — towering over me, his brown hair flopping into his eyes. I wonder if he remembers that?

3

Emerging from a café following a warm spring rain, I inhale deeply, and all at once recall a similar day three years earlier; the air now is as it was then when I fled Central Park, soaking wet, having been caught in a sudden downpour. I was on a bicycle pedaling after Philip, who was up ahead, leaning into a left turn. Philip, whom I haven't thought of in over a year. Philip, who was once so unforgettable. How could I have forgotten what's-his-name?

A person's memory is a complex web of associations. Mothballs remind us of grandmothers, popular songs cue up old heartbreaks, places are haunted by people we once knew, the utterance of a name can open on to a feeling, while a feeling can open backward onto a name.

But then names change, which can confuse things. For example, a person you once called your "boyfriend" becomes your "ex-boyfriend," and then there is your new boyfriend, who after a year also becomes your "ex-boyfriend," requiring the previous "ex-boyfriend" to shift down a spot and be renamed your "ex-ex-boyfriend" or your "old ex-boyfriend" or your "former ex-boyfriend," in order to distinguish him from your "most recent ex-boyfriend." It can get rather complicated, which is perhaps why it's best not to use names at all.

Philip used to call me by his ex-wife's name when we argued. "Katherine!" he'd yell. "I mean Iris." It bothered me, but I couldn't get too angry, as I'd done the same thing a few times myself. Just as Philip associated anger with his ex-wife, I associated love with my then-ex-boyfriend Martin.

We were in bed the first time it happened. Philip was on top when I rather affectionately cried out, "Martin!" because, as I explained after, I'd felt a sudden rush of love, a feeling I associated with Martin, who was my boyfriend for three years before Philip. "But, Philip! Martin was the furthest thing from my mind!" I insisted, for hearing his name had surprised me, too.

"If anything, you should take it as a compliment," I went on. "Had I called you 'chicken fingers,' 'tilapia,' or 'suitcase without wheels,' I'd understand your anger, because I don't much care for those things. But I really *liked* Martin! Don't you see? Which means I *really like you,* too."

"Katherine — I mean Iris — I don't want to hear it!"

After much discussion, his anger subsided, and we picked up where we left off. And then, what can I say? It happened again. "Oh, Martin," I sighed, before I caught myself and froze. He pulled away and looked at me, his eyes molten.

"I'm kidding!" I lied. "God, you're so serious all the time!"

He glared.

"Bad joke?" I asked, scrunching my face. "I remember what's-his-name," I said, forcing a laugh. "You know that joke?"

Philip left the room and I followed closely after, describing the symptoms of Wernicke's aphasia.

4

Aphasia is a brain disorder primarily affecting speech. The afflicted will substitute words like "blaff" for "glass," or "coutom" for "crouton." Sometimes called "cocktail hour speech," it's not nonsensical exactly, because it can still be understood, the way readers can glean meaning from Lewis Carroll's poem "Jabberwocky."

I'm not suggesting I have Wernicke's, but I think it's distinctly possible that I have Wernicke's cousin. While Wernicke's is caused by brain trauma, "Amatory Aphasia" results from a blow to the heart—a painful breakup or series of them—and presents as a trouble with naming romantic partners. It afflicts almost all single adults of a certain age. If you've dated around, you probably have it too.

That's where "baby," "sweetheart," and "honey" come in. They're pet names employed by the seasoned lover who'd never make a rookie mistake like mine, not again anyway. Had I cried out, "Baby," the debacle with Philip might well have been avoided.

When I was young, calling someone "baby" seemed vulgarly callous, as I hadn't yet grasped that a callus serves a purpose. Just like a person with a broken knee wears a cast, a person with a broken heart calls his new lover "baby." It's unfortunate but sometimes the heart mends imperfectly, requiring the injured to rely on a crutch. Saying "baby" is how the heart limps.

I could recall no name for the pain I felt when Philip left. And just as I'd become inadvertently poetic in my father's garden, describing objects when their names eluded me, I went on to friends, trying to describe my terrible feelings for which no single word sufficed.

The word I was seeking was on the tip of my tongue, I felt, and so I kept talking, like that annoying guy hanging over the jukebox at your favorite bar who won't stop hounding you about the lyrics to a song he can't remember but which he has, nevertheless, stuck in his head. "You know that song about the girl who's angry with the guy because he did something she didn't like?" he goes on. "Damn! What's it called? I'm not going to be able to stop thinking about it until I figure it out!"

If I could only name the feeling, I was sure I could let it go.

"Baby, you broke my heart," the guy says between swallows of beer beside the jukebox. "B'dm, b'dm, d'dm. It goes something like that."

5

Now I'm dating someone new. I've been seeing Sam for over a month and have in that time called him a variety of names: "Mr. Drummond," "Bird Flu," "Queequeg," "Octopus Lips," "Flounder Teeth," "One Hundred Seventy-Five Pound Cake," "Cold Cuts," "Chief Custodian of My Loins," as in "I hereby promote thee Sam to Chief Custodian of My Loins," "Orange Julius," "DDT," "Tempur-Pedic Mattress," "Wonderballs," "Shostakovich," and "Vitamin Supplement." Pet names, alternatives to "baby" and "sweetheart." Why not make my bandage words unique? Why not paint little drawings on each cast?

As Sam and I get closer, however, I find myself, much as before, on the verge of calling him the wrong thing. It's strange to say, but an intimate moment in the life of an adult is often a congress of previous ones. With the ghosts of one's past crowding around you in the present, a kiss is a haunted thing.

Like a song on the radio reminds you of your first slow dance; like the scent of damp grass brings back that high school pep rally; like the caress of an unseasonably warm day in winter reminds you of someone who broke your heart; like a storm of such triggers, setting off so many memories at once; like that, yesterday, with Sam inside me, all the men I've ever loved were all at once recalled, not because I was thinking of *them*, but just the opposite, because the whole of my history, everything I have ever known and since forgotten, was rising in me to mean *him*, Sam, whose name I could not remember.

The French call the orgasm "the little death." Approaching the big death, the rumor goes, one's whole life flashes before one's eyes. It makes sense then that with my little one, all previous loves should flash before mine, so that instead of crying out, "Sam!" I nearly sang a summary of my love life so far: I love you, Joey, I mean Martin, I mean Nicos, I mean Philip, I mean Max, I mean Glen, I mean Billy, I mean Sam . . .

> *"'Twas brillig, and the slithy toves*
> *Did gyre and gimble in the wabe;*
> *All mimsy were the borogoves,*
> *And the mome raths outgrabe."*

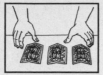

Today, after 50 years of its theoretical introduction, we have learned that the Higgs boson probably exists.

— CSABA BALAZS OF THE MONASH UNIVERSITY'S
ARC CENTRE OF EXCELLENCE FOR PARTICLE PHYSICS
IN MELBOURNE

LARGE HADRON COLLIDER

THE LAUNDROMAT IS A GREAT place to meet men, dating experts say. Also, sports bars. But what do you do when you have your own washer and dryer? When you quit drinking six years ago? What do you do when you want to meet someone who, like you, is not at that Super Bowl party, but home alone watching Science Channel, contemplating the certain collision of the Milky Way and Andromeda, and the romantic ramifications of quantum entanglement, what Einstein called "spooky action at a distance."

I was in my parents' kitchen, reading one of my dad's back issues of *Scientific American*, when my mother reminded me again of my hurtling headlong into a lonely void. "You don't have forever" were her exact words. I was reading about the possibility that time doesn't exist but is simply "emergent." Still, I didn't argue. I just nodded and turned the page, to an ad for a Bright Horizons educational cruise, this one with a physics theme.

"You're too picky," my mother went on, noting my age, "nearly forty!"

"Thirty-five," I corrected her, and continued reading the trip itinerary. After a tour of CERN in Geneva, home of the Large Hadron Collider, participants would board the *AmaDagio* for a cruise down France's Rhône River, enjoying twenty-two onboard lectures on the latest developments in physics and cosmology, punctuated by six tours of the port cities between Lyon and

Arles. *What kind of people take these trips?* I wondered. *Could this be my laundromat?*

The day before my flight, I'm still packing. The brochure suggests casual attire, but I'm not about to meet my soulmate in a T-shirt, and visiting the largest particle accelerator in the world where, after a forty-year search, the elusive Higgs boson (AKA "the God particle") was finally discovered, surely warrants a little dressing up. I settle on practical Hepburn-esque menswear for day and gowns for evening—perfect for a transatlantic steamer setting sail in 1925.

An overnight flight later, and I'm standing amid a crowd of T-shirted septuagenarian couples, waiting to board a bus that will take us all to CERN. Struggling to remain optimistic—if I can't have lived in 1925, at least I can rub elbows with those who came close—I keep my eyes peeled for a potential husband hidden within the group. I'm about to give up all romantic hope when a fantastically young man in his late fifties, an English astrophysicist, asks if he can sit next me. "Of course," I say, before noticing his wedding ring, fat and gold, shaped like the Large Hadron Collider we're about to see.

Three hundred thirty feet underground, a seventeen-mile ring straddles the Franco-Swiss border. Whizzing through it at speeds approaching that of light, particles smash into one another, causing mini "big bangs" and conditions like that of our universe 13.7 billion years ago. The Large Hadron Collider fills me with a sense of awe that follows me into the evening and is still with me the next day, as I stare out from the cold deck of the *AmaDagio*.

Swathed in secondhand mink—like an Edward Gorey character surveying the grounds—I watch the French countryside drift by. It's autumn and the trees along the Rhône are orange, and red, and then bare.

Below deck, I lunch with a couple from Greece who for many reasons remind me of my parents. "The *bœuf bourguignon* is delicious," I say, smiling. "The meat is tender, but none of that matters if you don't have a person to share it with," Eleni replies, after she hears I'm traveling alone. I'm grateful when her husband George, a gynecological pathologist, changes the subject. He asks if I've gotten the HPV vaccine. "My doctor says I'm too old." George nods gingerly before estimating my age, probable number of sexual partners, and the statistical likelihood that I already have the cancer-causing virus. Eleni beams and takes her husband's hand. "George's work has been honored all over the world."

For dinner, I select a dramatic houndstooth gown paired with my favorite polar bear earrings. But I'm the only one in formal attire and blush when I enter the dining room. The waiters all look at me, I think, pityingly. Quickly, I take a seat beside the roguishly handsome Mr. Taggart, a retired history professor from Bath and science cruise veteran—this is his fifth. Mr. Taggart has spiky white hair, thick black eyebrows, and a back problem that makes him look sulky and rebellious.

Immediately, we hit it off—I have a similar pain in my hip from too many hours at my desk—and I begin fantasizing about becoming the wife of Bath, about accompanying him on his sixth and seventh and eighth science cruise. Trying to scope out his marital status, I compliment him on his unique style—

a shirt with buttons—and ask if he has a stylist or if his wife and children dress him. Score: he is unattached. I probe further, asking after his other interests.

At this, he takes out his iPhone to show me photos of the clocks and barometers that he collects. He goes on talking to me about time and pressure when it hits me: I'm not being courted but visited by the Ghost of Science Cruise Future. With a start, I realize all his clocks are Grandfathers.

Like sands through Mr. Taggart's hourglass, these are the days of our cruise: On Monday we sit for lectures on the subatomic world—"Electrons come in pairs." On Tuesday, space—"We live in a time of cosmic collision, but eventually even galaxies have to settle down." On Wednesday, we tour the Roman ruins of Vienne—"The Temple of Augustus and Livia. What a pair!" And on Thursday, we are treated to a romantic night walk through the medieval ghost town of Viviers. Two by two we disembark, like Noah's animals, onto dry land. Mr. Taggart, gallantly, offers his arm.

The most unromantic view of marriage is that it's insurance against the future. "You don't want to end up alone!" my mother had told me in the kitchen. But here, on this ship, among the over-seventy set, I am with people who are pretty close to the end, and I am here alone. It dawns on me, I'm not sure on which day, that I've seen the end, and it's not so bad.

We stay up late after our night walk through Viviers. The captain, the married astrophysicist, George and Eleni, a couple from China who are celebrating their fortieth anniversary, and Mr. Taggart and I sit together in the lounge talking about ideas the way we did when we were in school, when we were still young, when we had forever. We talk about the Big Bang, about what came before the beginning, about what came before that, and what came before that . . .

On the last night, when I enter the dining room the waiters applaud. They've enjoyed my outfits, one of them tells me. They've never seen anyone make such an effort. I smile and adjust my turban. So what if electrons come in pairs? The Higgs boson, that special thing that took almost forty years to find, goes it alone.

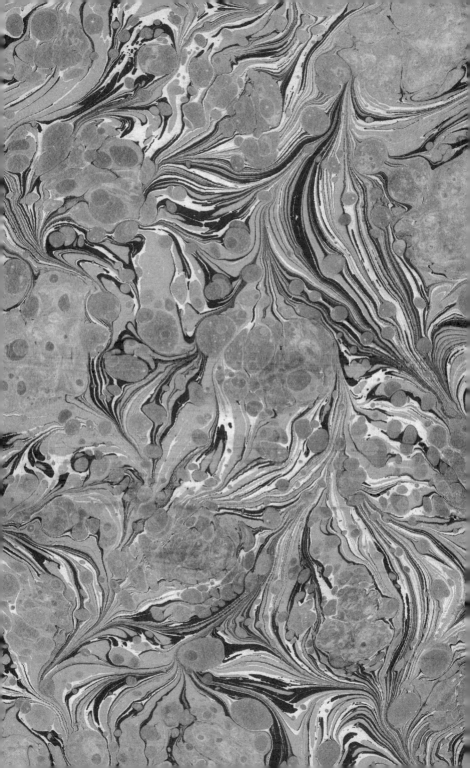

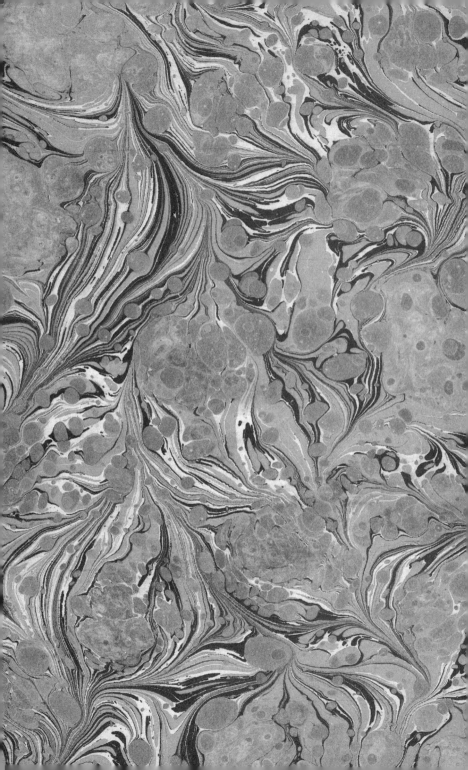

ACKNOWLEDGMENTS

THANK YOU:
Mike Solomon
Chris Stein
Arthur Smyles
Popy Smyles
Frederic Tuten
Irene Skolnick
Lauren Wein
Pilar Garcia-Brown
Russ Smith
Ann Hulbert
Scott Stossel
Betsy Sussler
Honor Jones
Erin DeWitt
Taryn Roeder
Rachael DeShano
Ayesha Mirza
Christopher Moisan
Arthur T. Smyles
Alexander Smyles

ADVERTISEMENT CREDITS

All advertisement pages, and the marbled paper pages, have been designed by Mike Solomon. Graphics, some of which have been modified from their original, have been licensed from or provided courtesy of the below-listed sources.

ADVERTISEMENT 1
divining rod Courtesy of Mike Solomon
book © Glandwr/iStockphoto
retro man © stocksnapper/iStockphoto
retro woman © incomible/iStockphoto
perfume bottle © ivan-96/iStockphoto
"before" and "after" portraits © Iris Smyles
storefront © Michael Valdez/iStockphoto

ADVERTISEMENT 2
map © touc/iStockphoto
bottles of alcohol © KeithBishop/iStockphoto
boy with hoop © nicoolay/iStockphoto
heraldry crest © ly86/iStockphoto

ADVERTISEMENT 3
cards in hand © Iris Smyles
dancers © IntergalacticDesignStudio/iStockphoto
playing spoons © Daniel Zalkus
paintbrush © BeylaBalla/iStockphoto
cheese © undrey/iStockphoto

ADVERTISEMENT 4
teapot © unalozmen/iStockphoto
ant colony © ilbusca/iStockphoto

ADVERTISEMENT 5
Chihuahua © maiteali/iStockphoto
scorpions © Grafissimo/iStockphoto
bottle © gruffi/iStockphoto
alarm clock © LEOcrafts/iStockphoto

ADVERTISEMENT 6
book (upper left) © Stephan Zabel/iStockphoto
portrait of a woman © nicoolay/iStockphoto
book (lower left) © tibor5/iStockphoto
baker's twine © neung-pongsak/iStockphoto
book (middle) © esseffe/iStockphoto
man ablaze © RBFried/iStockphoto
book (right) © Glandwr/iStockphoto
close-up of a chin © duncan1890/iStockphoto

ADVERTISEMENT 7
portrait of a man © ivan-96/iStockphoto
book © Joe_Potato/iStockphoto

ADVERTISEMENT 8
diner © CSA-Printstock/iStockphoto
book © Owat Tasai/iStockphoto

ADVERTISEMENT 9
book © Stephan Zabel/iStockphoto

ADVERTISEMENT 10
scales of justice © sh22/iStockphoto
mini golf course © Kaycco/iStockphoto
pyramids © 13, Adam Jones, Ocean/Corbis
snake handler © Daniel Zalkus

ADVERTISEMENT 12
doctor (body) © BakiBG/iStockphoto
doctor (face) © Iris Smyles
caduceus © Houghton Mifflin Harcourt, Clarinda-Academy Artworks
solar suit © Daniel Zalkus

ADVERTISEMENT 13
bait © StockPhotosArt/iStockphoto

ADVERTISEMENT 14
book © esseffe/iStockphoto

ADVERTISEMENT 16
three-card monte © Daniel Zalkus

ship and island © duncan1890/iStockphoto
jar © Big_Ryan/iStockphoto
mustache © Tairy/iStockphoto
portrait of a man © duncan1890/iStockphoto
T-shirt © rodrigofoca/iStockphoto

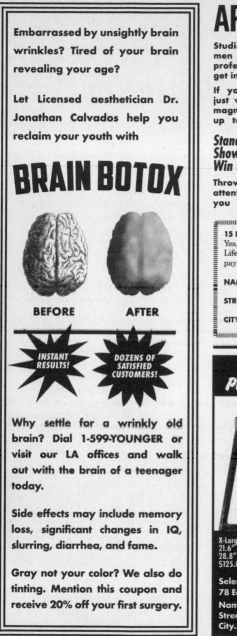
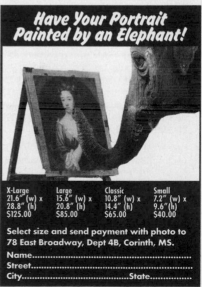

Are You Descended From Royalty?

NEITHER ARE WE. That's why we formed Ancestry Professionals Ltd. Our certified genealogists will investigate and then invent a glamorous pedigree to which you can reasonably lay claim.

Ancestors didn't come over on the *Mayflower*? Don't despair! Whether you come from a long line of chimney sweeps who emigrated to America after English child labor laws were put into effect, or Australia, we can help you cover up your ignoble origin story and concoct in its place the blue-blooded lineage that will help you get ahead.

Other ancestry services will merely research your background, uncovering a whole slew of unsavory characters you wish you never knew about. For the same price, our service will not only invent from whole cloth the fascinating distant relatives you wish you had, we'll change your name.

Whether you're a failure seeking an old-money background to make your current poverty seem genteel, or a bored housewife wishing to weave a touch of darkness into your otherwise bland history, we've got you covered. Just fill out and mail in the **Ancestry Professionals Ltd.** Questionnaire to help us identify your genealogical needs, and we'll spin a plausible and unique family history that you'll be proud to trot out at a cocktail party or over a pillow.

DON'T LET YOUR PAST STAND IN THE WAY OF YOUR FUTURE! APPLY FOR YOUR STORIED BACKGROUND TODAY!

Mail coupon to 239 Harbor Ave., Loughton, MD 10029.

Yes, I'm interested in genealogy and would like to receive more information about **Ancestry Professionals Ltd.** and their services.

Please send an **Ancestry Professionals Ltd.** Questionnaire and brochure to:

Name...

Street...

City...................................State..............................

YOU COULD BE...

A HABSBURG!

THE LOST DAUGHTER OF ANASTASIA ROMANOV!

THE MAN IN THE IRON MASK'S GREAT-GREAT-GREAT-GRANDNEPHEW!

A DESCENDANT OF THE DAUPHIN LOUIS-CHARLES!

GRANDBASTARD OF A ROBBER BARON!

THE DISAVOWED HEIR TO THE WHOOPEE CUSHION FORTUNE!

We don't know why some were born to the manor while others to those who sweep it. But there's one thing we do know: Nothing is more readily accepted as truth than gossip. **For an extra fee, we'll plant one of our actors at a cocktail party/special event of your choosing, who will refer to you in hushed tones from across the room:**

"Is that Lord Krichnau? I hear he's second in line to the Foreignian crown."

"Don't look now but Jaqueline D'Ripier is here. Rumor has it she's the great-great-granddaughter of Jack the Ripper. Apparently, he fell in love with one of the prostitutes he was planning on killing and that's why the murders stopped. They lived together for a while in a small cottage outside of London, until she bore him one child, a girl. It's said that they were very much in love. Fearing for the daughter's safety, however, immediately after giving birth, she took the baby and fled, turning up 17 days later at a convent outside of Paris where she thrust the baby into the hands of a nun before expiring from tuberculosis on the church doorstep. The girl was raised there, among the sisters, with no knowledge of who she was or where she came from. Jaqueline grew up here and was never told."